Naked at the Window

NAKED AT THE WINDOW

Bill James

Constable • London

First published in Great Britain 2002
by Constable, an imprint of Constable & Robinson Ltd
3 The Lanchesters, 162 Fulham Palace Road
London W6 9ER
www.constablerobinson.com

ISBN 1–84119–570–7

Printed and bound in Great Britain

A CIP catalogue record for this book
is available from the British Library

Chapter One

Although enemies and rivals sometimes called Ralph Ember Panicking Ralph, or even Panicking Ralphy, his panics were actually quite rare and only ever started from very particular causes, major causes. For example, a panic could never be touched off by the sight of three slaughtered people scattered higgledy-piggledy in a games room, no matter how well he knew them, and no matter how the bodies might have been mutilated and/or disfigured. Of course, hardly anyone ever used the name Panicking – either Ralph or Ralphy – to Ember's face, but he knew the rotten slur was around, and this grieved and angered him. In any case, he hated being addressed as Ralphy, even without the Panicking. He would tell people, 'Call me Ralph or R.W. or Ember.' Ralph W. Ember was how he signed letters to the Press, mostly on environmental topics such as air pollution and restoration to limpidness of industrialized rivers. He considered that 'Ralphy' sounded like somebody's retarded cousin who had to be made allowances for.

In fact, looking at these three bodies, what he felt almost immediately was not panic but a slight, brief but wholly genuine rush of shame. This came because his absolutely first reaction on seeing the untidy deads and identifying them despite the injuries had been: *Where the living fuck do I get my trade stuff now, then?*

More or less instantly he recognized it as a callously selfish response to a scene that could reasonably be regarded as tragedy – Barney and both his women destroyed like this and strewn about. After all, these three, operating together, with quite an obvious and lovely fondness for one another, must have been among the greatest bulk providers of prohibited drugs in Britain, if not all of the European Union. Barney, Maud and Camilla had long supplied Ember's own fine network pretty satisfactorily. All right, the women, Maud and Camilla, were not young and had never in Ralph's memory been anything but null sexually, as far as he, personally, was concerned, though clearly not Barney. But he knew this should not make the sight of them now like this any less poignant. And Barney? Yes, Barney certainly had times as the supreme posturing, grab-all, exploitive turd who tried to treat Ember as a serf, not a colleague. Yet in some ways Barney was also an affectionately regarded business connection, and surely something of a loss: a loss as a *person* as well as a commodity importer and super-wholesaler.

It had always been a worthwhile journey for Ember to drive all those motorway hours to Barney's place near Southampton and the Isle of Wight to negotiate delivery and payment of the next consignment for his, Ember's, fine pushing network back home. Tiderace, Barney's house, was a big, modern waterside place looking out on opulent sailing craft, and that fucking yachtsman's tan he always flourished like semaphore was holding up pretty well now despite the blood drain. There had been true depth to Barney if you could be bothered to look for it, and some of the darker blood might be coming from there.

Beau Derek was with Ember. Beau had sobbed one big terrified sob when they first entered the room and saw Barney, Maud and Camilla. Then Beau covered his eyes for a second with those lumpy red fingers. If you were not familiar with his cracksman career path you would never believe he could do safes. The thing about this room was that there was hardly any furniture, only a high-backed church pew against one wall, so all the bodies were totally in view at once, although not together. This was why Beau put those slab hands over his eyes, trying to lessen the shock. Beau could turn showy. He would know Ember saw him do it. Beau liked to be thought of as emotional.

It always used to enrage Ember that he had to bring Beau on these visits to Barney and the women, but Barney insisted. He would say it was crucial that both partners in Ember's business should attend, for the sake of continuity. The fucker meant, in case Ember was arrested or killed or coshed into gagadom one day and Beau had to take over and run things, and handle the deals with Barney. Beau running things? Jesus.

Oh, well, Barney boy, we can see now who'd get killed one day and cut about, can't we, and it's not Ralph W. Ember, thank you.

What Ember used to loathe was the implication that he and Beau rated equal. Ember had brought Beau into his quite distinguished pushing firm as a partner because he was loyal and spare, but it was as a dogsbody partner, not much more than hired help, really. Beau knew it. Naturally he knew it. Could someone always referred to except by relatives and his woman as Beau Derek be regarded as a full boardroom figure, for God's sake? His name was Derek and joky, cruel people had stuck the Beau on because of Bo Derek, the film actress, and because Beau looked a slob, not beautiful at all – that red cabbage skin and his random teeth. Yet Barney would always treat him like chocolate, just to unnerve Ember and push him down. When Beau sobbed in the doorway to the games room it could have been sorrow at realizing Barney would not be about any longer to offer him status. Barney was nothing now and Beau next to nothing, as ever.

There was no real trouble about identifying Barney, Maud and Camilla despite the treatment. After all, this was the house the three of them lived in. Who else could they be? Ember had visited often before, sometimes alone, sometimes with Beau, sometimes with previous partners such as Harry Foster and Gerry Reid, now very safely dead and for ever interred, oh, yes, surely to God, possibly even built over by a housing estate. Frequently Barney had led them to this room for meetings. There was a dartboard at one end, which was what apparently transfigured it from just any sort of damn room into a games room, or *The Games Room*. Barney always spoke its title with a holy boom to his voice, like he was talking about the Vatican. Discussions had been awkward because everyone sat strung out in a line on the church pew. Barney would be at one end and he usually managed it so that Beau and the women sat between him and Ember. This meant that when Ember wanted to speak to him he had to lean forward like a battery hen hunting feed. This was another way Barney had of making Ember feel subservient.

Yet Barney, plus Maud and Camilla, had been in Ember's view tolerable. You did not expect saintly egos in this game. Grab prevailed and you wouldn't find anyone better at it than Barney, except possibly Maud. Of course, what Ember saw now in these bodies was that some other dark team was going to take over and would immediately require Ember to start drawing his supplies from them instead. It was an uncomfortable idea. He felt minionized. These had to be savage people. Look at the deaths. Ember might have been able to understand why Barney and Maud required slaughtering – compare a foot-and-mouth cull – but Camilla always seemed to him almost decent, civilized and broad-minded. There could even have been a time far off when she did not look anything like as bad.

Gazing at this corpse tableau, Ember wondered whether it might be his cue to do something he had been considering for many months, even more than a year: to pull out from the drugs game altogether and go full-time and uncompromisingly legitimate. It was not impossible. He had other business areas to tend, all legal, and especially ownership of his club, the Monty. Ember's wife had lately been trying to persuade him more or less non-stop to go straight. He knew she craved that. He had even given some promises, sort of promises. You had to strive to be kindly to them. They did not always seem to understand how money was got, the kind of money Ember and his family needed. Skimping he hated.

But, yes, a sight like this at Tiderace was bound to make Ember wonder again whether Margaret had it right and now was the time to go pure. It could certainly be argued that a man well-placed in a commercial occupation should not be confronted with bodies on this scale out of the blue. Maud was on her side under the dartboard, her old, cruelly messed-up face towards them, legs slightly hunched on the cracked cream lino, and wearing one of those greenish pauper cardigans. This was a huge property in grounds and facing a stretch of river where *Modesty*, Barney's own grand yacht, and the yachts of several neighbours, lay moored. None of these boats was worth less than half a million and Barney's house must have cost at least as much. But when it came to furnishing and carpeting the place, or kitting out the women, it looked as if he had grown bored by wealth and did not care how scruffy the property and Maud and Camilla appeared. It could happen to the very rich. They began to feel contempt for their money and the ways they had collected it and refused to give any more evidence of surplus. In the magnificently large hall that Ember and Beau had crossed on their way upstairs to the games room, part of a car exhaust system was laid out on copies of the *News of the World* and the *Economist* across the mahogany-boarded floor. It had been there the last time Ember came. Behind this were an unconnected and dilapidated fridge-freezer and an open wooden crate containing what seemed to be the insides of a couple of television sets. Outside, the house was all gloss and capital gains. Inside, a scrap yard. Barney dressed damned nicely himself, though, usually with a casual, yachty theme: navy trousers, navy jumper in winter, smock-style shirt in the warmer weather, usually blue.

Even now, with his mouth sagging like that and his gear so stained, he had a kind of chicness, a dead kind, yet rich in pointers to how he was until really quite recently.

Beau whispered: 'Do you think whoever –?'

'You mean they're still here?'

'Could be, Ralph. But the front door was open.'

'What do you make of that, Beau?'

'A rushed exit and careless after this.' He waved feebly towards the bodies.

'Or they've left it open, ready for their escape.' Ember enjoyed his total coolness, the precision of his brain, the judge-like steadiness of his voice as he summed up for Beau. It was moments like this – leadership moments, dominance moments – that Ember cherished, and made him radically undecided about turning prim. He said: 'Yes, they could still be here.'

'Jesus, Ralph.'

'We need to search.'

'Or get out.'

'We need to search,' Ember replied.

Abruptly, then, he realized he could not have varied these words to Beau. At a monstrous gallop after all that confidence, the beginnings of terror suddenly began to move in on him. He loved to sound brave and collected, but wasn't. The repetition – that sort of chorus effect – gave him something to lean on, like congregation responses in the funeral service.

'Do you think any of them might be alive, Ralph?' Beau said, waving feebly towards the bodies.

'Touch nothing. We're a long way from home ground. The police here don't know us. We could be done for this.'

'Maybe best just get out then, Ralph.'

'We need to search.' Yes, yes, yes, naturally it was best just to get out, and he would have if he had been here alone, no Beau. But Ember was Ralph W. Ember, wasn't he, not Panicking Ralphy? He could not disintegrate in front of a dogsbody. Like everyone else he was more than one person, and he had to fight to be what he regarded as the best of these – the Ember who was Ember, or Ralph Ember or Ralph W. Ember, *not* Panicking Ralph, or Panicking Ralphy. Always it was a touch-and-go fight, no certain winner.

Chapter Two

'So, I'm leaving him, Harpur,' Margaret Ember said. 'If you're interested. You'll say, Why come and tell me – I'm not Marriage Guidance?'

'Will I say that?' Harpur replied.

'You can save Ralph. He wants to go legit, he really does. There have been undertakings.'

'Yes?'

'Oh, yes.'

'But?'

'But I've decided I can't wait. Talk to him, Harpur. Or you, Mr Iles.' For a moment she turned away from Harpur and towards the assistant chief, who was standing at the window. He seemed to make a small bow to her. She said: 'It might take a while, but talk to him. It's why I came, before I disappear. I'm going, but I want him happy, I want him safe.'

'Maybe *you* could save him, then. Stay with him, talk to him, Mrs Ember – Margaret,' Harpur said.

'I've talked and talked. He's promised and promised.' Her face seemed about to break up into weeping. Then she stopped all that. Harpur watched her deliberately harden her features, straighten out her jaw. 'This is the end now. Sort of end. I mean, if he really did it – went straight – I mean, really, really did it – I might still . . .'

'Think of going back to him?'

'Talk to him, Harpur.'

'That's not the only reason you're here, is it?' Harpur replied. 'Salvation of the Ralphy soul.'

Her face turned harder still. Her eyes rubbished him. 'Why do you call him that? Is it really how you think of Ralph?'

'He's various.'

'So are we all.'

'True, indeed,' Iles remarked.

'OK,' Harpur replied. 'So, why are you here – other than salvation of Ralph's soul?'

'I'll need protection. He adores his children. He'll come looking, Harpur.'

'I'm sure he adores you as well.'

'He can be extreme, Harpur, if he's pushed.' Harpur loved it, the routine absence of title when she spoke to him, no Mr, or Detective Chief Superintendent. When she addressed Iles it was with more formality. Harpur thought this directness with his own name seemed to give him solidity, as though he were a feature of the terrain, familiar, and without need of a handle. And he was, wasn't he? Iles, assistant chief constable, might seem a bit stratospheric to her.

Mrs Ember said: 'Ralph's away at present and I suppose you'll think it cowardly to walk out on him with the kids now, but –'

'Away where?' Harpur replied.

'What?' She seemed to find the question trivial and was offended.

'Is he down Southampton boating country way, the Solent, with his bulk man, Barney Coss?' Harpur asked.

'You have to show how much you know, don't you?' Small-voiced, small-mouthed, she was snarling just the same. 'On your patch or off.'

'He *is* at Barney's?'

'Do you have him under surveillance?' she replied.

'Not now. We did for a while. We like to keep up with

his procedures. I don't suppose they change much. Ralph's a status quo man.

'I don't know where he is. That's not relevant. It doesn't matter where.'

'Oh, I expect you know,' Harpur replied.

'I don't care where. I'm going, leaving, that's what counts.' She was small, blonde, boyish-looking, fierce and loud at the moment, in jeans, grey jumper and trainers, for travelling. Marriage break-up gear. Harpur said: 'Those Saturday-Sunday Yachtland sessions – bound to be golden days and nights in Ralph's calendar. I don't mean just the deals for his supplies, but the contact with a dirty eminence like Barney in a brilliant venue. And getting treated as a serious trader by people of that grade, Barney, Maud, Camilla – people known nationwide, yet so far still unprosecutable because of their cleverness and luck and government friends – sure to fatten Ralph's sense of self.'

'Perhaps I can't care very much any longer about his sense of self.'

They were in Harpur's sitting room seated opposite each other and drinking tea he'd made and served in mugs. His daughters were out, thank God. Mrs Ember had arrived alone without announcement driving an Escort, parked right in front of the house and knocked Harpur's door. Iles was on one of his visits to Harpur when she turned up: the assistant chief would often drop in on Saturdays. Of course, he stayed to see what she wanted. He remained standing now in the bay window, holding a mug of tea against his trouser leg. Sympathy glowed with a lovely fullness in the ACC's thin face, for the present. Iles liked to stand. This showed off his slimness and the exceptionally smooth skin of his neck, especially when the light came in from all angles as at present through the bay windows. It made a real meal of him. As ever, his clothes were a symphony. The ACC said: 'No, obviously it does not matter where Ralph is, Margaret. Colin Harpur invariably has trouble distinguishing between what's central in a situ-

14

ation and what's marginal. Accordingly, he's stuck at DCS.'
He bent forward confidingly towards her: 'Perhaps a
digression, but tell me, Margaret, do you think Harpur will
ever reach Staff rank? I would love to help him, love to,
but my attempts are continually stifled under the sawdust
tonnage of his supposed mind. All credit to him, he's very
much self-made, you know, but who would want to make
such a self? You come here, Margaret – you graciously trek
to Harpur's house in this white trash street – and all he can
ask, when you declare something as immense as the breakdown of your marriage to dear Ralph . . . yes, all he can ask
is to do with Ralph's whereabouts at the moment. You're
right, eternally Harpur has to show how damn informed
he is – the Solent, yachts, Barney and the women. Like a
kid, isn't he?'

'I've really worked to get Ralph out of . . . out of what
he calls business . . . what *they* all call it,' Mrs Ember
replied.

'A pinch from *The Godfather*. We know you have,' Iles
said. 'Even Harpur can recognize that much.'

She seemed to notice something in the ACC's tone.
'Maybe you don't want that, though, Mr Iles,' she said.

'Want what?' Iles asked.

'For Ralph to give up the substance trade. His firm and
Mansel Shale's, working in cahoots with each other, not
fighting for dominance, bring a nice bit of peace, don't
they? I heard you like that. Everything so steady. If Ralph
went, who'd come in to replace him? Would they abide by
the rules? Terrible street mayhem again, the way it was for
so long?'

Harpur thought it not a bad estimate of the ACC's
philosophy. Drugs he saw as inevitable, built into life for
ever. Policing was a matter of keeping the trade contained,
tidy, unviolent, with nothing hazardous or grim imposed
on the non-participating populace, or the participating
populace, come to that. In Iles's view, Ember and his trade

associate, Mansel Shale, helped preserve this fragile safety.

And, sometimes, Harpur did suspect the ACC's strategy might make sense in a rough world, even though it blind-eyed illegality. Iles used to say, 'Only *current* illegality, Col, totally nominal illegality. Ultimately, the law will adapt.' Iles stuck to this version of things, ignoring the chief constable, Mark Lane. He, with all his slight, wife-backed strength and standard ethics and vocabulary, struggled to oppose Iles's do-nothing stance. The chief backed those politicians who endlessly declared drugs an 'evil industry' and spoke of going to 'war' against them. Harpur saw, though, that the politicians then did nothing very serious to destroy the industry or win the war, because they were for the most part nicely educated and knew that demand produced supply. They noted there was mighty, continu-ously growing, cross-class demand: some were partici-pants. They had heard of the Prohibition farce.

Iles observed the politicians' helplessness and made his own workaday interpretation of their platform prêchi-prêcha bullshit. He hardly ever bothered to argue full-out or in detail with Lane. Simply, Iles let it happen on the streets. As ACC (Operations) he could do that, as long as he worked under a chief who had never discovered how to control him, and who wasn't going to learn this late in his career. Lane's attempts to reverse the policy were entirely sincere, useless and sad.

But the ACC seemed unlikely to discuss police methods with Margaret Ember now. He half raised his mug to drink and then lowered it decisively, as though signalling he wanted no further hospitality in this house, thank you, after Harpur had crudely failed to recognize the serious-ness of her visit. 'Mind you, Margaret, one can understand why Col might not fully register the importance of a marriage collapse,' he said.

Harpur heard Iles's voice take on again that victimized, frenzied, wailing edge it would assume now and then, like a Tehran street mourner's. His face suddenly had the suffering of the world in it, and the glum rage of the dispossessed. 'Harpur is not the most committed defender of marriage you'll ever meet, Margaret. I don't think he would dispute this. There's a kind of frankness to him, a big-headed kind. He was giving it to my wife, you know, over quite a spell, and ages before his own wife, Megan, was so tragically killed. Well, *naturally* you know. Every bugger knows. Excuse me – Everybody knows. My wife finds it incredible now that she ever let him get amongst her, and probably also his subordinate, Francis Garland, though not simultaneously, I'm convinced of that. Genuinely convinced. Absolutely. Some decencies. Of an evening now at home, Sarah and I will often chuckle over those strange episodes in her life and she will wonderingly list all Harpur's creepy, nauseating, flagrant defects. Nonetheless it did happen, didn't it, Harpur, you concupiscent, treacherous, uncontrolled –?'

'And your children want to go with you rather than stay with Ralph, do they, Mrs Ember?' Harpur replied.

'Would I leave them with him?' she said. 'If you can grasp in even the most basic way why I'm quitting you'll know I want them out of his influence. His influence as it is at present. That's key.' The small, immaculate features were firm.

Iles said: 'I think of Ralph as an exemplary father.'

'And he is, he is,' Mrs Ember cried. 'He will –'

'People are – what did you call it, Harpur, various? *So* various. Clearly, Ralphy is a villain – Ralph is a villain – almost all the way through, from arsehole to breakfast time. Plus, they say, spasmodically deepest yellow, and a shagger around almost to Harpur's standard. Yet he also strives to place one daughter in a fine private school, and the other, I believe, at an arm-and-a-leg French finishing establishment near Poitiers, to keep her from running pussy-wild here. I catch a whiff of nobility, don't I? Ralph doesn't mind spending on them.'

'Of course he doesn't,' she said.

'Admirable. Generous,' Iles replied. 'A pretty pony each, I gather, plus gymkhana fees and all the best clobber. Yes, there's a seedy, eternal grandeur to Ralph, and it's brave that you seem willing to sacrifice all this and quit Low Pastures. Or will you be able to keep in touch with his loot when you're gone? I admit I feel almost glad we've never been able to nail him for anything. Can one imagine Ralph celled? I feel for him as a man, as well as a piece of commercial enterprise.'

'I'm not here to finger him, Mr Iles, understand that, you devious sod,' Mrs Ember replied.

'No need,' Harpur said. 'We pile up our case against him. One day we'll do him. Just as one day Barney Coss and the women will be done.'

'I tell him that, all the time,' Mrs Ember replied. 'I tell him you tolerate Manse Shale and him for as long as it's useful to you, and then the both of them will be suddenly destroyed. Away for ever. But is this all you want? His eventual annihilation? It's possible to restore, reclaim him, Harpur. I swear you could do it. Not Mr Iles, but you I know could manage it, Harpur. He almost trusts you. You specifically.'

'I've heard of one or two people like that,' Iles said.

'Does policing have to be only a matter of persecuting people?' she asked.

'We call it *pro*secuting,' Harpur replied, 'and only those who deserve it. Like Ralph. And Barney. And Shale.'

'Harpur's been on a course in word-play,' Iles said. 'But, Margaret, I wouldn't be surprised if that daughter at the finishing school in France is turning into quite a bonny little thing by now. This would be Venetia? Gorgeous name. Poitiers – a region famed for bringing deportment to teenage girls. And for china. Ralph chose well. They'd show a girl how to make the very most of her whole pelvis and upper body. Yes, her pelvis and upper body.' The assistant chief exploded the p sounds like lust bucking its

18

controls. He grew breathless for a moment and seemed about to adjust the crotch of his trousers. He transformed this movement in time, though. It became, instead, a fond fingering of the upper reaches of the right leg crease in his magnificent tan slacks, part of weekend wear. With them he had on a brown, orange and green tweed field-sports jacket and crimson scarf, which he had loosened indoors. 'French women who've had deportment training are *so* fetching, but particularly when young, really young. What age would Venetia be, Mrs Ember? More than twelve by my reckoning. Glorious. I do think we have a lot to thank the French for, whatever people say about Maurice Chevalier.'

'Anything specific that's pushed you into your determination to leave now, Margaret?' Harpur asked.

Again he saw she resented his search for detail, exactitude, that cop habit. Her decision was enormous and she wanted it given scale. 'Specific?' she asked.

'You've been with Ralph for so long,' Harpur replied, 'and things between you have always been fine, apparently. There were his other women, yes, but you appeared able to see those for what they were, sidelines.'

'My wife was a Harpur sideline,' Iles screamed, and punched out as if to break one of the bay windows. He pulled back just when his knuckles touched the glass. Harpur hoped there were no neighbours in Arthur Street to see this and hear Iles's noise. It would be bad if someone reported a domestic incident and patrol cars came to neutralize and straitjacket an assistant chief.

Mrs Ember ignored his interruption. 'Yes, apparently fine. Apparently. Who can judge a marriage from outside?'

'Ah,' Iles replied.

'All the time my uneasiness built and built,' she said. 'His business involvements.'

'Margaret, I do understand,' Iles said. 'The gradual,

19

relentless drawing away from him. This is how good things die, slowly, unstoppably.'

'It might be difficult, giving you protection,' Harpur said. 'What reason? He wouldn't threaten. Ralph's too smart and polite.'

'Unofficially?' she replied.

'Difficult, especially if you go off our ground, of course, and I assume you'd want distance,' Harpur said.

She stared at him for a while. 'Did you somehow know I was coming to your house today?'

'What? How could I?'

'I mean, Iles being here. Like pre-arranged.'

'We're buddies, Margaret, despite his filthy betrayal and appearance,' the ACC replied. 'Forgiveness is big with me.'

'He comes over some Saturdays when there's no school for my kids,' Harpur said. 'I have two daughters, the same as you, Mrs Ember.'

'I hope I take an interest in a colleague's family,' Iles said, 'especially as he's single parenting. Hazel, Harpur's older girl, is hardly a child, anyway.'

'She's fifteen,' Harpur replied.

'God,' Mrs Ember said.

'Luckily they're out a lot,' Harpur replied.

'Hazel's a genuinely gifted girl,' Iles said. 'I hope I can bring some vitality, tenderness and humour to Harpur's household occasionally. Hazel appreciates it.'

'God,' Mrs Ember said.

'At Staff College I was often called Witty Desmond,' Iles replied. 'Heaven knows what Harpur would be called if he ever got there, which he won't.'

'Where will you go?' Harpur asked her.

'I might tell you when we're fixed up.'

'How can I protect you if I don't know where you are?' Harpur replied.

'You won't, will you, whether you know or not?'

'Difficult.'

'So, secrecy might be better,' she said. 'One thing I've learned on this visit.'

'You can't be secret from Ralph,' Harpur said. 'Not if you're drawing from his accounts and so on. Or was there an escape fund around the place? In the house? In the Monty? Cash? You've helped yourself? Prudent people like Ralph always have some bale-out treasure on hand. It could make him ratty if you've raided that.'

'I might let you know where we are,' she replied.

'We're not in league with Ralph, you know,' Harpur said. 'We wouldn't pass on your address.'

'No?' Mrs Ember replied. 'No?'

'If Harpur assures you of something you can more or less trust it, Margaret. Oh, definitely more or less.'

'Yes?' Mrs Ember said.

Chapter Three

Ember and Beau drove quickly away from Barney's place at the Wharf and back to a filling station. Ember wanted to pick up a couple of pairs of plastic gloves before starting to search the house and the three bodies. Naturally, he thought about never returning there. Naturally he still thought about driving away not just from the house but from the whole drugs game for keeps. Both ideas were big and sweet in his head. He could go home to Margaret and say he'd had a kind of inexplicable but conclusive revelation, like a Gospel Hall conversion. Forget the bodies, forget the trade, forget the yacht hopes. Turn clean.

Beau would not have protested about skipping the return to Tiderace and Maud, Camilla and Barney. Protested? Christ, it was going to take everything Ember had to get him into the house again, if they did go back. Almost certainly, though, there would be a safe and Beau might be needed, if the safe hadn't already been done by those who did the deaths. When business acquaintances were killed in the way Barney and those women were, Ember naturally felt an obligation, more or less, to clear up their paperwork and so on, quite apart from what money might be about. The paperwork should say something about how major drug importing functioned, and what the profits were like. Ember had an idea what they were like, of course. Look at the house, look at the bad good ship *Modesty*. But there might be account books available to verify in sparkling and uplifting detail what this end of the trade brought in. Ember could be interested, even though he was thinking of his exit. Only thinking. Possibly, it was fortunate after all that Barney had insisted on Beau's presence.

Ember felt ravaged by indecision. There were special opportunities, there were duties, there were dangers and fears. One of the duties was to Beau. He obviously longed to get home. Gently wheezing with dread he sat knotted up in the passenger seat, his face like a lost dog's looking for kindness. Ember did understand, wanted to pat him but thought it might seem an insult. Tiderace would be difficult territory and Beau was not built for this kind of stress. What *was* he built for? Beau could be fine when actually doing something, say cutting a fence or neutralizing alarms or, obviously, persuading a safe. He had skills and he had loyalty and a damned nice-looking woman partner somehow. There were many aspects of him to prize and Ember did prize them. Often he told himself that Beau might have been worse. Clothes and appearance were very secondary. All sorts of entirely capable people had vile face skin.

'Like a warning,' Beau said.

Ember could half agree, but you did not show nerves to someone like Beau and he said, 'What?'

'The bodies. The way they looked.' Beau's voice had almost evaporated through shock. Ember knew that kind of failure. During one of his own authentic panics he often found he could not speak or even scream. When they came, those times were appalling. He might have so much to tell the world then about his unique terror, his unique despair, his unique symptoms of break-up, and yet he had to stay soundless, unable to dredge anything from his voice-box or get his lips around words.

'Warning who?' Ember asked.

'Generally.'

'We don't cave in to that, do we, Beau?' Ember yearned to cave in, but true leaders didn't.

23

'We don't know who we're up against,' Beau replied.

'Neither do they.'

'Well, they might,' Beau said. 'They might know our moves.'

'They don't know what I'm like when I'm angry, do they, Beau?' He said it quietly, no swagger, but that question came out definitive and its own reply. Beau would get the imperturbability, Ember's sheer, damn track-proved power. You had to lifebelt people like Beau because he was worth saving, he was part of a tradition and a decent one. Ember carried a Smith and Wesson, .38, short-barrelled Bodyguard revolver in a leather shoulder holster. He did not much like the pressure of it against his chest. It seemed crude, but almost always when he visited Tiderace he went tooled up. They could be affable meetings, they could be very strained meetings, especially when Maud turned mouthy, and she had usually turned mouthy. Prolonged abuse by an uncle in her childhood? You had to try to understand women like that. Goodbye then, Maud, dear. Hellish to die in such a cardigan.

By going to the petrol station they might give any people hidden in Tiderace after the killings a chance to get out and be no longer a threat. Ember did not think this was his main motive for the trip, though. He really believed the gloves mattered, if they returned to the house, and they most certainly might. In any case, people hiding could think Ember and Beau had in fact left permanently and assume the house was theirs again, to do whatever they liked: search, strip. They might still be around when Ember and Beau reappeared. If they did. Ember played and played with options.

At the filling station they helped themselves to gloves from the dispenser and then filled up with petrol and checked the oil. Ember wanted ordinariness. It would be noticeable and memorable if they simply took the gloves. Three people dead and carved in a mansion would even-tually produce big police activity, even people like Barney,

Maud and Camilla: a lot of questions and dragnetting. All right, it would be a swedebashing police force for this kind of area, but brains and persistence could turn up in all kinds of surprising places. Beau flapped his hands like a shot swan, to show Ember how loose the gloves were. 'I won't be able to work in these,' he said.

'Keep them on for the general look-around. If you do a safe it will be a small area we can wipe clean.' Christ, did Ember have to tell him basics?

'They can find all sorts these days,' Beau said.

'You'll be all right.'

Beau would never carry a firearm. This was some absolute, temperamental block that he seemed damned proud of, as if it proved sensitivity, not daft squeamishness. Of course, this meant he would always expect Ember to protect him if a gun battle started. OK, Ember knew his responsibilities. You looked after your disciples, as much as seemed feasible, and Beau was constructed to be a disciple, nothing more, but a very faithful and very solid disciple.

Ember drove out of the filling station. There was a roundabout a couple of miles up the road and he could postpone route choice until then – back to Tiderace or home-bound on the motorway and, maybe, more than home-bound: bound for future solid lawfulness and decency, non-stop. This was take-your-pick-Ralph time. Like Beau, Ember also wanted to be away from here. He yearned for the security of his own place, Low Pastures. He craved the company and comfort of his family. Beau was companionable in his crawling way, but no substitute.

'You don't have to worry, do you, Ralph? They haven't got your prints. You've never been inside.'

'I don't know what they hold. I've given prints, and they should have been destroyed. But who'd bet on it?'

He hated having to wonder about miserable dossier matters like that when he had been enjoying thoughts of the family. Ember's older daughter, Venetia, had come back for a few days from her French school, and he felt a lovely completeness at Low Pastures since her arrival, a brilliant atmosphere of love and vitality. This warmed his soul. Throughout his business life Ember had striven to create that home ambience. He depended on it. Wasn't it a central need in all wholesome men? Margaret, Venetia and Fay would replace the horror of those three grotesque corpses in the mad games room. If Beau had not been in the car, Ember would almost certainly have driven away and forgotten about the shambles at Tiderace. That could be treated as just a closed episode, not even as an opportunity. But always there was this vital fucking officer-trooper aspect to consider. Someone like Beau needed an example, had to be shown how determination and courage and coolness operated when stress came. Ember could not be seen to fold. At the roundabout, he ignored the motor-way sign and turned back on to the minor road leading to the Wharf and Tiderace. Beau, still slumped, observed this, sighed and said: 'It could be a trap, Ralph.'

'I've thought of that.'

But Beau kept on: 'Like this: someone knew we were coming there today – one of our scheduled weekend trips – and has those three killed, then puts in a call to the local law while we're on the premises. Barney, Maud and Camilla might be only bait.'

'Who defaces bait?'

'For credibility. To make it look to the police like we had a hate going for them – about substance prices, or what-ever. Well, we *did* have a bit of a hate going for them about prices.'

Ember resented the way Beau kept saying us and we, as though they were a merry team of colleagues. Beau was great, but great in his place, like a Sherpa. Barney and his damned insistence on equal rating for Ember and Beau was dead now and Beau had better believe it. If there were any plot to trap someone it would be aimed at him, Ralph

Ember personally, not Ralph Ember plus assistant. 'I don't think so, Beau. Too fancy. If people wanted to get us as well as those three they'd have done an ambush. Easy.'

'They might still.'

'But we're ready this time. We've been alerted.' Ember tapped the pistol through his jacket. Not long ago he had begun a mature student degree – in suspension for the present – and, on the foundation course, studied some Hemingway. He had noted the special brand of courage Hemingway called 'grace under pressure'. Ember longed to display this. Oh, Jesus, yes. If he did a runner now Beau would have wonderful gossip to spread, real Panicking Ralphy stuff, grease under pressure. It did not matter that Beau was scared, too. Ember as the one at the top had to display greatness, dignity, poise. Much further back, he had learned the meaning of something else: the meaning of *noblesse oblige*. This message seemed to him indisputable.

Beau muttered: 'God, Ralph, they could be numerous.'

'Numerous?' It seemed a strangely flat, school essay word.

'All that junk about the place. They could come at us from behind it all ways.'

'The car exhaust in the hall wouldn't give much cover.'

Beau groaned. 'I admire you – your knack of joking, Ralph, regardless.'

'Part of our weaponry, Beau.' He deliberately brought him into it by saying our.

The risk in returning to Tiderace might be worth it. Ember still felt that at Barney's house there could be papers, ledgers, transaction records, estimates about future trading. These would be brilliant assets, suppose Ember decided to continue in the business, after all, but the business at a different, glittering level – Barney's level. Could he discover from the papers here the way to become an importer, not just a distributor, however distinguished? This was true status, true income. He loved the notion of people trekking to see *him* for their supplies, instead of *he* having to trek to Barney and kowtow. Ember didn't know whether he wanted a yacht, but he wanted the sort of *réclame* and social definition that came with a yacht. Entering the Tiderace drive, he was conscious of starry elation, he was conscious of fear. And of fucking horrible confusion.

Ember took the car to the side of Tiderace where it would be partially hidden by bushes. Pointless, this precaution? Their main worry had to be thugs perhaps already in the house, and it wouldn't matter whether the car was obvious or not. But to hide a car on a mission was a habit with him, and he needed the prop of habit now. They sat watching for a while, Ember still wondering if he should be here. Always he had seen total respectability and lawfulness as the ultimate career objective. He harboured a clear scheme for when this happened. He would invest his fine, built-up gains in blue chip companies and then concentrate on developing the club. He longed to take the Monty upmarket, gradually reducing and ultimately excluding the present slob, villain and slag membership, and moving it towards the kind of repute possessed by Boodle's or the Athenaeum in London. He had kept all the club's genuine brass fittings and mahogany panelling from an earlier existence as a social focus for authentic business and professional men. It was an obsessive ambition for Ember to transform the Monty, and perhaps the time had come to do it. He liked to visualize the day when the club admitted its first earl member or senior dentist or someone from the main board of Boots the Chemist. Ember was sick of crude parties at the Monty for people acquitted on a technicality, or just released from jail, although the spending excelled then. Margaret kept on and on about promises he'd made to respectabilize, and he did occasionally try to understand her frustration.

By his side, Beau remained very still. The scared oaf wouldn't want to seem impatient for re-entry, would he?

Even now Ember might have turned the Saab and disappeared, headed back towards Low Pastures and the Monty, and towards that new life, never mind what tales Beau spread later about Ralph's gutlessness. He could not do it, though. Could not, could not. He saw it would probably be a mad mistake to bolt from here now, and madder to drop the drugs trade altogether. All right, what they had found in the house shocked him – of course it did – but he could think of possible benefits. Yes, yes, the corpses were a kind of sadness. But didn't they also present grand career chances?

Ember climbed out of the car. He closed the door quietly, then took a few steps towards the rear of the vehicle and Tiderace's main entrance. He paused, waiting for dear, collapsed Beau. But Beau delayed longer, either because he was terrified to come out, or because his legs would not function, or both. Ember knew that feeling, too, and did not try to rush him. Ember's mind was working, and well. The thorough removal of Barney, Maud and Camilla must leave a gorgeous opening at the top of the trade hierarchy. Surely, surely, Ember had to fight for this role.

He felt now as if the Fates or even the good God had intervened brilliantly to stop him doing something hasty and miserably negative by quitting. Such a disgusting retreat could have been seen as panic, a panic brought on solely by dread that Margaret might lose patience, take the girls and leave him. But he had to resist, fight, defeat all panics. Lately, this had become the chief aim in his life. He must not disintegrate, *could* not disintegrate. He was Ralph W. Ember. Margaret would never exit, no matter how much she yammered, the weak, cloth-brained dependant. Never. They had too much together, she and Ralph. There was a kind of eternal holiness to it. And she must know he'd turn diabolical if she went off with Venetia and Fay, the cow.

Ember stood, hand on the boot of the car, surveying Tiderace, systematically searching the windows for movement. Once again he decided the risk was reasonable and manageable. Briefly, he put his hand under his jacket this time and touched the holster and gun butt direct. He still hated the feel of the leather and metal, but some unpleasant edges to life were inevitable. New business chances must produce major advancement and beautifully heavy wealth for Ember, and would improve the long-term security and integrity of his family, if it *could* be improved. This also was leadership. Leaders thought dynastically. Leaders looked long-term.

Sometimes, you had to ignore the tame advice of even a much loved wife because, as the one with flair and strength and vision – this above all, vision – as the one with these attributes, you alone saw that to benefit this wife and other cherished auxiliaries the man of leadership must act as he, only he, knew was best. Many said Ember's profile and physique recalled the young Charlton Heston's when playing supreme chieftains such as El Cid or Moses in films on TV. Especially women noticed this, luckily. He did not mind the attention. But Ember felt a duty to realize himself in full, and this, surely, meant more than letting smitten biddies with good bodies bed him. It meant behaving in line with his valiant, charismatic, commanding appearance.

The passenger door of the car opened and Beau came out. He stepped towards Ember, his legs reasonably all right, apparently. Looking at him, Ember had to wonder how Beau managed to get himself shacked up with his present very acceptable-looking woman, Melanie. 'I'd never let you walk into a place like that alone, Ralph.'

'Thanks, Beau. I knew it.'

'Did you honestly, Ralph? You were sure you could rely on me?' The prole face really shone for a second, so that Ember thought of that clay in the Bible which acquired a living glow when breathed on by God. Briefly, you might have imagined Beau had class. Ember felt he had created something here in this follower, and his eyes moistened with pride. It would not last, the glorious brave mood in Beau, but it had at least been brought into being and had lit up the moment with its beauty and verve, like the shortlived dragonfly. Ember found it good to think of Beau as a dragonfly rather than as a hopeless dog or a hurt swan.

Ember loathed the idea of entering someone's house with a gun actually in his hand, even Barney Coss's house, and even though it was a slaughterhouse, and a slaughter-house that might be looking for more slaughter. It seemed ungentlemanly to have the pistol on show. Just the same, he did bring out the Bodyguard and held it up on view across his chest, on view in case there was opposition in the house who needed to see what they could expect if, madly, they tried anything against Ralph Ember, and on view to keep Beau's bit of resolve alight. Although Beau wouldn't touch a gun, he knew the worth of firepower, the way Popes did. He also knew, of course, that the gun meant Ember must go in front and take whatever was coming first. All right, Ember also knew Ember must go in front, with or without the Bodyguard. Leadership. He felt sure nobody seeing them start towards the house would have doubted which one had the natural gift of command. It was not just clothes but bearing, looks, flair, the officer tradition.

They stood in the magnificent hall near the car spare parts and the spread pages of the *News of the World* and the *Economist* and listened. Or more than listened. They tried to take the feel of the house, whatever that meant. Would the flavour of the air have told Ember there were three deads upstairs if he had not already known? The flavour of the air told him that old bits of car exhaust kept their mileage stink no matter how long they had been strung out on newsprint.

But perhaps Beau could do better than this. Glancing at him occasionally, Ember saw that his previous appearance of collapse and terror was beginning to change. He looked much more collected now. Some parts of this experience would have been familiar to him far back, when a career burglar: the attempt to guess at and gauge whether he would meet any human resistance in a property. Ember began to watch him, as he might have watched a pressure dial. Christ, what could Beau hear, what sense? In his concentration, Beau's pitiably slapdash features took on something almost like refinement, something almost suggesting ecstatic trance. The shabby skin of his face seemed to tighten over the bone frame and become nearly translucent. For a second or two, his nickname, Beau, did not strike Ember as satirical. There was a beauty in his expertness and vitality.

Beau held up one hand. At first, Ember thought he was signalling to him to be quiet, and Ralph grew suddenly infuriated. Ember was already silent and, in any case, did not need orders from a fucking pointer dog. But then he realized that Beau was in fact pointing, pointing towards a door that should lead to the rear of the house, possibly through the kitchen. 'Someone?' Ember whispered.

Beau shook his head. So, why the alarm signal, Beau? His hand was stuck out like a crossroads finger post, but Beau began to bend one finger at a time slowly after each other, counting: not some*one*, more than someone. He finger-ticked two, then listened some more and in a while bent the third finger. Ember had heard nothing. My God, would it go to a fourth? What were they taking on here?

Ember waited, but Beau lowered his hand now and nodded. How could he be sure? Beau nodded again. He seemed to have picked up that Ember disbelieved him. Beau was saying, I'm telling you, Ralph. Then, very delicately, and with no sound, Beau moved slightly further back. Ember was already ahead of him, between Beau and the kitchen door, if that's what it was. Now, Beau wanted to concede unmistakably what was Ember's proper due – to head-up this sortie against the butchering enemy, three of them. Ember was in charge, Ember had the gun. Ember reeked of officer qualities and it was Ember's privilege to go over the top first. Oh, thank you, Beau, you fucking ugly, dodging sod.

Ember felt the galloping approach of a panic. His eyes began to cloud and a genuine juicy sweat started across his shoulders. He knew that in a moment his limbs might lose some or all their power, and he would grow convinced once again that the old scar along his jaw had opened up and was weeping gunge. It never did, of course, and couldn't, but in one of his panics – one of his kosher panics, not a half-cock, stop-start job – in an authentic, full carat panic, the barrier between the imagined and the real in his head got torn to bits, like the Berlin Wall. Oh, Christ, all that shit about his role and his obligations to inspire Beau and those stupid claims to natural leadership and flair. Wasn't he Panicking Ralphy? He longed to turn and sprint, sprint from the house to the car and, in the car, sprint from the Wharf to the motorway and to Low Pastures and warm security and holy innocence for ever. Sometimes, he used to adapt the Psalm: He maketh me to lie down in Low Pastures, He restoreth my soul. Beau nodded again, and again held up three fingers. Now he seemed to give a minute bow, like a maître d' respectfully requesting guests to take their places. And Ember's place was to first foot into an alien kitchen with three murderers in it waiting for him to open the door so they could jack the score up a bit. Ember, man of demon sweats, yet man of eminent and pre-eminent role, desperately fought himself, as he had often desperately fought himself in the past, each part of his soul looking for mastery. Was it true that victory in these interior battles most often went to the man of sweats and scampered retreats – to Ralphy? Many would say so. Was it true? Was it?

Today, no. NO. NO. Somehow, he lowered his gun arm from across his chest and held the Bodyguard pistol waist-high and ready. Now, instead of Beau nodding to Ember, Ember nodded to Beau. It signified acceptance of a task and risk, acceptance of command, like El Cid or Moses or like Winston Churchill in 1940, though Charlton Heston never played *him*. The fact that Ember could move his gun arm as he had was a glorious boost.

It meant his muscles and sinews were answering. If his arms worked, his legs might, and not just for running: to advance. He stepped forward – Yes, hosannas and alleluiahs, he *stepped* and it was *forward*. Oh, God, what a brilliant, magical combination. He wanted to sing. Gently, he pressed down the handle of the kitchen door. He could grip the handle, no slipping. The shoulder sweat was lavish and real, yet not torrential, and had not run down his arms and reached his fingers. SWEAT HAD NOT REACHED HIS FINGERS. Something like joy, something like triumph, merged with something very like absolute dread in him. But joy and triumph could prevail. They could, couldn't they? He had control and it was with magnificent, calculating control that he slowly pushed the door wide and saw the kitchen was empty, except that is for everything a super kitchen ought to have, all of it radiantly clean, like nowhere else in Tiderace. Not a murderer in sight. Had they fled jibbering through the other door at the far end of the kitchen and into the garden, knowing what they might have had to face otherwise: Ember armed, moving unswervingly FORWARD, morale unsplintered, almost steely?

He heard Beau gasp behind him. Perhaps he was desolated to find his intuitions so wrong. Or that was how the sound seemed to Ember at first. But when he turned to glance at Beau he saw that the gasp was not just surprise. True, there might have been some particles of surprise in it, because what had come at Beau had come at him from behind, not ahead and out of the kitchen, as half expected. Essentially, though, the gasp was more serious than surprise – an end-of-life gasp, one of those long releases of breath which might never be matched by a succeeding intake. Beau raised an arm and hand, almost in the way he had pointed at the kitchen door and signalled his culpably wrong guess at what lay behind it. This time, though, there was little strength to the movement and in fact he was not trying to signal but to grab at Ember and hold on and prevent himself falling. Ember did not object to this, no: if you had leadership you also had the dependence of others on you, and they would of course demand your support. Although Beau's fingers fluttered against Ember's right shoulder, they were unable to grasp it and slid off, skidding down the arm of Ember's suit coat as Beau began to crumble towards the floor, skewing away from Ember in a gradual forty-five degree turn. It seemed so much more in keeping for Beau, this catastrophic physical slump, rather than standing proud and allegedly knowledgeable, sign-languaging decrees at Ember.

He found he was expecting to see a knife handle protruding from Beau's body, but these days no one who knew anything about anything left knives in folk for possible tracing, and these were people who *did* know something about something, knew, for instance, how to baffle Beau's venerable and often infallible antennae. Although at first Ember saw no knife, there was a clutch of closely grouped and very unsuperficial wounds in Beau's neck, and a tumble of blood from them reached the back of his old brown leather bomber jacket, forming first a crescent, but changing to an imperfect circle, then a shifting, dripping, disintegrating rectangle as Ember watched. From somewhere fine and deep Beau got himself a small parcel of breath and, as his head went down past Ember's chest, he muttered what sounded like: 'Always, always with you, Ralph.'

God, they made Ember feel rotten, those words. Yes, Beau had seemed always with him at business deals, and Ember had resented it so much, thought that having Beau with him undid his own dignity. This view seemed intolerably arrogant to Ralph now. He must do whatever he could for Melanie, Beau's partner. Beau folded slowly on to Ember's shoes and, feeling his weight, Ralph thought sadly it might be the closest they had ever been and did not pull his feet away at once.

'In many respects this could be called a veritable House of Death, Ralphy, wouldn't you say? But four's enough, yes? Give us the little gun, there's a chum. You were never going to use it, were you?'

Us. Ember would have liked to ask who this sod with a long, red-bladed knife in his hand thought he was, and in fact who he *really* was. He stood half behind Ember, just into his peripheral vision, and so did the two men with him. At least Beau had the number right. But Ember could find no breath for questions, not even as much as Beau found for his farewell whisper. Besides, Ember knew he could not have forced his lips to get around vocabulary now. Plus, he thought the scar on his jaw line might be pumping out lymph or worse, and it would only make the filthy cascade fatten if he jogged his face about, chatting.

Chapter Four

Just before Mrs Ember left Harpur's house his two daughters arrived home with their boyfriends. All four youngsters had paint streaks across their faces, mostly green but some beige. Hazel and her boyfriend, Scott, had small beige smears on their clothes, as well. Some Saturdays the four worked free for a charity scheme, redecorating the homes of poor, elderly people.

Harpur never asked about it, because the Church organized this work. Charity was possibly all right, but contact between his children and religious organizations made him nervy, any contact, any religious organization, and he always tried to stop it. He did not want Hazel and Jill troubled. At fifteen and thirteen their minds might fall to dodgy, respectable pressures. Sunday School teaching used to torture his own early days, could still temporarily flatten him: texts and hymns would sneak back out of his kid memory box and crease Harpur. *And after this the judgement.* Or, *Just as I am without one plea.* His daughters had had enough downsides, their mother dead in the snow in a car park like that, guest semen aboard. This was a one-parent family now and he must be vigilant for them.

Iles had moved away from the sitting-room windows and lay sprawled on the hearthrug with his tea mug. He had taken off his jacket and crimson scarf and left them anyhow on the floor. He liked to think of himself as tumultuous socially. Immediately the girls and Darren and Scott arrived he stood, his breathing suddenly very laboured again. Oh, God, Harpur knew Iles would be driven feverish by the green paint across Hazel's forehead and beige stripes down her right cheek and thigh of her jeans. Always she could get him going, and unquestionably the paint would be a bonus thrill. It seemed to give a wildness, a primitiveness to her, squaw quality. Iles walked over to Hazel and fondly pulled some strands of her fringe back, so they would not touch the paint. 'There,' he said, stroking her head for too long. 'Yet green highlights could be magical, I suppose, given the right person.'

'Fuck off, Mr Iles,' Scott said.

'Yes,' Harpur said. He regarded Iles's interest in Hazel as genuine and intensely dangerous, not simply pay-back for what had happened a while ago, and for a wonderful while, between Harpur and Iles's wife, Sarah. The ACC would regard sex retaliation as miserably petty, anyway. Iles had a kind of undeniable grandeur of spirit, a slippery kind. 'Here's Mrs Margaret Ember come to visit,' he cried, a lilt to his voice. He introduced the girls and Darren and Scott.

Jill asked: 'Is your husband the one they call –'

'Ralph W. Ember, that's right,' Harpur replied.

'Who runs the club, the Monty,' Jill said, 'where all the –'

'A famed social club for business folk,' Harpur replied. 'Not your age group at all.'

'All sorts call on us here, Mrs Ember, and are welcome,' Hazel said. 'Please feel comfortable.'

'Many are women,' Jill said. 'Oh, yes, many.'

'Could you and the boys go into the dining room now?' Harpur replied. 'It's a private conversation for Mrs Ember, Mr Iles and myself.'

'Right, Mr Harpur,' Darren said.

Jill sat down in an armchair and said: 'This doesn't mean they're all *personal* matters, involving dad, Mrs Ember, just because the visitors here are often women. Sometimes women call because of police matters.'

'Has my dad been getting between you in that way of his, Mrs Ember?' Hazel asked.

'Come on, Hazel,' Scott said, 'this is your father you're talking about.'

'Between who?' Mrs Ember asked.

'You and your hubby,' Hazel replied. She also sat down. She got her woman-to-woman sympathy look on. 'Dad roves.'

'He does, but perhaps we should try to be tolerant, Hazel,' Iles replied. 'I know I do.' His voice rose towards an agony screech.

'Of course he hasn't been getting to Mrs Ember,' Jill said. 'Roved not roves.' She grew fierce and bitter, leaning forward and staring just past Hazel, over her shoulder, as if she was not worth noticing. 'Hazel *always* thinks something like that when women come here, Mrs Ember. It's not fair – not fair on dad. Hazel believes women only turn up because they've been what's called "foully wronged". Have you heard of that, Mrs Ember? It's in old books, "foully wronged". But dad's not like it now. He's got a lovely girlfriend called Denise, only nearly twenty. She's often here. His age and haircut and so on? They don't bother her so very much. And clever, too. She's at the university doing all sorts, French poetry in French about a mother pelican that bites slices from her own chest to feed her chicks. Dad's a bit like that. I don't mean biting his own chest, but really making sure we're looked after, now he's single-parent. It's a pain sometimes. I wouldn't be surprised if dad is really completely content with Denise now and doesn't go sniffing. All right, she's a bit untidy and she smokes, but she can make breakfast, a sort of breakfast. Probably she'll be here later on tonight. She stays a lot. It's steady. Steady for dad. Steadyish.'

'Into the other room now, please, ' Harpur said, opening the door for them to go. 'This is a personal matter.'

'Oh, God,' Hazel said, 'he *has* been –'

'I meant confidential,' Harpur said. 'It's part a police matter and part to do with Mrs Ember's private life. Absolutely not something we can discuss with you.'

'But is it part a police matter just because you happen to be a policeman? And is it part a private life matter because you're into her private life?' Hazel asked.

'You're so creepy and crude and smartarse, Haze,' Jill said. 'I've told you, it can't be like that – because of Denise.'

'Did you know about Denise, Mrs Ember?' Hazel asked. 'Didn't he tell you he had a steady, almost a live-in? He could probably be like that if he was making you. You're definitely attractive.'

'Hazel, stop it,' Scott said.

Hazel said: 'Dad's nice but crafty. Some of that's through being in the police, obviously. They learn it from manuals. But he's like it, anyway. He was born with it, I think.'

'There are two or three good elements to him, though, undoubtedly,' Iles said.

'Thank you, sir,' Harpur replied.

'Two,' Iles said.

When the children had gone and the communicating door was shut, Iles paced a little. He wore a plain blue shirt, probably made for him, and with the buttons covered by a fly pleat. It was a powerful, reassuring blue, like the wrapper of Cadbury's milk chocolate without the printing. He looked nourishing. He looked a carer. Iles could do this. It was thoughtful pacing. 'Mrs Ember, Margaret, I think I can say for Harpur as well as myself that we certainly recognize we have absolutely no right to infringe upon your marital decisions.' He paused for Harpur to speak. The ACC did like answers to his questions, but this was not one, and Harpur kept quiet. 'Oh, certainly not. None,' Iles said.

'Why not?' Mrs Ember replied. 'You think you run every-bloody-thing.'

40

Iles marginally waved his right hand. Perhaps it meant, Not at all. Or perhaps, That goes without saying. Responsibility darkened his eyes. Then his body jerked sharply. He staggered and uttered a tiny groan. It was as if he had been struck lethally by a sniper's bullet somewhere not immediately evident. Harpur thought the ACC must have accidentally spotted some part of himself he loathed in the mirror over the fireplace, probably his Adam's apple. He recovered at once and said: 'What I have to consider, Margaret, is the possible impact of your leaving Ralph upon police strategy here.'

'This is what I said, didn't I?' she replied.

'You did. It's what comes of being married to a kingpin. I expect you realized the break-up might have repercussions and decided to come and give us early warning. We're immensely grateful.'

Mrs Ember's small, neat body stiffened in her chair. 'I told you, I came because I might need protection and because I think if Harpur or someone equally straight – almost straight – and sensitive – half-way sensitive – spoke – and spoke again – to Ralph he could be persuaded to go wholly legit. That might change things for the good between Ralph and me – eventually. I'm not interested in the impact on sodding police strategy. *Is* there a strategy, a strategy beyond ensuring you two survive?'

Iles chuckled: 'I love scepticism in women. It makes all the s sounds whistle through their teeth.' He sat down on a straight-backed chair, stretched out his legs and looked for a while at his delicate brown slip-ons. 'It's famous, as you say, that Ralph and Manse Shale help bring a kind of business stability to this city.'

'So?'

'Harpur works at street level and is very appreciative of tranquillity there, aren't you, Harpur?'

It required a response and Harpur said: 'Has Ralph taken Beau Derek with him to the Wharf, Mrs Ember?

41

I gather Barney Coss and the women like Beau to be present, to ensure continuity. That's the talk.'

'You hear the talk and let it happen?' she asked.

'We wait,' Harpur answered.

Iles said: 'Margaret, you'll have no doubt read of the appalling turf battles and killings among drug gangs in London and Manchester and Liverpool. Daily, nightly mayhem. We've been able to avoid all that, lately, no trivial boon.'

'Are you saying I've got to stay with Ralph to make policing comfier?' she replied.

Iles gave a really good, humble frown: 'Lord, it *does* sound selfish, harsh, doesn't it? I'm sorry. But one thinks of Ralph, his pain. We don't dispute your right to leave – how could we? – but mightn't your departure be organized a little differently, perhaps made more gradual? He returns from a business trip and finds Low Pastures empty. The shock. The trauma. A note? *Thanks and goodbye, Ralph, your future's in the oven.* Devastating. He prizes you, Margaret. He prizes the children as well, but you supremely. And he depends on you. Men like Ralph, Harpur, myself – above all myself – we look strong, act strong, but we are terribly less if our women are taken from us. Myself, for instance, when Harpur was giving it to Sarah, I – Well, we can grow erratic. Yes, Ralph *is* liable to turn evil and do something extreme and grave. He's *Panicking* Ralph, after all. Panics usually paralyse him, of course. But there are other kinds of panics, panics where people grow frantically, defensively violent. It's conceivable in Ralph. You've said yourself he might come after you. He might turn on others. You ask for protection? But, no, Harpur's right, it's not really on, not off our ground, at least. And so . . . and so, who knows what? Possibly something ghastly. Then, we, or another police force, have to pull Ralph in and get him locked up – years, decades? It's the wrong time. What happens here? What happens here is a business hole and

42

God knows who struggling to replace him, fighting each other, slaughtering each other, maybe fighting Shale, too. Outside gangs. Yardies. Innocents hurt, killed. Ruin of an immaculate system. Chaos. We've had that kind of situation before.'

Mrs Ember began to weep noisily. 'Break from him gradually?' she said. 'For God's sake, Iles, this *is* gradually. It's taken me years to decide. You're looking at . . . well, at despair.'

Perhaps she thought the word lurid. She backed off from it and then only whispered it. Iles's pacing had brought him near her chair. He bent over and touched her briefly, lightly, on the shoulder. 'I know, I know, Margaret,' he said. 'A marriage – it keeps its sweet hold no matter what.'

'No, not no matter what,' she said.

'Almost,' Iles replied.

Her head was down and she did not look up now but nodded minutely. 'Ralph has goodness,' she muttered.

'We know that,' Iles replied.

'And weakness,' she said.

Iles said: 'He's villainous, sure, but not totally, and you are the reason for it, Margaret. For him to return from one of his happy, crooked business trips and find, or not find –'

Jill opened the door. 'I heard crying,' she said.

'It's all right,' Harpur replied.

From behind Jill, Hazel said: 'Has dad brought on some . . . well, deep, intimate tragedy, Mrs Ember?'

Harpur crossed the room towards them. Jill said: 'Ignore her, dad.' He closed the door again, then stood there.

Mrs Ember left her chair. She made her way quickly to the other door in the sitting room, the one to the hall and the street. 'I'm going,' she said.

'Going from here, going from Ralph?' Iles asked.

'Both. Now.'

'Despite all I've said, I admire your resolve,' Iles replied.

Perhaps he meant it. In a moment, Harpur heard the front door slam and then her Escort start up and drive away.

Iles said: 'We must go to him, Col. We owe Ralph that much. You think he's at Barney Coss's, Southampton way?'

'Possibly.'

'We find Ralphy and prepare him,' Iles said. 'Counsel him. Preserve him. Apart from anything else, he's an enduring element of the filthy landscape here. This has to be done with total gentleness, so leave it to me, Harpur. One day, when we've built a big enough case, we'll have to do Ember, obviously, but in the meantime he's valuable. He's often behaved with decent restraint.'

'We estimate he and Shale draw £600,000 each a year from drugs trading, if that's restraint,' Harpur replied.

'A lot for her to walk out on. This is courage, Harpur. The money's bought Ralph style, not guts.'

Harpur said: 'If there's any incident around Barney's place, we'll be intruding on another Force's ground without giving notice, sir.'

'What incident? Why an incident? Alarmist, Col. We're there only to see a friend, aren't we? Perhaps we could take Hazel and Jill, for the ride.

'No, I don't think so, sir.'

'We'll be back well before dawn. Sunday tomorrow.'

'No, I don't think so, sir.'

'You have your little quirks, Col.'

'Thank God.'

Iles grew grand: 'Scott, the boyfriend, a fine lad.'

'*I* think so.'

'But is he truly enough for her, Col? This is a questing girl.'

'Denise will be here soon. She'll stay with them.'

'Is Scott intellectually dauntless, has he insight, vision, aplomb?'

'Like?'

'Is he, has he, Col?'

'He's got eight GCSEs, one in Metalwork.'

Chapter Five

'So, why kill Beau? Reasonable question, Ralph, although you didn't actually ask it. It's the question you *would* ask if your talk box hadn't seized up for the moment. Oh, understandably. We heard about your panics, Ralph, and if someone gets panics I trust we know how to offer true sympathy. Think of shell-shocked Tommies muting in the Great War. You're the one who had the gun and Beau was harmless, yet we hit Beau. Why, why, why, you will certainly be thinking, and would have cried it aloud, but for the larynx seizure. And I'm going to answer. Actually, there's more than one answer. Top of the list, though – we kill Beau because he isn't *you*, Ralph. You're needed.'

'Who says I can't fucking talk?' Ember replied. *Thank God, thank God, it all came out audible, the k sounds really fighting brave. This was a man in trouble but a man in trouble who remained a man. This was that grace under pressure.*

'Oh, splendid, Ralphy.'

'I must tend him,' Ember said.

'Yes, tend him, do. We know you care for your people.'

Ember bent down to Beau. He was well gone, eyes open and duller than ever, mouth open, too, with the scattered teeth nearly all on show like a smile and a tank-trap, and not a tickle of breath. Just the same, Ember put his hand on Beau's neck as though feeling for a pulse. You had to do that. It signified hope, maybe hopeless hope, but a hope that would not expire yet because of the love you felt for this assistant, regardless of how he looked, even when alive. At home, Beau had that surprisingly presentable woman, Melanie, with a body at the edge of middle age, but *only* at the edge, and Ember would have to tell her of the death very tenderly, and provide some support, if he ever made it back.

'You'll be fine, Derek,' Ember said. He would not use Beau's nickname in the presence of this crew, although they referred to him as Beau themselves, the cheeky shits. That ought to be a name familiar only to colleagues and friends. There was mockery in it, yes, but also affection and even respect. In any case, it seemed wrong to address a corpse with a send-up name, like defacing gravestones. 'Help's near, Derek. Barney and Maud and Camilla will make sure the emergency services are notified and an ambulance comes.' He had decided it might be worth making out they knew nothing about upstairs. His mind was still capable of good deviousness. 'Hold on, Derek, friend. Summon that splendid tenacity we all know is yours.'

Crouched alongside Beau, Ember was able to gaze at the lower trouser legs and shoes of the three men who had come from behind them and were standing in a half circle on the far side of the victim now. None of the trouser legs was jeans. Ember thought they all looked like suit trousers, and the material at least decent and possibly more. Two of the suits were navy, one dark grey. These legs and feet kept very still, as though the men felt awed by his attention to Beau and by Ember's good, mad words. The shoes were all black lace-ups, of course, newish but not flashy new: excellent leather and shaping, possibly made for the wearers from a personal last, perhaps Charles Laity or Hayesbridge, and genuine stitching throughout, no damn glue. This all-round quality was bound to mean distinguished people of dark and established status, people who would take it in their stride not just to kill Beau but elite traders like the three in the games room, too, and chip away at their faces and so on before or after. Their hates had calibre. Perhaps they wore dungarees and plastic covers for their shoes then. Ember could examine very closely everything from the knees down and saw no staining. One of the pairs of shoes was pretty small for a man, a six or seven. Someone miniature? Often they were the worst.

Ember stood. 'Right,' he said. He wanted to show he was used to being in command, not just of himself but situations and folk. Everything in his body worked, legs, tongue, arms. He had no nausea or paralysis, his bladder and bowels were obedient, and the sweating stayed contained. He could tell as a certainty now that his jaw scar had not leaked. Unbowed was what he undoubtedly felt. He had not run. He had not opted out, despite pressure from a wife.

'Ralph, I don't consider we should ask you to undertake discussions with us here, in the presence of Beau's body, nor in the games room, clearly for the same reason. Look, don't give us all that bollocks about Barney and the other two turning up, there's a pal.'

'Discussions?' Ember replied.

'Entirely positive in nature. This was what I meant by remarking we needed one of you alive. Well, you, as it turns out.'

'Will Barney, Maud and Camilla be parties to these discussions? It's their property, after all.'

'I've said don't fuck us about, haven't I, Ralphy?'

He thought these men must be big city urban, probably London. If any of them were local there would almost certainly have been at least one pair of yachting shoes and leisure time dark slacks, the kind of gear Barney usually wore. Ember had heard no accent, and definitely not cockney or Hampshire. This one's voice sounded languid and good school, or imitation languid and good school. Three-quarters of whites in the profession talked like that and the other quarter like Beau or Mansel Shale, a slovenly disgrace. Of the three-quarters who talked nicely, half had genuinely been at good schools and, usually, one of the most chic universities, not Bangor, North Wales.

'Positive in the sense that Barney dead is not an end but the way to opportunity for you, Ralph. We're thrilled at your prospects. I thought we could go to the conservatory. It's as much a conservatory as the fucking games room is a games room.'

The four of them moved towards a door leading to the rear of the house, Ember ahead, the three very close behind. He had been in the conservatory on previous visits. Then it had contained no plants but a ruined trampoline, two disintegrating kennels and an age-old sewing machine worked by pedal. Barney seemed to want to make sure Tiderace never got into *Homes and Gardens*, in case the publicity caused questions about where his money came from. All this junk was still there, plus a couple of old, unconnected freezers, one with the door off the top hinge and hanging lopsidedly open. There were three deck chairs and two straight-backed canvas chairs. They all sat down.

'Loyalty to Barney and the two lumps might make you feel wary of us, Ralph. We know we must expect that.'

'Yes,' Ember said.

'Yet rapprochement is what we seek. My dear Ralph, if we are to replace Barney and his gals as bulk substance importers, what sense in eliminating a major, polished distributor such as yourself, with an operation running brilliantly in your area, and the police so understanding across there? Iles? Harpur? Those the lads?' He had kept Ember's Bodyguard pistol in his hand since Ralph gave it up and waved it gently now, not a threat, more a cheery conversational gesture. His voice grew apologetic. 'But when I say "we" – and I do, time and again – you're going to ask who is or are this we? Why imagine, here "we" are, knifing one of your noble team to death and trying to explain it away, yet there haven't even been proper introductions. I'm Bridges, as in the poet, but no relation, not that I know of: Andrew Cartier Bridges.' He had been holding the knife when they first spoke to Ember, but Ralph thought someone else had done the major work and that Bridges gave only a late, token jab, comradeship. Ember didn't know where this notion came from but it was strong in him.

'I've heard of that name,' Ember replied. His voice was still solid, no squeaking or paltriness. Ember had picked up tales of Bridges as a would-be high-flyer London way or the Home Counties. Well this was almost a Home County, and to kill Barney et cetera was high high-flying.

Bridges said: 'And then my associates, Charles Paul Merryweather and Cosmo York.'

'These names I know, too,' Ember replied. Yes, stylish sidekickery to Bridges.

'I was hoping you'd say so, Ralph. They're fond of recognition. They can be damn touchy, especially Cosmo.' He tapped York on the shoulder with the pistol butt, a jolly reproach for temperament. 'If you're called fucking Cosmo you expect to be fucking noticed.'

'And, of course, of course, we've all heard of *you*, Ralph, heard often,' York said.

'Why else would we be in this meeting now, you still alive and functioning, Ralph?' Bridges said. He was white, genial-looking behind thin-framed, square-glassed spectacles, over six feet, slim but not fit-slim, slim bordering on frail. His hands were wispy. Even the small gun seemed bulky with those skinny fingers around it, like string on a parcel. Ember considered that Bridges personally would not have the strength or vim to do Beau the way he had been done with the knife, not the original, deep blows. Either that or Bridges knew a lot about knives and the human neck and could stab with such finesse that no big power or commitment was needed. This idea scared Ember now, but definitely not a scare to panic degree. It was wise fright, healthy fright, fright that could also be

50

called alertness. He did not even get watery eyes. Bridges' lips and mouth were large for such a gawky body, as though Nature had spotted he would have to eat a lot to stay gaunt. The great double-breasted suit could not give him solidity. He looked like a single sick flower in a fine vase. You could see why he would be avid for the plus of occupational glory. Presence he thirsted for.

Bridges said: 'Ralph, we'll be proud of association with someone who has built the kind of social and commercial structure that lets him keep one daughter, Venetia – gorgeous name – at École Les Haies, 27–35 Rue Maisy, Poitiers, and the other at the smartest private place for girls in your locality, Corton House, Bay Street.'

Merryweather said: 'You see, Ralph, we do know you. We've put time in. Locations often tell a tale.'

Ember said: 'My children are –'

'Not involved at all with the business,' Bridges said. 'Well, we hope not, Ralph. Certainly too young for directorships.' He laughed quietly for a while. A laugh, even a quiet laugh, looked like a full day's work for someone so physically slight. 'But there's every chance they'll grow up – I mean grow up into people quite as gifted and mesmeric as their daddy.'

'We'll do every damn thing we can to keep them out of things, believe me, especially if things turn rough, as things can,' York said. He grunt-talked, the accent possibly Lancashire, and didn't seem comfortable opening his mouth, got stuck on one word. There was something cat-like about his face, the width and immobility, the sparse moustache. On the way to the conservatory, Ember had noticed a precision and nimbleness to the way York moved, also cat-like. He was middle height, about thirty-seven or eight, like Bridges. He had a fine, long head with gingery hair balding from front and back. His neck was thick and very smooth, and a quick vision came to Ember of a studded flea collar on it. The knife artisan?

'As a matter of fact, I'm about to pull right out of the

51

substance business,' Ember said. 'Sorry. Bad timing, but I'm at that sort of age. Early retirement beckons temptingly. My family – all that. This is not some casual idea. I've always planned to go about now.'

'Oh, we hardly think so, Ralph,' Merryweather replied with plenty of good nature. He seemed younger, not much over thirty.

'It would be much more than early,' Bridges said. 'Premature. Your daughters – schooling to be finished, university fees, wedding receptions.'

'We still think of you as like the young Charlton Heston, as do so many others, Ralph,' Merryweather said. 'Your best days now.'

'Chuck Heston? Me? That's a new one,' Ember replied. 'But I think I'm entitled to make my own decisions. I've been around long enough.' He was in one of the straight canvas chairs and sat very upright, assertively. The door from the house to the conservatory had been left open and he could see Beau's feet comfortably together, the soles of his shoes in view.

'Certainly right as to the first,' Bridges said, 'your decisions. Surely wrong on the second. You'll be around for productive decades, Ralph. You're indispensable to our scenario.'

Merryweather said: 'It's the very fact of your absolute right to choices, Ralphy, which we're sure will make you choose to keep trading, as part of our new network, and a crucial part.' Merryweather had a large, instructive voice and Ember thought that possibly, after all, *he*, not York, might have been the lad to do most of the work on Beau, and possibly the other three.

'Oh, at least crucial,' Bridges cried. He was sitting in one of the striped canvas deck chairs and looked insignificant there, like a crumb on a tablecloth. 'We think above all of trading opportunities via your club, the Monty.'

Ember was enraged. They would taint the Monty? They *thought* they would taint the Monty. If they had done so much research on him didn't they realize that the club was his most esteemed possession, the centre of all his finest ambitions? Nothing could be permitted to degrade the Monty's future. They must be made to know this. Ember said: 'For years it's been my ambition to –'

'Go totally straight,' Merryweather said, 'and upgrade that fucking sleaze pit club to God knows what standards – White's or the Carlton. Such nonsensical piss, Ralph. You must know it.'

Did he? Was it daft fantasy, his hope? No, by God. No. Ember said: 'The Monty will –'

'Obviously, the cleansing recently accomplished in the games room makes your projected retirement unnecessary and undesirable,' Merryweather said. 'Barney used to screw you and other wholesalers on deals – Barney, of course, only mouthpiecing that frenzied, tentacled greedster, Maud. So, naturally you'd grow disenchanted and think about an exit, and do reveries in your cosy, deranged way about the glorious flowering of the Monty.'

Ember cried out: 'Not reveries. This is –'

'We've grieved over your plight because the buzz claimed Barney treated you financially worse than any others, though who knows why?' Merryweather asked. 'It could be said, indeed, that one reason for our taking an unfriendly view of Barney and the girls like that, at last, was the pain we all felt on your behalf. I've often heard Andrew Bridges groan aloud in kitchens, aircraft, churches, newsagents, "Poor Ralph W. Ember!" He generally gave your full name. It was comprehensive sympathy.'

Merryweather seemed affected by his own words. He stood up from a deck chair and walked back and forth across the conservatory, picking his way carefully around the trampoline and freezers. He was black, lean, small, wearing similar unemphatic spectacles to those of Bridges. Behind the lenses his eyes had grown dark but brilliant with passionate resentment at Barney and the women's trade practices. York had nimbleness, but Merryweather had something else – an oddly heavy-footed, imperturbable tread for such a pocket figure. The small shoes were his. He walked like the New Testament shepherd, methodically scouring the countryside for Number One Hundred. He could kill all right.

'Your wife, Ralph, sharp in the very best sense,' he said.

'Charles handles all our research and fancy language side,' Bridges said.

'What do I mean by "in the very best sense", I wonder?' Merryweather asked.

'Tell us, do, Charlie,' Bridges replied. 'Don't tease, there's a pet.' From deep in the deck chair he playfully raised the Bodyguard revolver, stiff-armed, finger on the trigger, and pointed the gun without wavering at Merryweather's temple or right eye. Bridges spoke along the pistol's short barrel, but the words were for Ember now, not Merryweather. 'I don't want you to feel any ambiguity about who's Number One here, Ralph. Occasionally, people listening to Charles feel his wordage is bound to indicate leadership, like Kennedy – or Nelson Mandela, in the circumstances. That might confuse you, because if you've heard of us, as you say you have, you'll have heard that it's Andrew Cartier Bridges who's master, with Charlie Merryweather and Yorky as devotees. And this is indeed the case, regardless of Charles's sparkling bullshit.'

Merryweather continued, apparently indifferent to the gun and Bridges' chat on the Chain of Being. 'When I say "in the very best sense", Ralphy, I want to indicate that the sharpness I speak of as natural to Margaret is not some bossy, niggling, misery-making quality. I mean, she sees what's what and is intent always on your welfare. I think of her as the kind of lady who would bring a polished mind to bear on professional matters, and she would see the profoundly improper way Barney and the women

forced their savage terms on you. Consequently, it's possible she would want you to quit the vocation – give up. An
influence, Ralph? Indeed, *the* influence, Ralph? She might
imagine Barney's terms were the only terms available.
Now, though, in this new, sweet arrangement with
Andrew Cartier Bridges, Yorky and one's self – in that
fucking order, out of full, creepy deference to Andrew
Cartier Bridges – when your intelligent wife, Margaret,
hears of the delicate little shift of power there has been in
the mercantile tableau, she will appreciate that your future
and hers and the children's lies in a grand mutuality with
Andrew Cartier Bridges, Yorky and Charles Paul Merryweather. She will see this, I know.'

Bridges had lowered the revolver during the first part of
this address but raised it again to point at the same eye or
Merryweather's temple when the growling phrase about
deference to Bridges came.

Ember said: 'I think you boys know I'm not someone
who can be browbeaten or manipulated,' giving the three
of them a separate, personal smile, each smile different, yet
each containing geniality, manliness and non-compromise,
Ralph was sure.

'No, we didn't know that, Ralphy,' Bridges replied. He
swung the gun around and seemed to aim it at Ember's
temple or right eye, instead of Merryweather's. Bridges
held the Bodyguard like that in his thin-armed, stiff-armed
way.

'We need him, Andrew,' York said quickly. 'We didn't
need the two, himself *and* Beau – dangers of a harsh
alliance against us. All right. But, now, Ralph's the only
one in his region except for Shale, and Shale takes supplies
from elsewhere. From elsewhere so far. You need to consider all this. We've told Ralph that Beau had to go because
he was not Ralph, and this is like true. What I feel – my
own feeling as to deciding who stays alive, him or Beau,
my own feeling is that the decision turned out a reasonable

decision and that Ralphy might truly be the right one to keep alive and continue with. That's my true feeling.'

Bridges seemed to consider this. Christ, he *must* consider it. Ember felt the unmistakable onrush of the fullest, bleakest panic. All the traditional degrading symptoms battled to be tops. It sounded like a close thing between him and Beau for death, and Bridges might still decide in his deck chair they were both dispensable.

'That scar on your jaw seems to have opened up, Ralphy,' Merryweather said, 'and is weeping puce dregs.'

'What?' Ember muttered and put up a hand to grab at it. His fingers met total dryness. Of course they did. And he could still move his arm and hand and say 'What?' with fine precision, couldn't he?

Bridges and Merryweather had a smile, the same sort of smile, not meant to provide comfort. York seemed a bit ashamed of the teasing. Bridges said: 'Charles came across that in the research, the Ralphy stigmata bit. Charles has a gift. He unearths all sorts.' Bridges kept the pistol on Ember for another half-minute, then let his arm fall to hang over the side of the deck chair. 'Someone has to carry the torch in your diocese, Ralph, and who could equal you, except for Beau and Mansel Shale? And, as Yorky said, Beau has lapsed and Shale is fixed up with others, for now. You pick who you want to go back with you to keep a brotherly and constructive eye, Charles or Yorky. As we've pointed out, we utterly respect your precious right to choose. I'd recommend Yorky because Charles is sure to make a play for your missus – his style – knowing all her preferences and weaknesses through research and profiling, her kinks, such as on top or under or doggy.'

Chapter Six

Iles said: 'I think we'd better break in and have a quick look, Col.'

'The house is completely dark, sir. I've been right around. Barney Coss and the women are probably away boating. They do a lot of it. That kind of country. The house will be locked up, perhaps alarmed.'

'I think we'd better break in and have a quick look.'

'I can read you, you know,' Harpur said.

'I hope so. I prize transparency.'

'Ember's not here, sir.'

'We've come this far, Harpur.'

'Yes, and found the house empty.'

'This we do not know,' Iles replied.

They were parked near a river jetty a little way from Tiderace, the ACC at the wheel. Harpur had just returned to the car after a reconnaissance on foot. A huge blue and white catamaran lay moored nearby. Tied up at another jetty closer to Tiderace was getting on for a million pounds' worth of pretty yacht called *Modesty*, ropes clacking busily against its masts in the wind.

'We've done what we can for Ember,' Harpur said.

'He's important to us. I have to save him from the effects of appalling shock, Col.'

'Yes, sir, but it was always long odds against intercepting him here.'

'I can sympathize with a man who's losing a wife,

Harpur – this is quite apart from the policy aspect. Do you understand that – a man who's losing a wife?'

'I lost a wife.'

'You noticed?' Iles replied.

'It's becoming obsessive in you, sir, this empathy.'

'That's me, Col. My soul goes out to others. Poor Ralph.' Iles nodded a couple of times in what could be deep, engulfing sadness or tactics. 'Obsessive?' he asked. The ACC gazed with mild respect across his dark car, then breathed out lengthily and with a tremor, like someone who took on the pain of others: 'Are you saying I'm fucking mad, you ponce, Harpur?' he asked.

'Of course you are, sir,' Harpur replied.

'I do wonder about it.'

'But mad only now and then.'

'Thanks, Col.'

'Now.'

'Ever thought Ember might want to move into bulk distribution?' Iles replied. 'Displace Barney? Ralph would be bewitched by the sight of yachts. He'd feel humiliated when he came down here to call. Ember couldn't put up with that.'

'Ember might come out of it all, according to his wife. Remember?'

'Sometimes he and Beau stay here overnight, don't they?' Iles said.

'We used to do surveillance when they came on this trip. You stopped it – thought it could look like harassment, especially off our ground.' Harpur tried to recall whether inquiries done then named the yacht *Modesty* as Barney's.

'Sometimes Ralph and Beau stay here overnight, don't they?' Iles replied.

'Yes, occasionally, they would stop over,' Harpur said.

'I like policing to be humane, enlightened, pure, Col.'

'You're famed for it, sir.'

'That's why I pulled the tails off. We're not still in the

days of gumshoeing folk until they snap, I hope.' He looked towards Tiderace. 'Yes, better break in. Perhaps the household plus guests have gone to bed early. If Ember's giving it to one of the women it might be on condition the lights are out. Crumpled old pieces, aren't they?'

'You mean you want to break in there while the house might be occupied?'

'Are you saying I'm fucking mad, you ponce, Harpur?'

'Or you want *me* to break in.'

'Then let me in at the front door, Col,' Iles replied. 'Clearly, I can't take a direct part in totally illegal violence on someone else's property and in another police force's domain.' He had a chuckle about the preposterousness of this. 'I'm an assistant chief constable, operations, for Christ's sake. All right, this *is* an operation, but I have my integrity to think of.'

'I've heard of that.'

'If Ember's here we might be able to reach him without waking any of the others and tell him confidentially, gently, compassionately, about the death of his marriage,' Iles said. 'My only purpose, but a worthwhile one, I think.'

'It would need communication skills, if he's in bed with Maud or Camilla or both.'

Iles took a moment to visualize it. 'Oh, God, all that ancient breath. But I understand women of their age sleep damn profoundly after satisfaction,' Iles said. 'It's chemical.' He climbed out of the big unmarked Rover.

Harpur stayed in the passenger seat and while the driver's door was still open said: 'I can fucking read you, you know, sir.'

'I hope so, Harpur, I –'

'This farcical bloody expedition – you only wanted it because you hoped I'd let Hazel and Jill come. Or Hazel. Now, you've got to make something of the trip, anyway, and sod the risk.'

'She wanted to come, Col. Children adore night motoring. It stirs them.'

'I don't want her stirred,' Harpur replied.

Iles was bent at the open door to speak. The ACC's face looked sad again and thin with longing. He gazed at Harpur once more, now with eyes that said he might have regarded him as friend as well as colleague, if Harpur had only been able to get some style together. 'I pray I never become the kind of blankly obstructive parent you are, Harpur. You remind me so much of Edward Moulton-Barrett.'

'That right?'

'You've been told this before, I expect.'

'People shout it at me in the street.'

'You see the resemblance?'

'Did he break into someone's house at night trying to find a drugs king far from home and bring him marriage counselling?'

'Elizabeth Barrett Browning's monstrously repressive father,' Iles said. He stood back and struck the roof of the Rover two small, triumphant blows with his fist. A smile blazed in the night. 'You'll make entry to Tiderace seem simple, Col, I know it. You have my confidence.'

'Grand.'

'It's your kind of project, Harpur. You love breaking into villains' castles and reading all that can be read about them in the decor and fittings.'

'On my own ground, where I'm the law.'

'Where *I'm* the law. There'll be no alarms. Could someone like Barney risk an alarm, for fuck's sake? Would he want police to swarm if it went off and start nosing all through his home and papers?'

'Somebody will have noticed the car,' Harpur replied. 'People are vigilant in this kind of loaded area. Two men walking towards the house will be remembered. There'll be comebacks.'

'Still searching for a friend of ours, Col, that's all.' Iles hurried to Harpur's side of the car and opened the passenger door, standing back like a chauffeur. Harpur sat a few moments longer before joining him in the street. The ACC closed the door, then moved around and shut the driver's also. He locked up. They made their way towards Tiderace. The ACC said: 'If you inadvertently run into any of the people of the house in there, I expect you'll easily think up some tale to explain why you've forced your way into the premises so late.'

'Will I?'

'Do nothing provocative, Harpur.'

'Breaking in is provocative.'

Iles said: 'Any noise of trouble – gunplay, violence, calls for aid, anything like that, I'll abandon secrecy and probably come in somehow to help you, Col.'

'Probably? Somehow?'

'Would I let you down, Col?' No, he would not. Harpur had to concede this, just as he had to concede Iles possessed the integrity he spoke of: or a *kind* of integrity. They turned into the wide Tiderace drive. There was an old Astra parked near the house, no other car. Ember drove a Saab these days, didn't he? Iles said: 'Think of it as a political act, Harpur. Ralph means no bloodshed in the streets. The Government was definitely more or less in favour of reducing street bloodshed the last time I heard.'

Chapter Seven

Almost all the lights seemed to be on in Harpur's house when he and Iles arrived back from Tiderace at just before 1.30 a.m. Iles said: 'I think I'd better come in with you, Col. Some disturbance?'

'I'll be all right.'

'You've had enough stress tonight,' Iles replied.

'Yes, I don't want you in there flashing old hormones.'

Iles drove away. Jill must have heard the car and came out from the sitting room to the hall and opened the front door for Harpur. She stretched up to kiss him on the cheek. 'There's tea made. A visitor,' she murmured. She had an old tracksuit over her pyjamas.

'God, another one.'

'We were asleep. A Mr Gurd,' she said, still keeping things to a whisper.

'Who?'

'He's searching. Like a quest? It's urgent, dad. Really ringing the doorbell. Woke up all of us, Denise included.'

'Searching for what, who?'

'Shouldn't it be "for whom?"' Jill replied. 'For somebody. But won't say who. Not to Hazel or me or Denise.'

They went into the big sitting room, Harpur's favourite now all his dead wife's bloody books had been got rid of and the pushy shelving. Who wanted to live in a room where titles like *Edwin Drood* and *Journal of the Plague Year* were on show? 'Here's my father at last, Mr Gurd,' Jill said. 'He's quite often out late. It's duty and that sort of thing.'

Harpur did not recognize him. Gurd stood to shake hands. He was middle-aged, middle height, ill dressed by Iles's standards though not Harpur's, falsely confident, opaque, perhaps trained in ritual friendliness. Harpur thought possibly a cinema manager, financial adviser who needed advice or sub-postmaster. 'Can I help you, Mr Gurd?'

'I was just saying – my as it were *quest* is tragic, certainly, but then one sees and hears so much of it these days, doesn't one, the drifting apart, the failure of families to hold together?'

'Definitely a factor of our age,' Hazel replied. 'It's in Sociology. The nuclear family got nuked.'

'Of course, I don't mean *your* family, Mr Harpur. I heard from the children that this is a single-parent household, but because your wife, Megan, is unfortunately dead.'

'Was killed,' Harpur replied.

'If she hadn't been they'd probably have broken up,' Hazel said.

'You hard cow,' Jill replied.

'But right,' Hazel said.

'Right but hard,' Jill replied.

'I think you and Hazel could go back to bed now,' Harpur said. 'Thank you very much for what you have done.'

Jill asked: 'Didn't Ilesy want to come in with you, dad, when he saw all the lights and knew Hazel must be up?'

'Shut it, body odour princess,' Hazel said.

'Mr Iles was very keen to get home,' Harpur replied. 'He has a wife and child, you know, and hates separation.'

'My!' Jill said.

Gurd said: 'No real idea where Derek might be, you see, Mr Harpur.'

'Derek?' Harpur said. This man had something to do with Beau?

'Not with any precision – no street or even district. From somewhere his mother had heard he might be in this city. That's as far as her information went, and it's information based on not much more than rumour, I gather, and a rumour she heard several years ago. However, one acts on what one has.'

'Dad's not bad at finding people if he's interested,' Jill said. 'And sometimes he is. Watch his eyes. If they're like unchanged goldfish water he's not interested. If they're like burned toast he is. He's got what's called contacts, Mr Gurd. Heard of contacts? They see things and maybe tell him. The world's full of whispers. He might have to pay. There's funds. This is how being a detective works. People think it's just having rubber soles.'

'Then – and this is the tragic aspect, Mr Harpur – when his mother begins to sink towards – I must say it – towards death, really sink, she longs to see Derek once more, yearns to end the estrangement,' Gurd replied. 'Perhaps say good-bye to him, put things right with him, if possible.' The step-by-step rhythm of the phrasing might mean Gurd followed none of the occupations Harpur had shortlisted, but was a ladies' hairdresser or Baptist minister. Gurd said: 'She asks me to try to find him. Derek is not my son, of course. Not as it were blood. I've only met him twice, a long time ago. Although he's unusual, I didn't object to him. I'm his mother's second husband. But could I refuse her request? Could I?'

'Never, Mr Gurd,' Jill answered.

Gurd said: 'So you'll ask how I come to be here.' His voice was bright and confiding. 'Well, when I go to the main police station with Derek's pictures – ancient pic-

64

tures, I fear – yes, ancient and possibly no longer accurate, but a constable seems to recognize them all the same and says to come out to your house, Mr Harpur, because you might be in touch with Derek in the course of your . . . well, work. Naturally, I was hesitant, but he said it did not matter about the lateness, if the matter is urgent.'

'We have people here at all sorts of hours, believe me, Mr Gurd,' Jill said. 'This house is famous. We're in the phone book.'

'And it *is* urgent,' Gurd said. 'I don't know how long she'll last.' He lowered his head.

'I'm sorry,' Harpur replied.

'You did right, Mr Gurd,' Jill said. 'This is how marriages ought to be, even second marriages, especially when one of the pair is being rushed towards death.'

'We considered it very sad and a priority to look after our visitor, dad,' Hazel said. 'We tried to get you via the mobile, but it was switched off, as ever.'

Harpur said: 'I was on a – I didn't want a bell sounding.'

'Was this a hazardous, secret task, dad?' Jill asked. 'Aren't you getting doddery for that?'

'I expect it means Derek has fallen into crime if you know him, Mr Harpur – a detective chief superintendent.' Gurd's square, beefy face kept its mock-up amiable look, but was basically blank, unreadable.

'Dad knows many, many sorts, Mr Gurd,' Jill replied. 'Some *really* respectable, women or men. Quite a few trust him. At least quite a few. I did a list once.'

'I told Mr Gurd you were away,' Denise said. 'We didn't know where and for how long, but he wanted to come in and wait.' She had one of Harpur's old raincoats over her nightdress and was standing at the sideboard to pour Harpur's tea. The coat brushed the floor. Harpur had seen her dressed like this before when people called late and unexpectedly at the house and she was sleeping here. Once it was the chief and his wife. The coat did what it could to de-sex her but it could not do much, thank God. For Harpur, her bare feet relayed quite a charge, the symmetry of her heels. She sometimes said he had a fetish about feet.

'We prepared a snack for Mr Gurd because we were sure that's how you'd want us to handle it, dad,' Jill said.

Three photographs lay on the floor in front of where Gurd sat in a red leather armchair. Harpur recognized Beau. 'Yes, I know Derek,' Harpur said. 'To us, though, he's Derek Millward.'

'His mother's name before we married,' Gurd replied. 'He's entitled.'

Jill said: 'Dad, isn't this Derek the one they call –'

'Derek Millward, yes,' Harpur replied.

'The officer at headquarters said Derek might work with a man called Ralph who keeps a club, the Montgomery,' Gurd said. 'This could be a line in the search. Ember?'

'The Monty. Business colleagues,' Harpur replied.

'What kind of business?' Gurd asked. 'To do with the club?'

'This would be various enterprises,' Harpur said. 'Derek has some terrific skills.'

'Oh,' Gurd replied. 'Oh, I see.'

Hazel said: 'Under the terrible stresses of life many are driven into behaviour which is not, on the face of it, completely all right, Mr Gurd.'

'Hazel's *so* understanding,' Jill said.

'In the whirl of life's kaleidoscope some will come out like Mr Iles and dad, and some will come out like Mr Ember and Derek,' Hazel replied. 'This is well known. There's not really much difference between the two sorts. It's what's referred to as "nature and nurture". It's all in Sociology.'

'I'm sure Beau Derek's mother will want to see him, regardless,' Jill said.

66

'*Whose* mother?' Gurd asked.

'Dad will take you to find him,' Hazel said.

'I'm really grateful to your three daughters for looking after me,' Gurd said.

'Denise is not his daughter,' Jill replied.

'Oh,' Gurd said.

'She looks as if she might be his daughter, doesn't she, but really she's his . . . you know,' Jill said. 'Nothing sleazy. They're lovely with each other. It's quite mature. Denise was probably around before my mother died. But *mum* most likely had something going as well, Mr Gurd. You know how it is with people born in the sixties. Were *you* born in the sixties – the way folk seemed actually to start life with a non-stop sexual itch? Denise is nineteen and dad's thirty-seven, so it just about could be, father, daughter. She's a university student and will have a degree soon – so clever, but she still stays with dad. Habit is strong. She was looking after us while dad and Mr Iles went off on some police trip tonight. Confidential. But it probably *really* was a police trip. Sometimes Denise starts wondering and getting edgy when dad is out late, but it probably *really* was a police trip. Mr Iles wanted us to go, or Hazel to go, but naturally dad said no, because of Des Iles. Dad likes Denise to be sleeping here when he gets back from work at night. Like I said, he's sixties and needs all that. We think Denise is quite responsive, being genuinely in love with him and almost youthful. But no sleeping, anyway, tonight because of this crisis.'

'I'm sorry for waking you all,' Gurd said.

'Our role,' Hazel replied.

'It's over now, thanks very much, girls,' Harpur said.

In the old Fiesta from the police pool that he was using these days, Harpur drove Gurd to the flat Beau shared with his partner, Melanie, in Ambrose Street.

Gurd said: 'I would never tell his mother Derek's a villain.'

'That's a kindness.'

'How big a villain?'

'He's not too bad.'

'You mean he's not big enough to be too bad?'

'Like that.'

'When did you last see him?'

Harpur might have said he tried to see him tonight, him *and* Ralph Ember. But there was nobody at Tiderace, as Harpur had expected and had told the ACC before breaking in. Or there was nobody findable by Iles and Harpur in a good scouring of the premises: a house full of rubbish and rubbishy furniture and a smell of carbolic, no people.

There appeared to be nobody at Beau's place, either. Harpur rang the bell half a dozen times and rapped the door, but without an answer. He turned the Fiesta and made for Ralph Ember's club in Shield Terrace. Ember was usually there last thing, to close up and get the takings into his strongroom.

'Ralph!' Harpur called, as they entered. 'Here's a treat. The club's looking as ever, distinguished yet welcoming.'

Ember was sitting behind the bar at a small desk he used for working on his accounts. Harpur thought he appeared haggard and scared, but not near one of his standard breakdowns. The Monty *did* look good. Because of the care Ember gave the place, it would be very hard to find signs of damage from any of the hellish brawls and occasional shootings that happened here, about women or grassing or share-outs or mocked male wigs. Except for the clientele, the club could have been mistaken for an entirely decent spot in some wholesome quarter of the city. Ember stood now and took a bottle of Kressmann Armagnac from the shelf near him. He put two balloon glasses on the bar and poured. Then he brought a half-pint handled mug and made up Harpur's drink of a third gin and the rest cider. He pushed one of the Armagnacs towards Gurd and came around the bar to join them with the other balloon in his hand. 'Derek Millward's mother's dying, Ralph,' Harpur said, taking a good pull at his drink.

'Oh, dear,' Ember replied.

'This is Mr Gurd, his stepfather. There was a coolness lately between Derek and his mother.'

'That can happen,' Ember replied. 'So very regrettable.' He put a hand comfortingly on Gurd's shoulder. 'This must be an awful strain for you.'

'Mr Gurd wants to take Derek back to be reconciled.'

Ember said: 'How very worthwhile. I'd certainly like to help with such a good mission.' He was sitting on a stool alongside Harpur but stood now and looked carefully about the crowded club. 'I don't think Derek has been in tonight.' For thoroughness, Ember changed his position slightly, so he could examine the far corners of the big room. 'No, I don't think so.' Harpur saw a balding, ginger-haired man with cat-like face and thin moustache apparently watching Ember hard. The customer had been playing one of the fruit machines but stood back from it now and followed Ember's gaze around the bar, as if trying to guess what he was looking for. Ember ignored him, and ignored him. Ember called the barman and asked if he had seen Derek.

'Beau?' the barman replied. 'No.'

'Sorry,' Ember said. 'His flat?'

'No,' Harpur said. 'Nor Melanie.'

'Oh?' Ember replied.

'Beau?' Gurd asked. 'Your daughter called him that, Mr Harpur. What does it mean?'

'I've been away most of the day and evening, so I'm not altogether in touch,' Ember said.

'Ah,' Harpur replied.

'London. A tour of my vintners. It's the time of year for restocking the cellar.'

'And admirably you do it, I hear,' Harpur said. 'Derek didn't go with you?'

'Derek?'

Gurd said: 'I heard he was a business associate.'

'Derek? Associate?' Ember replied.

'There's some connection still, isn't there, Ralph?' Harpur asked.

'Derek will handle a job for me now and then, yes,' Ember replied. 'And handle it well. Intermediary work or transport. But nothing major or regular, obviously. And certainly not wine buying. This is something I have to do solo. All the blame's mine if it's wrong! Enjoyable but taxing. A very long day. I've come straight here.'

'Haven't been home?' Harpur asked.

'I like to be on the premises last thing.'

'Absolutely,' Harpur replied. 'One or two new faces about?'

'Are there?' Ember said. 'All properly signed in, Mr Harpur.'

'I expect so,' Harpur replied. 'It makes me uneasy to see people I don't recognize in the Monty.'

'But why?'

'How's Margaret, and the children?' Harpur replied.

'Fine, fine.'

'You haven't spoken to her this evening, have you?' Harpur said. 'I mean, in case Derek has been in touch.'

'In touch? Beau . . . Derek wouldn't ring the house. Why would he? It's not that sort of arrangement between us, you know. Casual. As and when.'

'Have you spoken to her?' Harpur asked.

'Margaret? It's late now. I wouldn't be popular ringing at 2 a.m.' He topped up Gurd's Armagnac and his own and added some gin to Harpur's glass. 'I feel really troubled about not being able to help you find Derek, Mr Gurd,' he said.

'Not your fault at all,' Gurd replied.

'Such sad circumstances,' Ember said.

'Not your fault at all, Ralph,' Harpur said.

'No, I know, but just the same,' Ember replied. 'You should leave an address and number, in case I bump into him. But presumably Derek would know where to come.'

'It's the shortness of time,' Gurd replied.

'Heartbreaking,' Ember said. 'Those of us with settled families should be thankful, shouldn't we, Mr Harpur?'

Chapter Eight

In their bedroom Ember gave a scream, a scream lasting for as long as his breath would hold, and which finished in small, pity-me, staccato gasps. This scream he longed to think of as a howl, but knew it was a scream. A howl would have suited the scale of his grief: desperate, larger, nobler, more animal. His voice-box – dried up and part paralysed – would only manage the scream for now, though, and it came out thin, tattered and childlike. Ember wanted to think of himself as a formidable, terribly injured creature, say a wolf or mountain leopard, but this scream sounded like something Panicking Ralphy might have uttered, if Panicking Ralphy could utter anything when panicking.

The bleak, neat emptiness of the bed should not have been such a heavy shock. In his hand was Margaret's letter, brought from downstairs. *I'm going, Ralph, for famous reasons much chewed over. It's time. You will have to believe this next bit. I asked the children separately whether they wanted to stay or come with me. Both said they would come with me. I will have to consider their schooling. In due course, I may be in touch about finance, but not at present. I have taken from the emergency fund. I think this WOULD be regarded as an emergency, wouldn't it? I know you could trace us if you wished, but don't, please. Bye, Margaret.*

Despite the letter he at once checked the children's bedrooms and in Fay's fiercely bit a teddy bear twice in its beige stomach, causing visible splits. The cleanness of the holes made him proud. This was real jaw strength and magnificent teeth. He thought that if he bit only once it would look like a kind of lunacy, but twice made the biting more intentional. Probably it would be only her second-string teddy, though. She had taken the main one. Any man should be prepared for betrayal by a woman, but disloyalty from children was hauntingly sad. All the same, as Ember used two fingers to clean some of the bear stuffing from his mouth, he did not sob. The scream had been enough.

Even without the letter, he should have anticipated catastrophe. *How's Margaret and the children? You haven't spoken to her this evening, have you?* In the club, Harpur's filthy, caring fucking words had made him uneasy, and he had wondered even then whether that second question meant, *You haven't spoken to her this evening, Ralph, and you couldn't have, because she's not there.* What did the sod know? The sod always knew a lot. Whenever Harpur came to the Monty he brought some unpleasantness, some threat. Of course, it would always be worse when that imperial yob, Iles, was with him, but even solo Harpur knew how to cause nerve-judder. Probably all police did, unless you were paying.

As soon as Harpur and Gurd left the club, Ember had rung Low Pastures to see things were all right. He got only the answerphone. That was disturbing, and yet normal enough: Margaret would often switch over if she wanted uninterrupted sleep. Nevertheless, Ember grew eager to leave for home and began to shut down the club several minutes early. Around the fruit machines, the Camrose-Horton family were deep into a champagne and vol-au-vent celebration marking today's Not Guilty for their grandmother-mother-wife on money-laundering charges. Ember ended this and gave them a couple of bottles of Bollinger to continue the party elsewhere. They were reluctant to be bought off, but Ember insisted. This was exactly

73

the kind of festivity he knew he would have to get rid of altogether one day.

He had not been able to leave immediately, even after that. Wasn't he required to report first to his ginger, double-balding, cat-faced, cat-moustached chaperone? Ember longed to dodge him and drive home to see everything was fine. Was it? Lately Margaret had spoken even more than usual about those continual promises Ember used to give over the years, to turn fully legitimate. Perhaps, after all, her patience had gone and she was determined to pull out. For some women of Margaret's age patience did get to be a shaky thing. *It's time*. Ember's assurances to her on going straight had always been more or less sincere and thought-out. He genuinely meant to do it, eventually. Yet to date the chance for implementation had always dodged away from him. And in the future it would be more elusive. There was Cosmo watching him now on Bridges' orders, to make sure Ember adapted nicely to the new supply regime. But, beyond and much above that, it had occurred to Ember that, if Bridges could get rid of someone as permanent and powerful-looking as Barney and the two women, it might be possible to get rid of Bridges and his aides by the same sort of rough coup, and capture the gorgeous sweetnesses of bulk distribution for Ralph himself. If he could corner that magnificent power, Margaret would surely see the glorious wisdom of staying in the trade, though at a more brilliant level than he had even come close to before. And, of course, there would then be no question of corrupting the Monty. The reverse. Ember could pour some of the extra money into it: he would improve the wines and the chef and facilities, and be able to afford the loss of membership fees from all the present dregs people he yearned to be rid of – must be rid of, if the Monty was ever to resemble the Athenaeum.

'Those two, who were they?' Cosmo York had asked at the club while Ember fretted to be gone.

'Which two?'

'The two talking to you.'

'A lot of people talk to me. I'm their host.' Ralph might want to leave, but he would make nothing easy for this lout.

'Those last two, like staring about,' York said, 'like, Oh, where is my wandering boy tonight?'

'Ah, those two.'

'One looked cop.'

'Vigilant, Cosmo.'

'Both?'

'No.'

'What did they want?'

'Looking for Beau Derek,' Ember replied.

'Fucking what?' York habitually spoke grunts, but this was a scared super-grunt. 'Why?'

'His mother's got a cough.'

'Whose?'

'Beau's.'

'Don't shit me, Ember.'

'Even someone who looked like Beau has a mother.'

'Police out at nearly 2 a.m. because an old woman's sick?'

'I don't know how old she is.'

'Someone's been gabbing,' York replied.

'You're one to cut through the frippery, aren't you, Cos?'

'Who'd gab?' York replied.

'Gab what?'

'That Beau was at Tiderace. Look, they've discovered Beau's missing and someone knows he went to Barney's with you.'

'Who'd know?'

'You talk to your fucking wife about how your trips are planned and who goes with you?'

'My wife's not involved in this.'

'You talk to your fucking wife?'

'My wife's not involved in this. Fucking listen.'

'You talk to your fucking wife?' York pulled out some papers from an inside pocket of his jacket. 'So, it was the police, yes? I've got stuff here on all the top law people in this Force.' From another pocket he brought a pair of Lennon spectacles and put them on. Ember thought he looked like an unambitious, non-mousing cat in glasses for an optician's ad. York began reading the top sheet. 'Not the chief, Mark Lane, was it? No doughy skin. Not Desmond Iles, the nutter. This one was too scruffy and big and no grey hair. Harpur? "Looks like Rocky Marciano but fair." Yes. I've seen pictures of Marciano. Yes, yes, yes. Colin Harpur? Detective chief super.'

'Charlie Merryweather been doing your research?'

'It says Harpur's wife, Megan, was murdered in some gang spat, a while ago. Right? Harpur, now giving it to a student, nineteen, and probably then as well. Denise Prior. "Lives in Jonson Court, university accommodation, but often sleeps over at Harpur's place in Arthur Street. Smokes. Tobacco. Parents in Stafford. Sister, Jane. Denise drives a Fiat. Doing a degree in French and English."' He skipped some paragraphs. 'Harpur might see other women. "Something with Iles's wife Sarah, at one stage, perhaps current." Iles knows? Harpur, "rough and crude and clever, non-purchasable, like Iles, also clever." That him? So, why's he here?'

'He white knights now and then. Harpur's certainly crude but he can do sensitivity. People go to him for help. This was a humane visit.'

'Don't shit me, Ember.' York moved the papers about and read from a later page. 'Beau's got a woman, too, yes? Melanie. "Not young but still shaggable."'

'I hate that kind of insulting label.'

'Beau talk to her? Would she go to the police if he was missing?'

'And he is, isn't he, Cosmo?' Ember nodded at the

papers. 'Do they say Beau's got a mother, Mrs Gurd who was Mrs Millward, and that she's poorly?'

'Beau might have talked?'

'Never. Beau knows the procedures. Knew. Anyway, Tiderace will have been properly spruced up, won't it?'

'Bridges wouldn't want anything that connects Beau with Tiderace. Neither do you, Ralph.'

'Nor you, Cosmo. Harpur noticed you.'

'Yes, it's been cleaned, but there'll be a real inquiry at the house once Barney and his team are missed. No knowing what could be detected. Blood specks in that fucking games room might have been overlooked, or in the hall where Beau went down. They're smart these days. If Beau was there, you were there. Andrew Cartier Bridges would hate that sort of shadow on you at a time of deep re-org. You're one of our assets. Perhaps you were getting some of that shadow tonight from Harpur.'

'This was a kindness visit.'

'I'll have to tell Andrew.'

'Really?'

'Listen, Ember, I thought you were into panics. So, why nothing when Harpur arrives and asks that kind of stuff?'

'Panics? Ralph Ember? Myth.' After this he had secured the club. The Camrose-Hortons still hung about the car park and Ember said a bit more to placate them, then left for Low Pastures. York drove to his bread-and-breakfast hotel. At Barney's place, Bridges had obviously assumed that whoever went back to watch Ember would move into his home, for closeness. But, although Ralph was terrified at Tiderace, he could never agree to let York, or anyone like York, into Low Pastures as more than a caller. This was fundamental.

Now, Ember pulled down the loft ladder and climbed up. What Margaret referred to as the emergency fund was kept part here, part in the Monty, all of it cash, naturally. Ember turned back a corner of insulation fibreglass. She had taken all the notes from between the rafters at this spot, about £40,000 as far as he could remember. Ember thought that reasonable. The children were expensive, no matter where they went to school, and renting a decent place would cost. He did not want them in some shithole. And Margaret had to be responsibly dressed. She still belonged to Ember. She had probably also taken the Volvo estate. It was not outside. That seemed sensible. They would have plenty of gear.

He calmed during this time in the loft. Although the emptiness of the house proper depressed him, up here he expected to be solitary, of course. He was hidden away, silent, £40K light. Few could be £40K light. The roof space was boarded in and he stood straight at the high point in the centre. Although he had been abandoned, his selfhood stayed indomitable. Thank God, he was Ralph W. Ember, with famed concerns about the environment and Nature and the possibility of getting into major scale substance distribution if he could devise something final for Bridges and the others. In a way it was even an advantage that Margaret and the girls had disappeared. It meant Bridges would not be able to squeeze him by threatening them.

Trees moving slightly in the wind sounded close through the tiles. Occasionally there came the light drumbeat of a shower. Ember felt comforted. He enjoyed the notion of being as tall as the trees. He felt a link with them – their durability, their unpushy splendour, the strength and suppleness of their chief branches. He came back to that term 'abandoned'. No, not abandoned. He had been fined down. His essence had been freed. His essence amounted to much more than biting a teddy bear, but biting a teddy bear showed that some inhibitions had fallen away. His loneliness was a strength. He could recall other occasions when he felt like this: once, standing in the wind at night on the foreshore seawall, he had imagined himself as a Viking warrior-king, an earlier, massive, ferocious, nordic Ralph, recipient of unlimited earned awe from his people. Positioned in the roof space now, he was not just tree-like but perhaps resembled an all-powerful aerial, alert and responsive to the world's calls for reassurance. Ember raised both arms, as though to harvest more of these tortured signals. He would give aid wherever needed. His generosity was massive.

He thought he heard something which was not the trees or rain or transmissions from the pleading world: possibly four footsteps outside the house, light, hesitant footsteps. Perhaps someone had come off the lawn facing the front door and moved guardedly on to the gravelled drive. Ember remained as he was, no movement, arms high. He knew he had locked the front door and put the bolt over as well. Christ, had Cosmo come out here after all, afraid of what Bridges might say or do if he discovered York did not stick non-stop to his charge? This idea enraged Ember, destroying his picture of himself as brilliantly solitary, brilliantly autonomous. He listened. Had there been the sound of a vehicle before the footsteps? Perhaps he was too tied up then with all those notions about himself as a tree or an aerial to notice. He lowered his arms, ashamed. *Ember, what a fucking bag of nonsense you can be sometimes: Ralph the mighty Dane, Ralph the timeless oak! God, he climbs a little ladder, and suddenly he's won a place among the mighty and can chuck forty grand!*

Thinking of the money edged him in a fresh direction, though. He smiled and turned, making hurriedly for the trap door. Margaret had come back, had she? Those footsteps could have been a woman's. York was nimble, but surely not as light on his feet as that. Perhaps she had parked the Volvo at the other end of the drive. She, too, might be ashamed and wanted to sneak in, return gradually, almost secretly. Possibly she had left the children sleeping in the car. Ember decided he would give her a total, understanding welcome, not even refer to her disgustingly savage letter or the filched cash. Largemindedness in himself Ember prized. He would more or less forgive. Carefully he went down the ladder and paused for a second or two on the landing. He listened again. Margaret had a key to Low Pastures, of course, but it would not get her in because of the bolt. She might be standing in the porch, wondering what to do. If she rang the bell and, supposedly, woke Ember she could forget any hope of making her return off-hand, non-confrontational.

Ember went into Fay's room again and tried to get the bear's stomach back to something like health. He thought that if he were told of someone under family stress biting a toy twice he, personally, would be sympathetic, but could not be certain everyone would feel like this. Even though it was only the second-string teddy, Fay might be upset to see the punctures, and Margaret and Venetia. There were bits coming out. He smoothed the split area with his palm, hoping to make the gashes less apparent, or at least less identifiable as tooth prints. But the tearing was severe. It could not be concealed. OK, so tell them that in his understandable surprise at the disappearance of Margaret and the children he had frantically searched the house and somehow dislodged the teddy bear from its shelf and trodden on it, causing a gut burst. He had seen something like this happen to a man once, though it had been the result of a kicking, not just being stumbled over. Ember considered the explanation might even be to his credit – the deep frenzy through acute loss, a temporary lack of balance. He put the bear back on the shelf, facing forward, its injuries obvious. An attempt at concealment would be miserable.

He retracted the ladder, closed the trap and went quietly downstairs. He refolded the letter and placed it where it had been on the kitchen table. Margaret would think he had gone straight up to bed and not even seen it. Obviously, she would have huge trouble explaining why she and the children were out so late, but whatever tale she offered he would not question. Ember was determined to treat her with understanding, especially as he would have to break it to her eventually or sooner that he was even more deeply concerned in the trade now, because of those forced undertakings to Andrew Cartier Bridges and the possible additional supreme opportunities. Margaret would be able to put the £40K secretly back in the loft and it would be as though nothing much occurred.

Bridges had returned the Bodyguard revolver to him at Tiderace just before Ember left, its chamber still full. Ember had felt outraged at that – the presence of the bullets. Bridges was saying he considered Ember incapable of using the gun against him or York or Charles Merry-weather. Their whole strategy had been to reduce him, reduce him, reduce him, turn him into a kind of franchised softy. You'd think they'd taken lessons from Barney Coss and that straggly old dominatrix, Maud. All the same, Ember was glad to have the Bodyguard now. He drew it from the holster and went and stood with his ear against the front door, his breathing silent. The door was real wood, a hefty job and in keeping with the property. A Spanish consul once lived in Low Pastures. For a minute or more Ember heard nothing through the door. He wanted to call out gently: *Margaret, love, I couldn't work out where you were. I searched the house and in my anxious rush I'm afraid I fell over Fay's teddy doing some damage.* He stayed silent, though.

Then Melanie said: 'Ralph? You there? You're home, Ralph, but where's Derek?'

Oh, God. He thought of staying silent even now. He could tiptoe to somewhere else in the house, ignore Melanie.

'Ralph? You *are* there, aren't you?'

All right, all right. Wasn't he obliged to treat her decently, her and Beau? Or her and the memory of Beau? There were standards of behaviour, and Ralph W. Ember knew them. He drew back the bolt, released the lock and opened the door. Melanie stepped into the hall. Ember put the revolver away. She said: 'Harpur's been around to the flat with Gurd, Derek's stepfather. What's wrong, Ralph? A gun?'

'You spoke to them?'

'I didn't answer. Saw them through the judas hole. I've met Gurd once before. What did they want, Ralph? I had to come. I didn't want to talk about it on the phone. I felt it had to be face-to-face, whatever.' Her eyes shimmered with brain. Dye still won against grey. She was whispering. Naturally she would think that Margaret and at least one of the children were in the house.

'We'll go in here, the drawing room.' Ember also whispered. Did he want to proclaim to the woman of someone like Beau that his, Ember's, wife had ditched him? In any case, Margaret might be back soon, once she found how damn much she needed leadership. She and the children would be just a rabble. Things could still be kept private. Possibly Margaret thought working the loft ladder for the cash meant she could cope alone with life in general, but there were bigger tests than that out there. Possibly she believed £40K had powers to put most things right. Didn't she know there were people who could smell a handbag wad across counties and would come looking and preying? He wanted to protect her and the children. Ralph would be protecting them twice if he could wipe out Bridges, Merryweather and York and incorporate their big new corner of the game: then, those three would not be around to do harm, and the extra earnings should set his family and the Monty right and impregnable for ever. He knew how founders of the great aristocratic British families felt back in the Middle Ages, or Joseph Kennedy in the States in the 1920s. Vision.

'I tried to find you at the club,' Melanie said. 'It was shut. Early? People in the car park said you'd been there tonight. You went to the Monty direct, did you, after coming back from Hampshire? But what happened to Derek? Wasn't he with you on the trip?'

'Did he say he was going to Hampshire?'

'Was that wrong?'

Work with someone like Beau and you had to expect mouth. Where else did he talk? Had the ripples reached Bridges, and so the Tiderace reception? *Beau, old blabberer, did you do for yourself?* 'Which people in the car park?'

She shook her head. 'They seemed to be having a party. An old woman climbed on to the roof of an Omega and sang "Shrimp Boats". She was taking swigs of champagne from the bottle.'

'They were –'

'I wouldn't have worried about Derek – a bit late, so what? – but it's Harpur calling and that Gurd. The people in the car park said Harpur had been at the club tonight with another man. It sounded like Gurd. What's it mean, Ralph? Why the search? These days, nights, I understood Harpur doesn't stir from his student unless it's something big. I'm worried. Well, you can see. Would I be out here troubling you at this time if not? They said Harpur couldn't touch them, whatever.'

'Who?'

'The people in the car park.'

'No, Mrs Adele Camrose-Horton was acquitted. She'd be the one on top of the vehicle. She's known for joie-de-vivre and fight although sixty-seven.'

'Why were Harpur and Gurd there, Ralph? To see you? It's about Derek?' Mostly, she continued to whisper, but so urgently that some words crackled at nearly full sound. Her teeth looked like her own and still good. Her tongue busied around them intimately. He felt a big, wholesome compassion for Melanie. She was a bit older than Beau, say thirty-eight or even forty. This was a woman doing damn well against middle age, and still capable of the impulsiveness that had brought her out to Low Pastures after 2 a.m. On the whole Ember liked impulsiveness. How had she stuck with Beau? Her anxiety about him definitely seemed genuine. Ember envied that bond, although it was broken now, of course. She must suspect this. Ember knew she needed him.

Ralph went to the long, Regency sideboard and poured a couple of good Kressmann Armagnacs. Melanie sat down on a chesterfield. He took her the drink. She swallowed half of it at once, the way Americans drank spirits, like for thirst. Ember found this coarse, especially in a tastefully furnished room, but did the same. He was bound to feel a link with her. They were both alone in life now, though she did not know this as a certainty yet. He sat opposite Melanie in an armchair. She had kept her hips manageable. She said: 'I begin to feel as if I've behaved really stupidly, badly, coming out here, disturbing you and perhaps disturbing your family.'

'It's all right,' Ember replied. 'Not much wakes up Margaret and the girls. I arrive very late from the club most nights and they've learned to sleep through it.'

She looked approvingly around the large room with its bulky period furniture, bought bit by bit by Margaret and Ember in markets and antiques fairs. Her eyes on the mahogany sideboard, she said: 'Derek's dead. They've sent for the stepfather.'

They were not questions, statements, but statements seeking denial. Ember hesitated for possibly three seconds. Her instinct was right, her reasoning wrong. Should he comfort her for now with lies? 'Yes, I'm sorry, but Derek's gone,' he said. Would he have told her if she hadn't told *him* first? In his mind was the warning from Cosmo York that nothing must connect Beau to Tiderace. *If Beau was there, Ember was there.* Did Melanie know how to stay quiet? She was not part of a firm, had no training in silence. Beau had training in silence, but still yapped. Harpur might come to Melanie again. Gurd might come to her again. So, perhaps Ember should have tried to block her off, delayed the knowledge: buried the knowledge for good, maybe. Who knew whether Beau's body would ever be found? It would not have been right, though, to play ignorant with this woman. There were standards. Fuck York.

Perhaps the certainty had been with her for a while. At any rate, she did not disintegrate in front of Ember. 'Dead – not hurt and lying low somewhere?'

'Dead.'

'I've always thought Derek had a doomed quality to him.'

'He didn't invite this. Nothing stupid, nothing hasty.'

'What I'm sure of is that you didn't betray him, Ralph.'

'Thanks, Melanie.'

'I don't believe it's in you to betray a friend and sub-ordinate. Regardless.'

'Thanks, Melanie.' What did that mean, fucking *Regardless*? The word came out so naturally, like formula, as if everyone knew Ember had pitiful faults but could some-how occasionally escape a few of them. 'I never thought of Derek as a subordinate,' he replied.

'Derek always said you'd never betray a friend and subordinate. Regardless.'

'It could have been me,' Ember replied. 'It really could have.'

'But you always get away with it. Regardless. People say that.'

Could he have saved Beau? Christ, he'd had a gun in his hand when it happened, actually in his hand. What had neutralized him? Was it just that eternal, brooding factor – a resounding Panicking Ralphy panic? He felt ashamed. He always got away with it. *Regardless*. 'I've been sort of lying to you,' he said. 'My wife's gone. I've just found out. She's had enough. With the children.'

'Oh, God, Ralph.' She was still whispering, but then realized the pointlessness of this and spoke the words again, normally.

'It doesn't rate with her.'

'What?' Melanie asked.

'That I get away with things. That I always come home.'

'And always bring the bacon.'

'There's a lot of bacon now.' Yes, a lot of bacon, but a lot of lurking panic and weakness in him, too, and a lot of risk about. What the fuck did he mean, dispose of Bridges, Merryweather, York? Who was he, Rambo? He said: 'But Margaret wants me to be somebody else. For a long time she's wanted that. I can understand it.' Now and then humility felt comfortable, even natural. It was so undemanding. He drank, smiled: 'Look, this shouldn't be about me, it's about *you*. I'll be all right. You, you've lost a terrific man. Melanie, do you want me to tell you how it happened? This kind of thing can be valuable. It helps locate and so contain the grief.'

She made a bit of a face, almost comic, almost into break-up and weeping, the kind of complicated response that Beau dead was bound to produce. 'I don't think so,' she said. 'Or not now. He's finished. I'll cry, when I realize it properly. I know you'd have done whatever you could to stop it. Perhaps tell me in the future. Weeks?'

Yes, great, but he wanted to feel guiltless and manly straight away. 'All right,' he replied. 'I'll just say at this moment, an ambush. Outnumbered. Hopeless. Perhaps I should have anticipated it. I'm supposed to think, and think ahead, not only for myself. I've got people dependent on me, Melanie.'

'Don't let self-blame torture you. Derek used to say you worried too much about your staff.'

'Nobody can worry too much about staff.'

She leaned across and touched his wrist momentarily with the base of her brandy glass, a weird intimate, impersonal gesture. He thought his skin looked gorgeously tan through the drink. Her breath fiddled mildly with his face and neck. For most of his adulthood Ember's neck had been very sexual. Melanie said: 'Not, not, NOT, a criticism. Derek saw it as very much part of your wonderfully reliable, expansive humanity, regardless of what some say. Enemies. Fools.' She pulled back her arm and seemed about to drink the rest of the Armagnac, but then put her glass down on the floor alongside the chesterfield. It was as though she did not want any clouding of her mind. 'I feel it would be wrong to leave you alone, Ralph, after your suffering.'

'Mine?' he cried. 'Oh, Melanie, *you* –'

'No, *you* – seeing it happen. Then cut adrift,' she replied. 'Have you found a message from her – a note, a cassette?'

'Nothing.'

'So, there might be some ordinary explanation of why she's gone,' Melanie said.

'I'm sure she's left.'

'This is despair, Ralph. Her mind's askew temporarily. It's so difficult for a woman to think of another woman leaving you.'

He could see this might be true.

'You mustn't be alone, Ralph. Can I stay? Don't we both need support?'

'Stay?' he replied.

'If you would like that. Only if you would like that.'

'I don't even know where Derek's body is,' he replied.

'I don't want to go home. Suppose they visit again, Harpur, Gurd, make a bigger effort to get in.'

'How did you come here?' Ember asked.

'Taxi to the end of the driveway. Then I walked. No noise and no car to be spotted outside. *Can* I stay?'

He had left the light on in Fay's bedroom and the door open and as they passed Melanie glanced inside and noticed the teddy bear on the shelf. With a little cry, she entered the room and took it down. She was in velvety black trousers and a short black jacket over a silvery blouse. Ember did not mind this combination. 'I'd say that shows they'll come back, eventually,' she told him. 'Clearly a precious chum.'

'She's taken another.'

'But isn't this the important one, the established one? She's kept him, although he's become so worn and even broken over the years. He's the one that counts.' Gently she put a finger into one of the clean bite wounds. 'There's a poem I heard of once about a pelican that bites into its own innards to feed its young.'

'Yes?'

'Did Margaret take money?'

'Money? I don't know,' Ember replied. 'I'll have to check.'

She replaced the bear. 'This is what I mean about your humanity – a sort of grand indifference to that supposedly practical side, cash.'

Low Pastures was not made for solitariness. All the exposed stone and black-painted beams became hostile-looking, dungeon-like, if you were here by yourself. You might want to bang your head to jelly against a wall. But when you had smashed up the dull tidiness of the bed by having a woman in it you could look out now and then at the naturalness of the decor and get to be all right with it, get to be supremely heartened by it, not jailed by it. And, in any case, you did not need to look at it all that much because you would want to look mostly at the woman. Melanie was still fine to look at – that wide, warm face and up-to-the-mark body. And as a sort of widow, she fiercely needed the tribute of a kindly gaze. Gladly he would supply one.

He was awoken by the sound of a car on the drive before dawn. Then he was not sure whether he had dream-wished it. He said: 'Melanie, the family's returned.'

She had been sleeping heavily but became instantly *compos mentis*. 'Is there a back way out?' she said. She rolled from the bed and began to dress.

'No good. The bolt's over on the front. Margaret would try the back. Stay here. I could be wrong.'

'Get me out of this bloody house, Ralph. I'm in bed with

a man the same night *my* man was killed. People won't understand. It looks flippant.'

'Yes, I'd thought of that.' Ember had – flippant and barbaric, especially to be in bed with Melanie in the house which his own wife had quit so very recently. A pause was expected before this sort of activity. There had to be standards. His children would be damn puzzled. 'Stay here,' he replied.

'Why do people say you panic?'

'Idiots.' He went quietly downstairs again and once more listened against the door and once more heard nothing. He edged away into the library which had a bay window giving a view of the front door. The curtains were over. He went to the side of the window and carefully looked out from around the edge of the curtain. It was dark but he could see a Subaru Impreza parked in front of the house. A map light was on in the front of the car and he made out Cosmo York behind the wheel, apparently scanning some papers. But, instantly, he seemed to sense Ember's presence. York looked up from his reading to the library window, and at once waved in considerable friendship to Ember. Eagerly, York left the car and hurried towards the porch and front door. He moved at such a rush that he left the driver's door of the Subaru hanging open and the map beam still bright.

Ember put on the hall lights and went to let York into Low Pastures. He seemed breathless. 'Thank God. All well, Ralph? I was damn anxious. When I drove from the club you were talking to that mad gang in the car park. I thought afterwards I should never have left you. They could be unpredictable. They could be a plant. *Were* they? Something sinister there? I'm supposed to look after you. You're one of our investments. Andrew Bridges is right, I should be living in.'

'You'd find it a bore, Cosmo. So remote. I'm fine. Everything's perfect.'

'Possibly.'

'Well, just look,' Ember replied. He waved a hand around to show how ordinary everything in the house was.

'I was scanning our research notes just now and they say a Volvo estate should be outside with your car.'

'In dock.'

'Ah.' York appeared to lose some of his tension. 'Fine place, Ralph. I love the obviously extremely stony exposed stone. The wood.' Admiring the structure he moved around the hall and opened the door into the kitchen. 'May I?' He stepped in. 'Grand. But here's what looks like a note for you, Ralph.' York picked up the folded piece of paper from the table and handed it to Ember, without seeming to read it.

Ember took the note and glanced down. 'From Margaret, saying she's videoed a water-colouring programme for me.'

'Kind.'

'I sometimes watch a bit when I come home from the Monty. I need to get relaxed.'

'Well, I can imagine, Ralph. Harpur there. That partying crew. Anything odd about them – that old capering woman? A show? But you missed it.'

'What?'

'The note.'

'Tonight I actually went straight to bed. Yes, exhausted.' He tried to listen in case Melanie came down the stairs while they talked and made a run through the front door. He loathed the idea that someone like this grunting York with his stony stone flair for words might discover Margaret had gone, and that Ralph W. Ember was finding express consolation with slaughtered Beau's woman, and, almost certainly, giving it.

York said: 'Yes, well forgive me. You'll want to get back to bed. I hope I didn't wake any of the family.'

'Not at all.' Ember thought that excellent long balding head really invited bullets. When it came to bullets and the wounds they gave, Ember liked the word *cluster*. It suggested precision and thoroughness. Ralph felt he could give York's head a cluster when it was due.

'Lock *and* bolt on the front door,' York said. 'I like that.'

'Good,' Ember replied.

York left and Ember heard the Subaru pull away. He secured the door. When he went back upstairs, Melanie was asleep again in bed but fully dressed. He climbed in with her. For lovemaking, it always excited him most to start when the woman had all her clothes on and work towards nakedness. But he could not ever remember sex with a woman wearing a complete outfit bar shoes actually in bed, and to some degree quite a formal outfit. This really got him going. The awkwardness of it, the tugging and wriggling and throwing of garments anywhere made things so office-like and physical.

Chapter Nine

Harpur watched the grey Subaru Impreza RB5 pull away from in front of Low Pastures and progress sedately, sedately for a Subaru Impreza RB5, down Ember's fine tree-lined drive. Drive? An avenue, more like. Low Pastures and its grounds were on the Ordnance Survey map. If there had been an Ordnance Survey list of distinguished local people, Ember might have been on that, personally. He and his property helped compose the landscape.

Harpur was hidden among a clump of trees and bushes, or he hoped hidden. Rain banged down in occasional long, grey, unslanted showers. Hell, but this was no work for a detective chief superintendent, especially a detective chief superintendent in fashion boots. At his rank he should be co-ordinating things not doing them. But it would be hard to explain to a subordinate why this thing needed doing at all. Oh, God, he recalled the lovely heat and beautiful dryness in that Subaru, even with the door open.

Harpur did have a hooded, navy, waterproof coat on, glinting now from the downpours. Ember's drive was long, wide, gently curving and stately. TV costume drama would love it for coaches-and-four. Or it might give a rest home first-class cortège scope. The ground-floor lights in Low Pastures went out. An upper-storey light still shone, perhaps on the stairs and landing. Soon, that was extinguished, also. Ember must be going back to bed, or at least signalling he was going back to bed. Ember would be edgy. Ember's edginesses were usually big and might involve keeping an eye over the approaches to the house now.

It was worry about him that had brought Harpur out here tonight, maybe part of the same anxiety which took him and Iles to Barney Coss's place. Iles probably felt such concern more than Harpur: Ember, after all, was central to the ACC's balance-of-power policing, and this chic strategy obsessed Iles, brain and body, possibly almost as much as Hazel did. Iles battled unscrupulously and long for his policy against the chief and would not allow it to be weakened. On top of that, though, the ACC genuinely revered Ralph Ember as an established and eminent regional feature, like a county regiment's colours. Ralph had a stained and torn grandeur. The ACC would take it as an affront to himself if anyone from outside tried to fuck up Ralphy, police or villains. It was safest not to affront Iles, though Harpur had risked it now and then.

He found he had come to share at least some of the ACC's uneasiness about Ralph's safety. Harpur also felt a kind of affection for him, and after the visit with Gurd to Ember at the Monty, this uneasiness grew fast. When they left the club, Gurd had driven back to Beau's mother, presumably, to report no luck, and Harpur went home to bed and Denise. At just after 5 a.m., he awoke suddenly with the thought, half formed or even less, but jaggedly uncomfortable, that Beau Derek must be in a very bad way somewhere, that Ember knew it, and that Ember himself might be menaced: Ralph, wifeless, persecuted and possibly short of Beau – this was a tough mixture for someone so temperamentally frail. Harpur had decided it would be cruel and possibly dangerous to let him meet such agonies alone.

Denise still slept and, disentangling himself delicately from her arms and legs, Harpur had left the bed and begun dressing. A rain squall spat against the window. He went downstairs and put on the waterproof, then quickly returned to their bedroom in case Denise had awoken and needed an explanation for his absence. Or in case she could persuade him to take all the storm clobber off, leave whatever it was until later, and get back in bed with her. He stood by the bed and she did stir marginally, made a minor, silent explosion with her lips, like a mild bubble in simmering stew.

'A sortie, love,' Harpur said.

'What?' She opened both eyes, but only just, and let them move slowly across the waterproof. She frowned and tightened her chin muscles, marginally drew away from him, pulling a pillow against her as though for defence, like a sandbag or her mother: 'Listen, Col, I'm not doing bloody rubber romps again at this time in the morning. Quieten down, for God's sake. At your age. I've got an *explication de texte* test in less than five hours' time.'

'I felt a call.'

'Where from?'

'My soul.'

'Where's that?' she had replied, burrowing under the pillow and getting fast back to blotto.

Now, watching Low Pastures from his hide, Harpur thought he would remain an hour longer, perhaps until full daylight seemed imminent, when concealment might be tricky. Leaning against a beech, he wrote the Subaru registration number in his notebook, using large script and trying to keep the page dry. Even so he could hardly read the letters and figures and had to hope they would be intelligible, or that he would remember them, anyway. He would have liked to make some more notes, about what he had seen when inside the steel blue Subaru for those three tense minutes half an hour ago, but this would be impossible in the dark. He must try to get it all down as soon as he had better conditions. Or not exactly *all*. He realized he would remember none of the figures. And, of course, he did not need the stuff he'd read about himself. He knew that already. It was mostly accurate, mostly devilish. Some gifted detection had been done to provide that material, not by detectives.

As to conditions, the conditions he wanted for the moment were total invisibility. Harpur was bulky and did not merge easily with foliage, especially wearing a navy coat. He would have preferred an absence of rain, too, but that was not crucial or likely. Ember might still be alert and watching from an upstairs window after saying goodbye to the Subaru driver, especially if his wife really was gone as she had threatened, and he had nobody to climb back into bed with. Now and then, Harpur had known that kind of unholy deprivation, the dim neuterness of sheets as just sheets when he was between them alone. Possibly he would be able to manage a couple more hours alongside Denise later this morning before she went academic. At worst alongside her.

Harpur considered the trees shielded him pretty well, he was not a jungle war expert. He had watched the Subaru until it disappeared around a bend in the drive, and then thought he heard it proceed and finally get on to the road and accelerate away with the authentic growl of the RB5 turbo. Once more he squinted through the soaked greenery towards Low Pastures' gravelled forecourt. He did not keep a list of Ember's cars in his memory. An error. It was basic policing when doing a log on someone major. A V registration Saab stood to the right of the very authentic wood front door, which he thought might be Ember's own main vehicle. But Harpur had an idea, a vague one, that a Volvo estate should be present, too. Perhaps, then, Margaret actually had vamoosed with the children. It was true the Volvo might be garaged somewhere. Low Pastures had plenty of outbuildings and stables, right for its rural scale. Although Harpur had seen Ember in a dressing gown when he came out into the front porch to end the Subaru driver's visit, the view was imperfect. Distance and darkness made it difficult to spot whether Ralph looked shocked over Margaret's absence. At least he seemed physically all right, had done himself no panicky damage and could still conduct business: Harpur assumed the Subaru lad was on some kind of a trade call. Why else would he have those thorough and sickeningly accurate profiles of Harpur, Iles, Barney Coss and Ralph himself in the car?

Harpur had found these in a pink folder on the Subaru's back seat. Reading them was a very nervy scamper. Well, obviously. If you were sitting uninvited in someone else's car, illuminated by the map lamp and utterly uncertain how long the owner would be away, you galloped. Harpur was pretty sure he had seen the driver earlier in Ember's Monty, that stranger idling near the fruit machines and possibly watching Ralph. Ember had very, very noticeably not noticed him. This man must have some status if he was given confidentiality at the Monty and allowed into Low Pastures. Harpur still did not recognize him. Large commercial changes in the drugs network were under way, were they? Above all, Harpur had wanted an identification and thought the car cabin might tell him something about the driver, and about any trade revolution. This would make it a more valid police call, not just a mother-hen concern for Ralph. So, Harpur had risked leaving his den among the trees and bushes and sneaked to the Subaru. A car door had been left open when the driver hurried into Low Pastures. Deliberate? A ploy? A trap? Harpur decided not, because his curiosity had compelled him to decide not. The car registration could give an identification, of course, as long as the vehicle had not been stolen. RB5s did get targeted. It was one reason Harpur recognized the model. He did not know much about cars but he did know about cars that got nicked as getaways. The 'owner' of the car outside Low Pastures might not be.

Harpur had hung on in his cover watching the empty RB5 and the house for at least a minute before making his little push towards the car, despite the open door and guiding light. He did not altogether understand why the driver had left the Subaru so suddenly. The man had sat there in the vehicle for about a quarter of an hour before getting out, apparently studying Low Pastures and quite settled. Had he grown impatient? Had he seen some movement in the house? Harpur thought the driver might have made a kind of small, hesitant wave towards the big, curtained bay windows to the left of the front door, as if he had spotted someone spying from there. Harpur had seen nothing, but he was further off, his attention split between the car and the house, his view interfered with by leaves and rain. At any rate, the driver must have had it right because Harpur heard a lock turn and a bolt pulled and the front door of Low Pastures was opened almost as soon as Subaru man reached the house. He went inside. Harpur had waited, though, in case whatever transaction was taking place should happen quickly and the driver return. Or in case Ralph gave the driver the bum's rush.

After this minute's pause, Harpur had taken a couple of smallish steps forward, away from his shielding trees. He stopped and did another long look and listen while he thought himself still reasonably covered by the bushes. Then, he had gone out into what must be full view from the house if anyone were looking and, as fast as he could on the muddy lawn, made his approach towards the forecourt. Once clear of the grass and on to the gravel he had to go more slowly and carefully, in fact, for fear his footsteps crackled. There was no question of running and he had walked across the gravel like a caricature Mr Plod on the stalk, putting his feet down very flat, very softly. He had stared towards the house, not the car, alert for any activity, ready to retreat, if he had time to retreat. He was still listening hard for the sound of the Low Pastures door opening again. Ember himself might be prepared to allow Harpur a bit of tolerance, even on Ralph's own soil and at this rough hour. The other man would not know the way things were organized in this area, though, and might regard an intruder as an intruder, no messing.

When he reached the car Harpur had taken a one-handed hold of the top of the open door. He found he wanted contact with the metal. It would signify he had reached this far, and Harpur liked such tokens. But he also needed the feel of its shiny toughness under his fingers, after the greasy mud and shifting gravel. He was used to metal. He had sat down in the driver's place, then swung his legs in, leaving the door as it was. Some blessed warmth lingered and the rain had not blown in on to the seat. At once he began to survey the inside. Generally, as Iles had reminded him at Tiderace, Harpur loved penetrating other people's property in secret and without authority. Often, the inside of a house examined like that could tell him so much. At first, though, the Subaru had no information. There was nothing useful he could see on the windscreen shelf or the passenger seat. He tried a glove box, but it was empty.

A bit desperate, he turned and examined the back seat, and immediately found the pink envelope file. He had picked it up and, leaning forward so it lay under the map lamp, opened to the first page, which was a scatter of ink figures he did not understand. There were three more like this. His inability to make anything of them infuriated him. He was usually fairly good with numbers. Not these. Then he reached the sheet about himself. The typed heading said, *HARPUR, Colin, Det. Chief Super., age 37, head of CID.*

In a sense, of course, he had wasted very scarce time reading this profile. But, God, it was a facer, unexpectedly to pick up your own chronicle. A facer, and flattering. Momentarily, Harpur was thrilled to think anyone could be so interested in him, could get his name spelled right, with a u. There were sentences about Denise and he felt pleased they knew how educated she was. He found himself stupidly searching the page to see if they'd caught up with her knowledge of that French poem about the pelican who fed itself to its young. Soon afterwards, though, he had found they were interested in Iles as well, and this brought Harpur's pleasure right down. Anyway, he knew all this personal stuff, naturally: the long-time closeness with Denise – degree-material, nineteen, smoker, probably promiscuous, family home Stafford – and the car park murder of Megan. Yes, you could say he knew it. He had found himself pleading silently, *So, tell me something fresh, something fresh. Make this ludicrous, sentimental trip out here tonight worthwhile, worthwhile by accident.*

The notes on Barney Coss did help more, and Ember's dossier confirmed that Margaret Ember used a Volvo estate. Harpur had been struck by the apparent preciseness of a calculation that Barney Coss made *£671,422 last year untaxed from substance importing.* Part of the precision was crazy though, wasn't it? Who expected drugs income to be taxed? He read that *Maud Cheverley-Cheverley and Camilla Battisto, neither of them young or obviously attractive, have nonetheless worked an exceptional influence on B. Coss's policy thinking, and have been important in reshaping strategy as drug quantities in Britain soared and prices eased.* Who wrote *nonetheless* these days? Villain researchers? Harpur liked *eased*, too: a Stock Market euphemism for fell.

A faint ink line had been drawn down the page through the whole of Coss's biography, and shorter, separate lines through Maud and Camilla's names. Was it wasted time to be reading their profiles, too, then? Maybe another call at Tiderace was required, more leisurely and penetrative, preferably not shared with Iles. What went on? What was the carbolic smell there? Why this small hours meeting now between Ralph Ember and someone who might have put a cancellation line, however faint, through Ember's famed, brilliant, and brilliantly monopolistic, suppliers since . . . well, since Ember became mighty in the business, and magnificent in the county? That would be three years, maybe four – something like for ever in drugs trade terms. By then major people were usually dead or jailed or Life Peers or transformed and reformed into Nonconformist ministers.

In the Subaru, Harpur could not find full answers to his questions and had felt it would be stupid to stay much longer pondering them. The driver might be dangerous, and not just only if behind the wheel. So, Harpur had speeded his skim of the profiles and when he spotted the entry, *perhaps an executioner, and seriously deranged by congenital malice, VANITY and frustration, favouring VERY YOUNG ethnic whores (exceptionally generous payer by all girls' reports)*, he knew he had reached the expertly rounded character sketch for the assistant chief. Harpur did not linger on this page. Again, he knew most of it, the name of Iles's house, *Idylls, a literary reference from Tennyson, Alfred Lord (1809–1902), poet*, and the terse, inspired account of Idylls' interior, *MUCKY*.

Very quickly, though, Harpur checked there was no mention of Hazel. There was not, not yet. Harpur would, of course, agree with the concluding assessment on Iles: *gifted, ungovernable, incorruptible, sexually avid, ruthless (possibly slaughtered two men cleared in court of killing an undercover policeman but probably guilty), ARROGANT, cuckolded, unpromotable, maudlin, pragmatic, SELECTIVELY LOYAL, tirelessly narcissistic.* All the same, this left out Iles's flair at head-butting and *entrechat* and *pas de chat* ballet steps, practised around headquarters whenever the ACC could get spectators. Harpur was puzzled that some words had been capitalized. They were important words, yes, but he would have considered *executioner, ungovernable* and *tirelessly narcissistic* at least as important, and spot-on. Unpromotable to chief? Yes. Harpur often thought Iles had gone as far as he wanted to, though the ACC occasionally complained of poisonous cliques holding him back. Iles needed a boss to kick against and defer to.

Harpur had given up searching for identification, replaced the folder on the rear seat, and quit the car then, driver's door still open, map lamp still on. He returned to his retreat among the trees and bushes. Had he left a load of give-away mud on the driver's mat? Fairly soon afterwards, Ember and the driver had appeared and parted. Their handshake seemed brief, uncomradely. The Subaru driver closed the door, switched off the map lamp and left.

Harpur would be writing up a description of him later, not as sharp or in-depth as the profiles in the car, but a start. Harpur had managed only a few glimpses, hindered by darkness, yardage, rain and leaves. He thought the man seemed about his own age, or maybe slightly younger, middle-height, athletic, a wide, deadpan face, the long head with what could be fair or ginger hair, receding in the front and not too thick at the back, either. There might be a moustache, but flimsy. He had on dark slacks and a black woollen jacket, no hat. Could Harpur make a guess from this appearance and the car at the visitor's role? Probably not someone seeking commodity supplies from Ralph. He looked too fit and prosperous for a junkie. A supplier himself, offering bulk consignments? A confidential messenger for someone who did not trust telephones or e-mail or fax, or who wanted the message accompanied by a heavy presence? An enforcer?

Harpur speculated and waited and stared at Low Pastures. Ember was alone in there? Rain seemed to have further softened the mud and it now pretty well enveloped Harpur's Charles Laity boots. The cold of the clay jabbed through to his toes. He would have liked to do some pacing, to keep the blood on the go, but could not risk movement. He felt like pictures he'd seen of troops in 1917 trench war, and standard police self-pity gradually put a hard hold on him. Sometimes, like now, like now, he would wonder about his career choice. Why the fuck hadn't he picked the Diplomatic Corps or Hollywood or snail farming? Naturally, he had an idea of the answer: because he could never have survived in any of them, supposing he'd even been allowed to start. Diplomatic Corps, with an open and gentle nature like his? He would have fallen at the first interview.

101

So, now here he was, wet and fairly addled, aged thirty-seven and accelerating hellishly towards thirty-eight, crouched among rhododendron bushes and trees before dawn, snooping on someone else's architecturally distinguished property and grand surrounding spread. Unless there was the windfall of windfalls, Harpur knew he would never own anything comparable to Low Pastures, and probably not even anything comparable to the departed Subaru Impreza. Normally, this kind of thought troubled Harpur little. Cars did not preoccupy him, and he felt he could do without the fret of keeping intact acres of old roof and big crumbling chimneys: in Harpur's greenhouse sour grapes flourished all-year. Besides, he could usually console himself with the notion that criminal wealth like Ralph Ember's was deeply precarious: if Harpur did his work well, Ember and those like him would eventually, or sooner, lose their magnificent homes and everything else and finish in small, locked, unstylish rooms where the views, if there were any, would be broken up by bars. Today, this consolation was not available. He had come out to Low Pastures to make sure Ralph was all right, not to nail him. Call it enlightened policing. Call it welfare. Harpur knew about the sudden loss of a wife. *Ralphy, it's all for you: the acceptance of mud, the battering by rain, the stress, the wanton separation from Denise's bed-resting limbs and so on.*

This – the wanton separation from Denise's bed-resting limbs and so on – began to get to Harpur. He told himself, and more or less believed it, that he would discover nothing about Beau here this morning. And it might be better for Ember not to know Harpur was around, in case Ralph had to be put under watch again soon. Harpur decided that a full hour more would be unwise. Dawn was swimming in fast on the rain clouds and it had become too light for him to go prowling around outbuildings in search of a Volvo estate. After forty-five minutes he began to walk towards Low Pastures' magnificent ironwork gates. For the first hundred metres, he tried to keep himself screened by the trees. Once he rounded a main bend in the drive, though, he was out of sight of the house and could leave the cover and make more speed. The gates were never closed. High on the left one was fixed a slate tablet with a Latin inscription in faded gold lettering which Iles said meant, *Me, I'm here because I'm here and don't ask how I did it.* Harpur had left his car about half a mile away in a lay-by and he walked quickly to it now, head up, like someone joyously approaching a new day, or someone soon to be back in bed with a girl who could recite bits of old French rhyming plays, yet genuinely seemed to feel he mattered now and then or even oftener.

And, when he was alongside Denise, she turned at once towards him with a long, joyful, probably English-language gasp, eyes virtually open, and held him to her, arms around his shoulders, with all her lacrosse player's strength. 'When you go out like that in the night I can't sleep for worrying, Col,' she said.

'Is that right, love?'

'No.'

'No, I thought not,' Harpur replied.

'But if I *could* stay awake I definitely would.'

'I know.'

'I'd really worry about you then. I don't care what they say, you're worth it.'

'Who?'

'Which who?'

'What *who* say?' Harpur replied.

'You know.'

'No.'

'The mischief makers. The envious,' she replied.

'Which?'

'The kind of worry I suffer is what is called in philosophy the *Ideal* form, with a capital I,' she replied. 'It's Plato.'

'I heard he had a lot going for him, ' Harpur said. 'You

mean it's higher quality because it doesn't actually exist?'

She yawned and scratched her neck for a while. She said: 'Once it takes on Being, the Ideal becomes merely measurable and finite. In some ways it is enhanced by form, and yet it's also encumbered by form. Cheapened. My worry for you, Col, is immeasurable and infinite and eternal. Yes, the Ideal. I don't have to stay awake for it to be present.'

'I was all right. There's a hood on the waterproof.'

'Do *you* worry about *me* like that?' she asked.

'You mean in the Ideal form – by *not* worrying about you at all?' Harpur replied. 'Oh, yes. Why should I worry about you? You're here, warm in bed, definitely prepared to worry a lot, but *not* worrying, and not worrying so much you sleep like Mogadon.'

'Was it dangerous?'

'You were mentioned,' he replied.

'Good.' She smiled, full of vivid smug bliss.

'Why?'

'It shows a link with you,' she said. 'I figure in the total range of your life.'

'We're in bed together five nights out of seven. You make gourmet toast for the children's breakfast. Doesn't that show a link?'

'More than five out of seven. What was said about me?'

'Oh, tit, bum, face, hair, mind,' he replied.

'In that order?'

'Bum might have come first.'

'But mind last? I'm glad. I'd hate you to feel backward.'

'I don't mind your mind,' Harpur replied.

'Do you worry about *anyone*?' she asked.

'Yes.'

'Who?'

'Hazel.'

'Of course. That's serious worry.'

'Thanks, Denise.'

'However, I can see the pull of Des Iles sexually,' she replied.

'You fucking what? He's had crabs, you know.'

'Ah, you *do* worry about me.'

'About your neck muscles and lip muscles. You look around and grin at people too much – Iles, students, lecturers, pub landlords, students, lecturers, Iles. I don't say giving them the eye necessarily, not all of them, but *perceived* as giving all of them the eye and, as you know from your studies, what's perceived can become what is.'

'A university education encourages the widest kind of vision.'

'When you're having wide visions –'

'You're frequently in them, Col. Oh, yes, frequently.'

'How frequently?'

'Five out of seven. Who else do you worry about?'

'Beau Derek. Ralph Ember.'

'Why?'

'They've picked hazardous lives. I'm not sure they're up to it. Ember dithers about the future and could be saved.'

'Is it your place to worry about them?'

'No. I do, though,' Harpur replied. 'A tic.'

'This Beau's a man, isn't he? And Ralph Ember, of course. The Monty? Do you fancy them? Which one more? I hadn't realized. Sexually, you must have the widest kind of vision.'

'They're part of what's known as the fabric,' Harpur replied.

'What fabric?'

'Oh, you know. Our area.'

'Whose?'

'Mine, yours, the populace's, the chief's. The whole locality.'

'Iles's?' she asked.

'You get your tongue around him very nicely.'

'Him?'

'His name. You like referring to him.'

'The two you mentioned are crooks, aren't they?' she replied. 'I've heard you talk about them to . . . to your colleague.'

'I only give them some rudimentary, actual worry, not the Ideal sort, of course. They've never even heard of Plato.'

'What's wrong with them?'

'Apart from that? I don't know.'

'If they're crooks wouldn't it be good if something bad happened to them?' she asked.

'Bad is good? What kind of thinking's that? Not Plato, I bet. No wonder your mind came last after tit and bum et cetera. No contest.'

'If they're crooks wouldn't it be good if something bad happened to them?'

He sighed, like persecution: 'I'm afraid I really can't discuss police matters with you, Denise.'

'If they're crooks wouldn't it be good if something bad happened to them?'

'Ralph's wife might have left him,' Harpur replied.

Her arms twitched and she gripped Harpur even harder, a scared child clutching a solace toy. It always terrified her to hear of break-ups, although she liked a reasonably free life for herself, because of youthfulness. She pushed her face against him and rubbed her cheek slowly up and down on his, as if merging their essences through friction. What would she want with his essence, for God's sake? It was old and catastrophically diluted. 'Oh, God, that's so savage, to ditch Ralph,' she said. 'How can people do that to each other? He's just a nothing, isn't he, Col?'

'He looks like the young Charlton Heston. He's rich. He writes worthwhile letters to the Press. He thinks about salvaging himself. He's worth helping, maybe.'

'Without her he's just a nothing, isn't he, Col? Would he be utterly inconsolable?'

'Probably utterly.'

'I can understand this.'

'Don't ever ditch me, then,' Harpur replied, 'or I'd be probably utterly inconsolable.'

'I'd never ditch a man just because of his haircut and looks and age and clothes.'

'Thanks, Denise.'

'And the other one?' she said. 'Beau. Is he dead? A victim?'

'What? Why do you say that?'

'Is he?'

'I'm afraid I really can't discuss police matters with you, Denise.'

'He's dead?' she replied. 'And does he have a woman, too, a wife? Dead where? Does she know?'

'I'm afraid I really can't discuss police matters with you, Denise.'

She held a finger up, as if to signify some considerable statement due. 'This talk about separation and the smashing of relationships is clearly going to set up desire in me for a monumental, reaffirming, a.m. fuck,' she replied.

'I wouldn't ever rebuff that kind of offer – from you only I mean, of course, of course –'

'Yea, yea.'

'– but I don't need to reaffirm anything. Nothing has ever been at risk.'

'Oh, it's so loyal of you, Col, to say that.'

'I *am* loyal.'

'Sometimes I feel vulnerable, that's all,' she said.

'*You* feel vulnerable? I don't understand it.'

'An *ordinary* monumental fuck then.'

'Not so much ordinary as apt, and full of indestructible commitment to each other.'

'Yes, yes,' she cried, 'more or less all that.'

'Which?'

'Which what?' she asked.

'More? Or less?'

'Yes.' She used the grip she had on his shoulders to pull herself aboard him, like someone reaching a mountain ledge, or a lifeboat in freezing waters, and doing a desperate clamber. He wanted to be both of these for her: the timely ledge on which she could pause and then be afraid to move off from, or a saving lifeboat, one with high sides so that, once in, she could not get back out. This was a girl made for permanency, permanency with him. Denise had never quite agreed yet, only more or less. She was a more or less kind of person. Universities probably taught fussy little distinctions like that. He was not sure he would encourage Hazel and Jill to go. Harpur could not remember so far back but he supposed that when you were nineteen permanence looked like quite a while and naffish.

Denise had nothing on and lay very flat on him, remarkably no ciggie in her mouth, her cheek rubbing his again, her knees cool and sweetly unbony against his thighs. Denise's legs were together. This was an intimate position but a position that could grow additionally intimate, given adjustments. As her body moved slightly in harmony with the faces contact, her breasts badgered his chest, as if with a sort of contempt for its totally dud flatness. This mockery Harpur could put up with. Although he did not feel he suffered breast envy yet, he could see that Denise's breasts in a situation like this might be a plus, whereas his own chest was not much more than basic. He considered Denise's aggressive nipples a kind of aggression that could be put up with, also. You would not see many nipples more suckable than these, and each equally suckable, equally prominent, no egocentric pushing ahead by one. At first, Harpur used to resist doing this to either. It had seemed crude to him for a man approaching forty at such a fucking helpless rush to be tit sucking a girl not even twenty yet and most likely nearly able to remember innocence. But Denise had lifted a breast one night and stuck it cheerfully into his mouth, saying she really needed some of that, it would put a tremor down her vertebrae. So, how did she know it would? But he had not asked. Universities probably encouraged students to get in touch with all parts of themselves for the sake of wider vision, including vertebrae.

Afterwards, when he could speak all right, he had explained to her about his reluctance, saying it was absolutely no slur on her body, the opposite. Denise had eased his worries then by mentioning some quite decent American novel where a much, much older man than Harpur who's starving sucks the breast of quite a young woman for nourishment and symbolism. She had said 'much, much older' in a big, defiant voice, as if it took some believing that anyone could be much, much older than Harpur. On the whole, he was not keen on books, but now and then he wished he had read more, because literature seemed to have blasted all sorts of hang-ups. And this was only American literature. God knew what she got from French stuff.

'I suppose I'm at my happiest when I'm with you, Col,' she said.

'I don't know how I do it.'

'You don't. You don't have to *do* anything. It's just like that, that's all. In a way it's a pain, really, taking into account your condition.'

'This can be soft-pedalled,' he replied.

'Yet every day, as you say, I'm surrounded by all these other people, many of them interesting and presentable, and younger.'

'It's a pain.'

'I cope. And when it comes to lovemaking today, as it possibly will, very soon –'

'Yes, possibly. I've had a strenuous –'

'When it comes to that, what I require is lovemaking that makes it really obvious you'll always want me, Col.'

109

'Of course.'

'Which of course, damn it?' she asked.

'What?'

'Of course you'll always want me, or of course you'll make it obvious.'

'Both. They're the same.'

She reached out to the side table, apparently for a cigarette, but then seemed to change her mind and pushed two fingers up his nostrils for a while instead as if to give her hand something to do and so make smoking redundant. 'You find me a sad little puzzle now and then, don't you, Col? Sometimes I'm all brassy and selfish and clever-clever, and sometimes all weak and needy.' She dragged her fingers clear. 'Is it daft to talk about "always"?' She did the word very big and breathy, like the song.

'I love it,' he replied. 'Always, always, always.'

'But is it daft?'

'It's built in,' he said. 'I *will* always want you, mainly because of your mind, of course, but with tit, bum, face and hair as subsidiaries, so this is bound to be there in the lovemaking.'

'Yes, we can say it, can't we?'

'What?' he asked.

'Always.' She gabbled, too: 'Always, always, always.'

'I like it.'

'But is it –? Oh, anyway, Col, this doesn't mean the lovemaking has to be too damn considerate and gentle.'

'I should hope not.'

'This is a man and woman matter.'

'I'd heard that,' he replied.

'Mature bodies.'

'I think so.'

'And not me on top.'

'No?'

'That's fancy,' she said.

'Right.'

'Although you don't need the help of gravity yet.'

110

'Thanks, Denise.'

'Something wonderfully caring, cleverly paced, but ferocious, unmatchably deep in all senses.'

Harpur turned her over slowly on to her back. One of her hands waved feebly for a moment, as though she might again seek a cigarette or his nose. Then it folded down to her side. Denise's hair fell across her face and Harpur carefully moved it away bit by dark bit. Her mind might be crucial, but he did want proper sight of her. In a while he said, 'Like this?'

'That's deep.'

'In all senses?' he said.

'Oh, yes.'

'Unmatchably?'

'I'd damn well like to see anyone who could match it.'

'I'd rather you didn't,' Harpur replied. 'Do you mind?' Or he would have liked to reply like that, but the chat time was well over and words not easy to form.

Just after eight o'clock, they were sleeping again when Jill, wearing school gear, knocked once and came in carrying two mugs of tea. Harpur's daughters loved it if Denise was at the house for breakfast, and especially if she *made* the breakfast. They could think family. That pleased him. 'Were you out in the night, dad?' Jill asked. 'I saw the wet waterproof downstairs.' She placed a cup on the floor at each side of the bed and gave Harpur and Denise a good morning kiss on their foreheads.

'Surveillance,' Harpur replied.

'Gang-related?' Jill said.

'Possibly.'

'Were you tooled up?' she asked.

'Please, don't talk like your rap caff,' he replied.

'But were you?'

'It was sort of marriage guidance,' Harpur said.

'From *you*?'

'And a sort of attempt to save a soul,' he replied.

'I'll come down and do the cooking now,' Denise said.

'Great,' Jill replied. She sat on Denise's side of the bed and began to tidy up the little table with one hand, closing the cigarette packet. Jill had a copy of the *Daily Mail* under her other arm. She often brought this up for Harpur but would not hand it to him unless he actually asked, as if not yet ready to believe he really wanted to read that kind of paper.

'What have we got to eat?' Denise asked.

'Bacon, sausages, eggs, tomatoes, black pudding,' Harpur said.

'Did you give up on the surveillance because of Denise in bed here waiting, dad?' Jill asked.

He chuckled pretty grandly for a while. 'Police matters could hardly be run like that, Jill. In this kind of operation there are certain objectives and once those have been achieved the operation is terminated.'

'Did you give up on the surveillance because of Denise in bed here waiting, dad?' Jill said.

'Can I have the paper, please, love?' Harpur replied.

Chapter Ten

Ember woke up again alongside Melanie conscious that he had been muttering something as he came round, but not what it was, not the words. This enraged him. If he had committed himself to a statement he wanted to control it. Statements defined one, and it was important that any declaration from him should be of the Ralph W. Ember flavour now, not a Panicking Ralphy squeal. He had stress, didn't he, and this meant the fucking Panicking element in him would be pushing for attention, maybe getting his mouth working while he was asleep and imposing Ralphy-type gibber. Everybody had multiple identities, and it followed that you should prefer one of these to another. Ember recalled something else from his university foundation course, a line by Descartes: 'I think, therefore I am.' It had not gone down well with the lecturer when Ralph suggested it should be: 'I think, therefore I'd like to be someone else.'

Melanie must have been half awoken by whatever it was Ember had said: 'Ugh?' she replied.

Ember lay silent for half a minute, his breathing steady to suggest continuing sleep. Obviously, you could be in bed with a woman without its meaning you wanted to give her your inmost aspects. The whole thing about the dick was it was very outward, if it was working properly.

'Ugh?' Melanie said. She was on her side, turned away from him.

He quite liked backs, the length and blankness of them.

They were an expanse that did not seem to commit you to anything. 'It's all right,' he muttered.

'What's it mean, Derek, love?'

'Not Derek,' Ember said.

'Oh? Oh.'

'Ralph,' he said. Christ, Ember might yearn to be someone else, but it was no treat to be mistaken for bloody Beau, and in a love bed. If you wanted to be someone else you wanted to be someone with vim and acceptable features. Ember could have said to her, 'Derek's dead,' but that would be monstrously harsh, even though she knew, and it had merely slipped her sleep-blurred mind. In any case, more major differences existed between him and Beau than that Ember was alive, for God's sake. Status, polish, skin, money, repute.

Now, *Melanie* went quiet for a while, maybe trying to get herself back to clarity. It would be quite a thing to work out not only that she was not in bed this time with Beau, but that she *could* not be in bed with him. Still facing away from Ember, she said: 'Yes, Ralph – obviously. Oh, obviously, of course. This is your house, your bedroom, isn't it? Fine old-fashioned picture rail.' She must have an eye open now and be looking around for landmarks. Did she mean that only his fucking picture rail distinguished him from Beau for her? Jesus, he'd made love to this woman twice, once not all that long ago. Didn't she register *anything*?

Ember was on his back. He said: 'Last night and then again towards dawn, because of terrible sadnesses affecting us both, Melanie, we –'

'What did you mean?'

'When?'

'Just now.'

'What?'

'I think you said, "I'm a good man,"' she replied.

Did he? Ember was proud of this, if so. Even in his sleep, then, he kept unwavering contact with values and worth, with a concern for merit. To some extent the sentence was

114

egotistical, but the subconscious *was* naturally egotistical. It had to be private, individual, untroubled by inhibitions. 'No, not just "I'm a good man,"' Melanie said. '"*But* I'm a good man." Yes, "But". Dreaming?'

'I must have been.'

'You can't remember what? Were you at the Judgement Seat, making your plea?'

'Judgement Seat?'

'I was a Sunday School girl.' She turned towards him in two slow stages, first on to her back, like Ember himself. Then, as if accepting that she was in his bed on his property and therefore could hardly pretend to distance, she did another swivel and faced him. There was a kind of modesty to the movement, no vamp scamper to confront him with her looks and tidy breasts. She was naked again now, her clothes around the room on the floor and chairs. Melanie's chin lightly touched his shoulder. She kept it there. He did not mind this. In exchanges between man and woman in bed, a chin was nothing much, especially when the pressure remained only minor. In any case, she might be entitled to some closeness with him. There had been intimacy beyond your unavoidable bed-refuge intimacy: there had been true, emotional conversation.

After not too long, though, he must get her out of here – not just out of the bed and the bedroom, but out of Low Pastures, in case Margaret came back with the children. He needed a private look at the sheets. He hated to think of the sudden arrival of the three, and his daughters finding not just the bite holes in the teddy bear's stomach but another woman in their parents' bedroom and bed with Ember. These things amassed could easily perplex a child. It looked unkempt, the way Melanie's clothes were spread in the room. And Fay was not going to swallow that tale about pelicans tearing their stomachs out to feed offspring. She might ask exactly *how* this was similar to the bear's wounds.

Most likely, Margaret *would* come back today. Probably

115

she thought, in her little, harmless fashion, that staying away overnight even only once was a pretty meaningful gesture, sure to get to Ember and say brutally, definitively, what she had been trying to say to him for . . . for how long? A year? It could be even more.

Melanie seemed comfortable against him. Ember disliked the way that apart from her first confusion she seemed to regard the present scene as fairly all right, even routine. For God's sake, she was a widow of twenty-four hours, and widow of one of Ember's most familiar work flunkeys.

'What's it mean, Ralph?'

'What?'

'"But I'm a good man." Why "but"?'

It was said in a level, unflirtatious voice, her chin fluttering against his collar bone as she spoke. She seemed truly interested. Ember felt very used to women being interested in him and he almost always wished to respond. He said: 'I don't go much on dreams and all that. I expect I –'

'Perhaps in your dream, you were saying it to Margaret. "But, I'm a good man – so please, please, don't leave me."'

Melanie was very bright, plus a lovely face and fine body originally, and acceptable even now. Yet she had lived with Beau. Women were so powerless – weren't they? Was why Margaret would be back soon.

'Didn't she like your commercial side, Ralph? Is this what the "but" was about? I remember Derek said there was a buzz you were coming out, wanted to go . . . well . . . legit. He said one reason was you looked like Charlton Heston in noble roles – which is true, obviously, *so* true – and because of this you had decided you should *become* noble now and quit big-time drug pushing. Derek was scared – scared you wouldn't need him then. *Could* you go legit, Ralph? I don't mean just Ralph W. Ember letters in the Press on worthy, bullshit topics. Could you? Is that what Derek's death is about? Is it impossible for you to go

116

legit now? Are there new, intense people? Was it one of them who called last night? They kill Derek to make you terrified and obedient, willing to stay in the career, so they can maximize use of you and your grand network? Understandable. Derek said you were esteemed in the trade. Now they send someone to hold your hand and twist your arm if required. A foreman.'

This woman was a gorgeous brain, regardless. This woman could analyse. Once in a while, Ember had run across such a thing before: a woman who seemed devoted to emotions and fucking could turn out to have a thought or two, also. He did not object too much to this, although it could confuse him. 'I'll make sure you get him back, Melanie,' he replied. He could speak with true concern. Didn't he know about separation?

'Who?'

Lord, *who*? 'Derek.'

'His body?'

'You'll want his body – a proper funeral, though unpublic. A funeral helps draw a line, doesn't it? All say this – grief counsellors and so on.' God, but it was possibly off-key to be discussing a man's funeral with his wife in bed so soon after the death. They had solaced each other, that was all. Surely, it could be understood? The circumstances had almost forced it, hadn't they?

'Poor Ralph,' she replied.

This set his fury alight again. She was a woman who should have been distraught through loss and yet she wanted to treat *him*, Ralph W. Ember, as the needy one. Also in that university first year, they had glanced at a modern woman poet, Stevie Smith, or something like that, who had written a couple of lines the feminist lecturer there really adored, especially as the woman's name sounded like a bloke's:

> Man, poor man,
> is he fit to rule?

117

They had made Ember want to spit and point out all the great male rulers, Attaturk, Caesar, Alexander. Ember knew what would happen soon. Melanie would reach down and put her hand on his dick, as if everything would be tidied away again by instilling a focus there and getting some juice primed: a disgraceful trivializing of his pain. This was how women could be now and then. They thought carnal because they thought a man lived only carnal, and often the male's very severe mental suffering remained incomprehensible to them. In his case, it was partly because of that resemblance to Charlton Heston as Moses and El Cid: some women expected Ember to be forever craggy and indomitable. They discounted his nick-name. Well, of course they did. That name was founded on malice only. Women and many men, too, could see his worth. This worth would never allow him to be shoved around by Bridges, Merryweather and York, would it, even if Barney and the women had messed him about pre-viously, and he'd put up with that? Ember saw better now, though, and sharper.

'Ralph, you would have gone sweetly lawful so as to keep Margaret – and I think this is really lovely, even if it meant Derek was made jobless – yes, lovely, but now you *can't* go lawful and get her back because there are people who'll kill you if you try. They've told you that. It's a battle for your very core, like Faust.'

Stuff Faust. She did not comprehend the full furl of what they wanted from him, and what they would never get, *could* never get. They might not be the only ones who could kill. Had this bonny, ferreting mind in his personal marriage bed thought of that? His knowledge of guns was from a long time back, but he'd forgotten nothing. If Bridges and his disciples shoved too hard he would remove them. He, Ralph Ember. They were shoving too hard already. These sods intended moving in on the Monty, *his* Monty, and on the trade network, and they wanted his agreement. *His* agreement. *His* participation. God, were they lunatics?

He had planned for so long to elevate the Monty, and now they meant to pollute it by making it a drugs emporium. The Monty was their aim. That's why they killed Beau and kept Ember alive, although Ember had been the one with the gun and, on the face of it, dangerous. No, dammit, more than on the face of it – *truly* dangerous. They needed Ember. They had him designated personally to run their drugs game in this city because of his flair and strength, and to run it mainly from the Monty. It must look a brilliant site to them. It *was* a brilliant site. They could not have it. Nobody could, for that purpose. Always, he had struggled to keep the Monty apart from his own trading activities. Oh, there was crookedness among the present membership of the club, he knew that, a massive, almost pervasive crookedness. But never had he permitted dealing to take place there. People were familiar with his feelings and by now respected them. And, in time, he would prune the membership of all its villains and slobs and bring the Monty up to the qualities he craved for it. He had selected this as his main life task as soon as he quit the trade.

When Melanie said there was a battle for his core, she probably meant for his allegiance, his soul, something in that area. She had it right, the battle *was* for his core, but his core was the club, the dear, gloriously potential Monty, and none of them would touch that.

Melanie said: 'They gave you their message by knocking over Derek. You're parcelled up. You say to me and Margaret and the world, "But I'm a good man." It can't be done, though, can it, Ralph? You're not allowed to be good.'

It would be done. When he said – *if* he said – 'But I'm a good man,' what he meant was he would make the Monty good and that this proved his own worthwhileness. A new, transformed Monty was his grail and had been for

119

years. 'Things won't be allowed to slide, Melanie,' he replied. He almost allowed himself a small laugh: yes, it might be good for now that Margaret and the children had disappeared. Bridges could not touch them, use them as a way to bend him. At Tiderace these sods had played with the names as a threat, shown how much they knew. They wanted to pile on the persuasion, the pressure. Killing Beau had been part of that. Talking about the family was another part. He saw why.

Melanie's hand started to creep knowledgeably lower. *Things won't be allowed to slide, Melanie.* He left the bed, not in a silly virginal rush, and not clutching himself protectively, but stepping with determination. At the window he drew back the heavy blue velvet curtains. This was the thing about a country house in grounds: you could be naked at the window and it did not matter because there were no gawping, little-people neighbours. Here, then, stood Ralph W. Ember, entire, as he wanted himself, in his own elected setting, dick at wholesome rest – no plaything or distraction or starting handle – eyes proud yet kind, physique intact, not dismally folded down in an alien house and swiftly nothinged, like Beau Derek's. *Poor Derek*, she should be saying, the fuckable, insolent genius, not 'Poor Ralph.' Ralph was available unstintingly to console her and to save the Monty.

But she kept on at it. 'Suddenly, you're just a minion,' she said. 'Oh, poor, poor, Ralph.' He could remember Merryweather or one of them at Tiderace chanting 'Poor Ralph W. Ember.' Did she want to line up with that doomed trio? 'Come back to bed, Ralph. There's comfort to be had, for both of us. The good God would accept this.'

Good God. He dressed, went down to the kitchen and cooked full breakfasts. If you were going to chuck a grieving woman out, it was humane to offer black pudding et cetera. Women did need compensation for the loss of him. He'd seen other lovers upset when he ended things. It would not look bad if Margaret and the girls arrived during a grand breakfast. Melanie might have been at the house trying to trace Beau, that was all, and Margaret would approve hospitality.

Margaret and the girls did not arrive, not during breakfast or later.

Very late next night Ember drove by himself to Tiderace at the Wharf, Southampton way again, to find Beau for Melanie. In his tableau of priorities this was well down, but it did matter, all the same. He had his Bodyguard .38 revolver in a shoulder holster and also hid a reserve gun, a 9mm Parabellum PO18 Bernadelli automatic pistol, under the passenger seat of the Saab. He had checked both magazines and made sure they were at max. This gave six rounds in the Bodyguard, sixteen in the PO18. Never skimp on bullets. You might need to cut someone more or less in half to be sure he did not keep coming. He took a mild and wholesome pleasure from loading guns. He liked to observe the precision and untwitchiness of his fingers, and generally stayed untwitchy in this act.

His mind was cloudy about where danger might originate at Tiderace, but he knew he should be armed. Perhaps he could recover Beau's body and safeguard the Monty and its lovely prospects at the same time. God, how fulfilled he would be to recreate the Monty. Some of the major London clubs had exchange arrangements with provincial spots of similar character, and he would be aiming for this. He longed to see the reciprocity written down in both clubs' brochures: say, *The Athenaeum, Pall Mall, with the Monty, Shield Terrace (prop. Ralph W. Ember)*.

Would Bridges and Merryweather still be at Tiderace or perhaps have it under watch? Ember had only a sketchy and dangerous plan of how to move Beau's body from the house and bring it home. Obviously, he would need to take the Saab close to the front and drag Beau to it if Beau were

121

still there, perhaps lift him into the boot. Ember had the strength. He was not El Cid, but his physique remained workable. Thank God, Beau had been killed downstairs in the hall and not all that far from the main door. Ember would not have liked to cart him downstairs from the games room, where Barney, Maud and Camilla were. Games could be hazardous, couldn't they, Barney? There was something uncivilized about bumping a dear body like Beau's down stair-by-stair, one at a time.

All kinds of risks might come from entering the Tiderace grounds. Didn't he recall his own doubts and Beau's when planning their approach on that last visit? Yes, very much the last for Beau. Perhaps Beau had been right. Had they run, he would be alive still and Ember might not be encompassed now by the rough ambitions and powers of Andrew Cartier Bridges. Ember would not be on this idiotic trip. If he failed to flee the trade and failed to bring the Monty up to honour, virtue and weight – and also failed to displace and replace Bridges, Merryweather and York – would he have to whine when he arrived at that Judgement Seat Melanie spoke of? It would be something like: 'I wanted to become either pure, oh Lord, or reverently rich in the business, but Bridges was an immovable obstruction to both.' Ember reckoned this would not get him anywhere. Judgement Seat staff might ask why the fuck he hadn't disposed of Bridges and his aides. Ember believed in personal responsibility. A man had to prove himself admirable, and especially a man such as Ralph W. Ember. Was it, then, to prove himself admirable that he devised this piffling mortician's hunt for the body of Beau? 'I wanted to become pure, oh Lord, or become a trade rajah, but there were snags either way, so I went looking for a lower-class corpse instead.' Pathetic. Yet generous-spirited, too?

It was just after 2.30 a.m. and he would be at Tiderace reasonably soon. He was passing turn-offs for Winchester and fortunately these always helped improve his morale

122

on trips to the Wharf. This was partly to do with wonderful old Winchester College, which Ember regarded as a symbol of the most glorious aspects of British heritage. But, also, in woods near the town, he had buried those two difficult colleagues so successfully a while ago, Harry Foster and Gerry Reid. That was after a visit to Barney at Tiderace. Or, at least, it had been woods then. Development might have encased them. He liked to think of Harry and Gerry under a double garage used for really prestige cars. They deserved that kind of distinction. Only one of them Ember himself had personally killed. The other had done the other. Ember decided now not to detour to see the place. He was unsure he would be able to find the site of the common grave, even if it were not built on yet. Possibly he could have a look on the way back. It might be light then, and a small delay in delivering Beau would not be serious. Of course, he and Melanie must discuss where to put him. Clearly, there could not be an official funeral, nor even notification of the death. It would be slack to invite questions.

Ember, cruising nicely with some Brahms on the CD player, was glad of his Winchester memories and the assurance in them that private disposal worked. He felt sure he and Melanie could agree a spot not too far from their home, and a confidential, loving, respectful send-off by herself and Ember would be fine for Beau. No vicar was needed and certainly no crowd. Melanie should be able to visit the grave now and then as long as she was discreet and left no flowers. He would visit it himself. Beau had been not very much, but he had been Ralph's. He drove on to the Wharf and, with the car windows closed, cried out, 'Here I am, Beau. Ralph has returned. You knew, knew, he would.'

There had been some changes in the river craft, but Barney's yacht was still moored there. Of course. Who would shift it? A.C. Bridges was not into boat theft. He thought bigger. He thought of the Monty. Ember knew he must not stop the car but go on straight to Tiderace. If he did pause, he might never get his nerves smoothed out enough again to take him forward. Even during his jubilant shout just now a segment of his mind was telling him he could easily U-turn near the yachts and get on his sweet way back to Low Pastures or the club. All right, Low Pastures would be a lonely home, most probably. Safe, though.

But he kept the Saab on its course. This was Ralph Ember still, not Panicking Ralphy. He could feel a sweat patch across his shoulders and reaching up towards the back of his neck, yet it was no copious sweat, no omen. Anyone would have suffered stress coming into this kind of situation. That was only sensible and healthy, and the sweat was healthy, too. It smelled but smelled normal.

He could enjoy the rage he felt looking at Barney's fucking boat and at the gates of Tiderace. These gates were bigger than the ones at Low Pastures and the grounds were bigger, too, and the house itself, although modern. Ember had no yacht. People like Barney and perhaps people like Bridges occupied a different wealth caste from Ember's, and he had loathed Barney for this, and would loathe Bridges for it, also. He hated anything that made it appear he had been idling, or had settled for an easy career target, especially now he might mean to quit: wouldn't it seem as if he were giving up, incapable of fighting at the top, like a QC who turned judge?

Ember drove through the gates. It was an undoubted moment. For a second he saw himself in the Ben Hur chariot. He thought he felt an actual spurt of sweat, like a water pistol jet. It broke out from the small of his back and ran down over his left buttock in a neat, chartable arc. He ignored it. He could do that. As with Low Pastures, the house was not visible at once. There had to be a bend and then the full exciting view of the property. It would be 1970s or '80s, mansion dimensions, mock Georgian, lots of antiqued red brick and dinky windows. How had Barney managed to keep himself out of that list of the rich they did now and then in the *Sunday Times*? Probably he would have beaten some of those soccer players and softwear ginks. At least Low Pastures had some true fucking age. A Lord Lieutenant of the county lived there once, and, later, a Spanish consul. Ember believed in true fucking age and in antecedents, class. The jumped-up was that, jumped-up.

As he expected, Tiderace looked dark. There had been nothing in the media about discovery of the bodies, so the house must have stood unvisited since he left with Bridges and the other two that night after the deaths and the discussion in the conservatory. Very precise in his head somewhere, he still had all the stages of what happened then, and one day he would go over it, detail by detail: the conversation across Beau's body, continued in the con-servatory, the foul, imposed business agreement, the departure.

Obviously, he did not mess up his mind with all that now. Only an old hop-about Astra stood near Tiderace tonight. Gravel crackled under the Saab's wheels as Ember parked. He decided this crackling was louder, mellower, more expensive-sounding than the gravel noise at Low Pastures. Did Barney, with all his sailor-Billy know-how and stout wallet, have access to superior gravel? This helped Ember's anger further along and made Barney's death seem pretty just, and even the defacement. Barney had really loved his looks, although they were damn ordinary.

Ember pulled in under the shadow of some tree, maybe a eucalyptus. There was an awkward bit of moon tonight. At the Monty before leaving he had burned the ends of a couple of corks and brought them in an envelope. Quickly, he blacked up and pulled on dark gloves and a tan wool-len hat that sat low. Did Heston ever do a commando role? Ember recovered the PO18 from under the passenger seat and put it in the pocket of his navy pea-jacket. His first plan had been to leave the automatic in the car, in case he had to retreat and turn the Saab into a last stand fortress. But now he decided he wanted both guns on him, because the dark and silence troubled Ralph. *He* was the fortress here. Beau would not look at guns and was dead. The crude logic of that might be, make sure you went into any dodginess with all the weapons you had. Ember tried to readjust his body so the sweat-wet shirt was not pressed so widely against his skin, nor his underpants so sticky on his behind. Never would he cave in to moisture.

He left the car. From the boot he took a tyre lever. Most probably, he would have to break his way in. The house style might be phoney almost right through, but the front door and frame he knew were genuine heavy wood, and not jemmyable. Or not jemmyable by Ember. It was an age since he needed to try anything like that. This had been Beau's kind of job, an employee's task. But Ember would cope, though probably not via the front door. He did not despise Beau's rough skills.

He also took a flashlight from the boot. Treading as quietly as he could on the elite sodding gravel he made for the left side of the house, the furthest from the road and obscured by tall bushes. There should be a small window he could do there. The fact that Bridges and his boys were able to get into Tiderace and see to Barney and the women suggested there were no alarms. Those three must always have expected attacks – weren't they standard at their level of the business? – but they relied on personal radar. As a matter of fact, antennae would have suited Maud – beige. A slip-up to be so confident, wouldn't you say, Barney, Maud, Camilla, if you could?

Two or three times Ember had watched Beau break into a place by smashing a window. This would usually be at a house where it did not much matter whether the forced entry were apparent afterwards: for instance, the home of some pusher who refused to operate to Ember's rules, making it necessary to snatch leverage photographs of him in bed with twelve-year-old girls or boys or both. That kind of colleague was not likely to go to the police and report a break-in.

Normally, Beau would be subtler than glass cracking, and work on a door or the window catch. Just occasionally, because of time or where a door or window were impregnably secured, Beau had to do the pane. His method was to use a tiny toffee hammer to make a small hole first, big enough only to let his hand in. It was an exquisite art, this ability to keep the pane from shattering totally. Looking at Beau you would never have expected such delicacy. But even this method did entail having glass fall on the inside and possibly cause noise. Beau would keep it controlled, though, by ensuring the bits were not large and very few. Then he would stick his hand through with a thick gardening glove on and push the glass from inside outwards. Often he put his coat under the window and the remaining splinters dropped noiselessly on to that. He could clear a whole window like this, providing a space big enough to admit a man. Ember meant to manage it the same way. His gloves were not as heavy as the one Beau used, but they would do.

He found a window. Although the curtains were over, Ember guessed there might be a small side room behind. He took off the pea-jacket and spread it under the window sill. Then, very gently, he began tapping with the tyre lever on the glass. Quietness might be unnecessary here, if the house were empty, but he liked the methodicalness and the rudimentary, artisan process. It soothed him. With his darkened face, woollen hat, gloves and tyre lever he felt part of a skill tradition, like membership of a livery company. Although the hole he created was probably not as small and rounded and neat as Beau used to make, Ember thought he carried out the task all right. He did hear glass fall on the inside, but nothing startling.

He waited for a while after that small din, in case of some reaction in the house. Or in case lights came on.

Nothing. He proceeded: hand and arm through the hole, a turning of the hand back on to the interior of the glass, then firm, steady pressure to persuade the rest of the pane in pieces to tumble outside. This was educated vandalism. When he had finished, he lifted the pea-jacket and shook the fragments on to a bit of lawn. He put the jacket back on and made sure the butt of the PO18 was upwards in his pocket and easy to grab. He left the tyre lever under the broken window. He would need one hand for the flash-light and the other ready to go for the PO18 or the Body-guard. He still didn't know what kind of enemy he was expecting to be here. Did he think A.C. Bridges feeble-minded enough to come back and lurk? He and his people had moved their plans forward: earlier in the evening Cosmo York had called at the Monty, allegedly to check Ember was all right but really, Ember reckoned, to eye up the club for future use. Yes, they were pushing the push-ing, fucking fools.

Swiftly, Ember climbed through. He had all his athleti-cism still and felt he could have done every one of Chuck Heston's *Ben Hur* adventures without a stunt man, not just the chariot scenes. Women could get very fond of Ralph's body. Never did he take offence at this. They were entitled to their rampant needs. For a few seconds he stood behind the curtains in the dark among glass fragments. He must walk carefully. Barney's house was such a tip there would be obstacles everywhere. He still felt strong and proud. He had behaved with dash tonight, leaving the Monty in the charge of a barman for the last couple of hours, and getting out on to the dark motorway in a totally selfless cause. Selfless, yet supremely Ember-like. Plainly, it was not important to him, personally, to recover Beau's corpse. But he had always felt that if you fucked a woman in overtone conditions you did have responsibilities, and the condi-tions last night and this morning with Melanie were surely overtone. Wholly casual sex with widows or anyone else he regarded as a disgrace, no matter how much they craved him.

Ember eased the curtains apart and edged through the gap, like an actor in a one-man stage show. He had been right. He was in some kind of small sitting room. Ember did not use the flashlight yet but could make out a number of mixed period armchairs, naturally all cheapo, and a couple of straight-backed kitchen chairs. There was a coffee table on which stood the grass box of an old lawnmower and jam jars containing what looked like sticks of liquorice root. This would probably be the garden room, because of the grass box, like the games room was the games room on account of the dartboard. He moved forward slowly towards the door, still without showing a light. He tried to remember the shape of the house. This door should lead out into a corridor which, on the right, would take him to the hall where Beau had been abandoned on the floor when Ember and Bridges and his people moved the little distance into the conservatory for talks that night. The door from the garden room was not quite closed. That pleased him. He could pass through without the sound of turning a handle.

He did not do so immediately, though. Once he was out of this room and into the main area of the house he'd be committed. Second thoughts almost always gave Ember a jumpy time. At the moment, he could still turn, nip through the broken window and reach his car. His head began to swing away, seeking a glimpse behind him of the window space and escape: Low Pastures, the Monty, the world, non-hazard, quiet, earned eminence. He tried to fight it, got his eyes back from there and made himself concentrate on the door and on the daft righteousness of his narrow mission. This house had to give up its dead, or one of them.

Ember moved into the corridor. He wondered if he ought to have one of the guns actually in his hand now. Would this seem purple? Anything melodramatic, he detested. He might look like an acting star but despised theatricals. This was a house of corpses, wasn't it? Wasn't it? Why wag a pistol? And if it was not *only* a house of corpses, he might scare someone into shooting first by having armament on view.

Again he appeared correct about the layout of the house. The corridor did lead towards the big hallway. The darkness seemed less thick there. Perhaps light from the moon shone into some of the upper parts of the house and reached the hall down the wide stairwell. He tried to see if Beau still lay where he ought to be. Ember would have liked to use the torch beam now, but one thing he remembered about break-ins at dark houses was you did not switch on your lamps for anything but very close scrutiny. Probe far ahead like a searchlight and someone outside might see and start wondering, and start looking.

He shuffled forward. All at once, the idea came that he was not the only person in the house. At first, this delighted Ralph. He thought it must mean Beau was in fact there and that Ember had sensed the presence before he actually saw it. But then he corrected fast. Second thoughts. He realized he felt he was not the only *living* person in the house. Oh, Jesus, where did this certainty come from? All right, by packing two guns he had been saying, hadn't he, that there might be people here? This was different, though, from actually *feeling* someone might be near, perhaps more than one.

He stopped and tried to listen, tried to squint further into the blackness and the greyness. Now, he would have loved to bring the PO18 from his pocket, or even the Bodyguard from its holster. He thought mainly of the PO18, not so much because it carried more rounds but because Ember doubted whether his suddenly palsied fingers would be able to free the Bodyguard from its buttoned holster. He found he could not move his arm and hand for the PO18, either, though. All the hellish symptoms of a full-out panic took crude hold of him again: more

130

sweating, the paralysis in his limbs, a break-up of vision, the conviction that the jaw-line scar had suddenly opened and was weeping muck. God, had he been demented – all that shit about himself as Ben Hur and the young Heston? The project to take on and kill Bridges, Merryweather and York! Who was going to do it? He, Ralph Ember, alone? Come on come on, Ralphy. And then that barmy life mission: salvation, elevation, canonization of the club. The Monty was a villains' roost, and would be for ever, grimy and irreclaimable. Ember wanted to raise his hand to touch his jaw scar and investigate, but knew he could not do it, and knew in his brain that the scar must be fine, as it always *was* fine, panics or not. This was not a brain situation, though.

But he did still *have* a brain somewhere, didn't he, buried for the moment under great welters of terror, yet only in suspension, surely? Surely? He leaned against the wall and tried to force it – force his brain – force it to go back over the last couple of minutes and reveal what had made him sure someone else was in the house. Just fright-juiced imagination? He could not recall anything definable: not seeable, hearable, smellable, touchable. So, how else?

This was a quality lean, with intelligent, quiet, measured breathing. A therapy lean. Ember did not, could not, time it. He had no strength yet to raise his watch arm, and even if he had been able to his eyes would probably fail to manage the dial, especially in the part-dark. But the leaning definitely took a while. He felt good about it. At least he had not turned and bolted. His legs would probably not have let him bolt, anyway, but he had not even tried. Resolve. A kind of resolve. Towards the end of this leaning period, Ember could trace the slow return of strength to his limbs, and a quicker return of good sense about the scar. Of course it was all right. Often his panics showed this gradual changeability. They would swamp him, then pull back gradually like a beach wave. *Look out, Bridges, Merryweather, York, I've got you marked. The Monty will never be yours*. Soon, Ember found he could bring the PO18 from his pocket, and hold it more or less effectively. The sweat remained on his body, but did not build. Although his shirt was soaked it continued to feel like a shirt, not a dish cloth or porridge. Yes, by God, yes, he would transform and purify the club. Yes, by God, he was Ralph.

He could still not recall anything tangible to make him think someone else was in Tiderace, and had still not seen, heard, smelled or touched anything definable during his helpful lean, or the lean would have had no chance of being helpful, regardless of good breathing. Probably, he would have fallen. He kept the automatic in his hand, all the same and went gingerly forward into the hall. Beau was not on the floor, nor were there marks or traces of Beau that he could see. He switched on the flashlight and holding it very low examined the oak-boarded floor. He did not find anything. Once more he felt proud and strong. He had taken a lean, but only a lean. There had been no run and no full collapse either, physical or mental. A lean, after all, was almost upright. Gymnasts might lean when they were grabbing a rest. Ballet dancers used a barre, didn't they? There were times when Ralph thought he might have excelled in ballet.

Now, he wanted more evidence of his victory here in Tiderace. Ember's heart sang in triumph at his staunchness and courage and bravura. These were the qualities that would cleanse the Monty. All right, he would go upstairs and look at the games room, too. Perhaps Beau had been heaped there, a mausoleum. Leaders of Ember's sort did things thoroughly, or might be stricken with shame and self-condemnation later. Dereliction he could not despise more. He went to the first floor and opened the games room door. His approach had been without pause or timorousness. He knew now – *knew*, didn't he? – that there was nobody else alive in Tiderace. It had been a contempt-ible rush of make-believe terror.

In the empty games room he decided there was nobody

dead in Tiderace, either. Of course it depressed him that he must tell Melanie he had failed, so far. But he had tried and tried well. As he went deftly back out through the cleared window he had never felt himself to be more completely Ralph Ember – or Ralph W. Ember, when necessary, for statements in the public prints. Integrity and acumen glowed in him and he remembered to pick up the tyre lever left under the sill: he'd had gloves on when holding it but these days you never knew what the fly bastards could discover from something left behind.

He had brought a sponge, soap, flask of water and towel and, in a lay-by not far from Tiderace, washed the black from his face. He used the vanity mirror to confirm he was spruce and noticed of course, of course, that his jaw scar looked as it always looked: like a scar, what else, dry and eternally sealed. He removed the woollen hat. His duty was through.

Dawn had begun to show as he turned with pleasant nostalgia off the motorway towards Winchester. For nearly an hour and a half he drove around but could not find the spot where Foster and Gerry Reid lay so neatly under-ground, both reasonably dispensable. In a way he was glad he did not have Beau in the boot after all, because this might have made Ralph nervy and intent on getting home quite fast to be rid of him: it would have been difficult to explain Beau if Ember were stopped by police on the road for something and they started going over the car. Police could be damned intrusive. Always Beau had seemed pretty superfluous, though this obviously did not make his woman a dog. How damned harsh it would be to think this! He could not see that widowhood should be entirely negative.

There *was* new building around Winchester, and poss-ibly the landscape had been drastically altered and become baffling. However, Ember could hardly consider the detour a waste of time as he was able to see Winchester College again, gauntly fine at first light, a splendid emblem of culture, decency, tradition and learning. Oh, heavens, he was such a fan of all these. He stopped the car at a good viewing spot and gazed. Although he had turned off to see Winchester three or four times before on visits to Barney, his heartbeat still mounted at the thrill of this sight, and Ralph suddenly realized very forcibly that he would love to think his grandchildren might become pupils at the College eventually. Perhaps the idea had been in his subconscious for quite a period and reinforced without his knowing it each time he saw the buildings. Today though, aided perhaps by this splendid dawn, the notion took hold of him with real urgency and definition.

Apparently, people who attended the school were known as Wykehamists. He liked this. It was an awkward, complicated word to say, a better mouthful than Etonian and more ancient-sounding, perhaps because of the hardness of the k. He did like k sounds, if they were suitable. When he was old, Ralph would enjoy being able to tell folk that this or that grandchild was a Wykehamist and not at some fucking supposedly improved Comp. So many truly distinguished folk had been pupils at Winchester in history, such as Hugh Gaitskell and Richard Crossman, but not only Labour people – bishops, considerable chefs and all sorts. Ember would, naturally, pay the fees, though he did recognize at once that this might mean he certainly would not be able to come out of the substance trading scene as quickly as he wanted, or ever.

God, this whole situation had abruptly become very intricate. He wanted to provide his grandchildren with the best, with the most brilliantly traditional – certainly, certainly: what else was a grandfather for? – but, to get the best for them, did it mean he must risk his marriage and perhaps risk the Monty's transfigured future, by tolerating Bridges' dirty plans for the club? Which of these two did he care about the more, his marriage or the new Monty?

Confusing. If he stayed in alliance with A.C. Bridges, what would Ember lose in his general life to secure the necessary trade profits?

Or then again, if he removed Bridges and the other two, trade profits would mount brilliantly. He could become a bulk importer himself and would easily be able to afford Winchester for the children as well as a yacht like *Modesty*. To Ember now, gazing at the College, this seemed the most intelligent compromise – kill Bridges, Merryweather and York, possibly beginning with York. After all, he was around the Monty and Low Pastures solo and careless, full of gross self-belief, and had that exceptionally shootable head.

Of course, if Ember had not been who he was, he might have considered another method of removing the three. He had seen them kill Beau, hadn't he, actually witnessed it? He believed they had killed Barney and the women. He could tell the police about this, couldn't he? Could he? Ralph Ember did not grass. It was a soul matter, and a trade matter. He felt almost certain he had never grassed, not even in one of his most jabbering, brain-dead states. Although he gave Harpur and Iles cringe drinks at the Monty now and then, he did not talk, except about things everyone knew. On one side there was the tactical business of keeping the law sweet and on the other there was informing. Different, different, deeply different. He would not be alive to run the Monty if he had ever let them overlap. He was trusted, not by Harpur and Iles, obviously, but by his members, by *people* – the crucial dregs people he had his life among, pro tem. Democracy he approved of.

Ember turned the Saab towards home. Grassing was perilous. It would be especially perilous if implicating Bridges, Merryweather and York. Did Ember imagine he would survive to give evidence? Was he sure the police would regard him as only a mouth? He might come out of things tainted, disqualified for ever from running a club and from making it socially and intellectually topnotch. Or he might not come out of things at all. *How is it you were in Tiderace at the time of the deaths, Ralph? Had Barney been screwing you on price, so you decided to finish him? Were you scared Beau might crack and broadcast about the little slaughter session some day? You silenced him? Carving women? That bitch Maud made you really cross? We all know you're big, Ralph, and resolute, big, resolute and bloody.* His brilliant status and strength could go against him, might make him seem capable of extremes.

He drove only at cruising speed, so he could continue to think, plan. The kind of years-ahead school provision for grandchildren might be beyond Margaret's mind, though she was definitely no thick bitch. Virtually the opposite. Now and then she had quite a mental grasp. Would he be with her still, if not? When she returned crestfallen he was sure to enjoy explaining about provision for the grandchildren. Of course, she might argue that a lawful existence immediately, today, rated more than the possible schooling of children who did not even exist yet and might never exist. This was what he meant about women's sad blindness on long-term matters.

In this new millennium, Winchester College most likely took girls as well as boys, a break with traditions going a fair whack back, probably, such as the Middle Ages. 'Manners Makyth Man' was the school's famous motto, and Ember agreed. He always stressed the need for good behaviour. These days 'Man' did not mean only man but girls and women, naturally. Good. A woman with bad manners – loudness and interrupting and so on – was worse than a man. In those early days as was well known, most girls did not do much in the academic line, poor things – just not their role. They were for breeding and nursing and decoration and skivvying. Ember felt pleased conditions had changed, and he longed to see all his

grandchildren, girls and boys, get true schooling, if possible with the Classics in the original languages, Latin and
Greek, not just fuckwit tales about fucking golden apples
done in fucking English. This was already a big topic with
Ember in the education of his own daughters. Authenticity
he craved. Barbarism he abhorred and feared.

Chapter Eleven

When Harpur fed the registration number of the Subaru Impreza RB5 into the computer, the owner's name came up as Daphne Charlotte Trueblood-Maine, seventy-two, unmarried, dead. The number had belonged to a Ford Mondeo, not a Subaru, and four months ago this car was written off after an accident in the Solent area. Following the crash, the Mondeo had gone to the crusher. Daphne Charlotte Trueblood-Maine had gone to the crem. It was the kind of answer to his inquiry that Harpur expected. The Ford is dead, long live the Subaru. He had hesitated about making the search. The computer recorded every question it was asked and who asked it, and at this stage he wanted to sit on what he knew, and what he did not know, which was a lot more. He feared leaks, he feared pressures. He had any detective's hatred of sharing. He put out no general call to patrols for the Subaru to be harvested. Explanations would be required.

Harpur could also have fed a description of the Subaru driver into one of the system's other computers: that is, the driver who was not and never had been Daphne Charlotte Trueblood-Maine. He drew back from this. It would really risk giving too much away, if someone trawled the computer to discover what colleagues were doing. By someone, Harpur of course meant Iles. Iles might nose. He was entitled to nose. He was assistant chief constable (operations), and he operated by trying to stay ahead of subordinates' operations. Iles believed in freedom of information, for himself. Harpur wanted the ACC excluded above all. Iles was one of the pressures to avoid. The ACC had his own darling maxi toleration drugs game strategy, and would insist it prevailed. Iles knew how to insist. In any case, Harpur's portrait of the driver was sure to be so vague it would probably provoke a list of five hundred possibles. And the driver would be on it only if he had form. Although the way he acquired the registration suggested he had seen some life, he might not have a record.

Harpur drove over again to Beau and Melanie's place in Ambrose Street. He felt a responsibility to Gurd and Beau's mother. Perhaps it was too late to feel a responsibility to his mother. Besides these welfare considerations, Harpur had powerfully in mind also, of course, the sight of Ralph Ember searching for something, for somebody, conceivably for some *body*, in Tiderace the other night. Upstairs in the house alone on that second visit which he'd promised himself, Harpur had heard a ground-floor window shattered. It sounded a crude job, not the work of a professional burglar. Harpur could do better himself, much: that night he had used the same forced catch as on the visit earlier with Iles. When he heard the breaking glass, Harpur at once hid in one of the smaller bedrooms. Through the part-open door he could watch the central hallway down the stairwell. After about a minute and a half, a man had appeared walking very slowly and carefully from one of the downstairs rooms. There was only moonlight through a landing window and at first, because of shadow and distance, Harpur did not recognize Ember. He thought he could make out, though, a flashlight in the man's left hand. It was not switched on, and Harpur decided then that perhaps this visitor did after all know something about burgling and its basics. Perhaps the man was familiar with the state of the house and worried about stumbling in the dark over the kind of junk Harpur had found strewn across the hall and several rooms on both visits. Although Harpur knew Barney Coss from photographs only, he felt pretty certain this figure was someone else, someone taller and more athletically made.

Suddenly, the man stopped, seemed to freeze, staring forward. Had Harpur made some sound and scared him? Harpur might even have been glimpsed from the lower floor up the stairs and through the door gap. With what appeared a vast effort, the man broke his immobility and moved a couple of steps so he could prop himself against a wall. He leaned with the whole width of his shoulders, as if needing big help to stay upright, his face out towards the hall. He made tiny, spasmodic movements with his right hand, possibly wanting to move it up towards his pocket, but he lacked the strength.

Now, Harpur recognized Ember. Although he appeared to have smeared his cheeks and forehead with soot, and wore a dark woollen hat pulled low, his face was fully towards Harpur and unmistakable, the back of his head against the wall to gain more support. Yet it was not so much this open, stationary sight of his features that identified Ember. Harpur realized he was witnessing one of those ransacking panics that continually reduced Ralph and were unique to him. Until now, of course, Harpur had never been present at an Ember fit. Usually, they occurred during a difficult and perilous and private piece of villainy – a raid of some kind in Ember's earlier career, or a gang fight. Only accomplices and enemies had seen these breakdowns close to, and some accomplices were dead or in jail because of that closeness to Ralph when he dissolved. The symptoms, though, had become part of criminal folklore, and so of police folklore: physical paralysis, loss of speech, noisy and laboured breathing, splintered vision, Lake Michigan sweats, the Vesuvius scar. Harpur had heard criminals speak of Ralph with loathing for his failures, and with admiration for his ability to fight back from these attacks and come out in credit. In money credit, at least.

140

Enemies referred to the plus balance of Ember's bank account as 'in the yellow', not 'in the black'.

After several minutes, as Harpur had watched at Tiderace, he saw the slow beginnings of recovery in Ember. This, apparently, was also standard. Harpur had felt joyful relief, as a doctor might seeing heartbeats pick up on a screen. Ember still leant against the wall but his body looked stronger, less likely to fold down to the ground suddenly. In a little while, Ralph was able to get his right hand and arm functioning slightly. He worked on this, as if bringing muscles back to usual after a fall or cramp. Soon, he could reach into the pocket of his coat. He produced a large automatic, perhaps a Bernadelli Parabellum. He waved this in a slow back-and-forth, belligerent arc, a sort of 'So-who's next?' arc. There was murderous exuberance in the movement. Ember grinned. It must have been a huge grin for Harpur to see it from that distance in the dark and despite the blacking. To Harpur it appeared a victory grin, though he could not be certain what the victory might be. Ember had not physically collapsed or turned incontinent: did this constitute the triumph? There was courage here. There were almost farcical cowardice and terror as well, yes, but Ralph could soar above these. Give him a four- or five-minute lean against a sound wall and he would gloriously reclaim dignity and normal breathing.

Ralph straightened up, gingerly flexed his legs and prepared to move forward again with the gun in his hand. Harpur could see the Heston resemblance once more, despite his smudged face and the shadows, and could appreciate the full Ralph W. Emberness: his mighty, ever-aspiring crooked status and durability. These qualities were what Iles prized in him, too. He called them 'Ralph's validation'.

Ember reached the main part of the hall and gazed about, obviously searching. Now, he did switch on the torch but kept it against his trouser leg so the spread of the beam was limited. He bent very low, examining the wooden floor. For what? Had he dropped something valuable or potentially dangerous on a previous visit here? Had some incident occurred at this place in the hall and was he now searching for signs of it? The area of floor that interested him seemed very limited. He kept the light on a section not more than four or five square metres. Did he expect to spot damage to the boards? Stains? Harpur decided that whatever Ember had been hunting for he failed to find.

He abandoned the hall and suddenly came very quickly up the stairs, the light switched off again, legs stalwart, pistol still in his right hand. He had to pass the part-opened door to the small bedroom and Harpur tried to quieten his own breathing and crouched a little to give less of a target, in case Ember came in and fired. Probably he would never have knowingly shot at Harpur, but Harpur would be only a blurred and threatening outline for Ember in hostile territory and, despite the vast, fiendish grin, he might still be jumpy.

He did not enter this room but went on along the landing. He was out of Harpur's sight now. Harpur heard a door open and for a few seconds could see the gleam of the torch. Harpur thought Ralph must have looked into the strange, almost bare room at the corner of the house, containing a dartboard and a high-backed church pew against one wall. Old cream lino covered the floor. When Harpur first examined that room with Iles, there had been a strong smell of carbolic and areas of the lino looked especially clean. Harpur had already been back in there tonight, before Ember's arrival. The smell had subsided. Harpur found nothing then that helped him, and found nothing that helped him in the rest of the house, either, just as on the previous trip with Iles. Perhaps the continuing lack of occupants should tell him something, just as it would presumably tell Ember something. All it signified to

Harpur, though, was that Barney, Maud and Camilla were absent. Possibly it signified more to Ember.

Ralph had not hung about in the dartboard room. Harpur saw him pass the bedroom door again and heard him go down the stairs. Soon afterwards a car started up close to the house and pulled away. Harpur had not stayed much longer, either. His examination of the house was more or less complete before Ember broke in, a useless exercise. Harpur went back to the patch of hall floor which had seemed to preoccupy Ember and gave it his own close look. He could find no damage or marks on the boards, not even high heel pits: Maud and Camilla were probably into the flat shoe era. Harpur went to see where Ember had come in and climbed out that way himself, then walked nearly a mile to his car. The old Astra was still parked near the house, presumably a knockabout car for Barney and the women. Using the same window as Ember had given Harpur a mild and happy sense of bonding with Ralph, what guidance from someone's sledge tracks would be in an ice waste.

Driving to Ambrose Street now, Harpur might have liked to describe to Melanie what he had seen at Tiderace if she was at home, but of course he would not. Detection was not about telling, it was about being told, about inhaling, not blowing smoke rings. It was especially not about informing someone that a senior police officer broke into private property, even if the cause were good, and Harpur did not know whether it had been. Mostly, he did prefer the cause to be good, though other causes could be to the point now and then.

In Ambrose Street Melanie opened the door of the flat. Harpur said: 'I was hoping to see Beau. Something personal.'

'Derek's not here now.'

'Can he be reached?'

'What personal?'

'I'm Harpur. Detective Chief –'

'Yes. I've seen you on TV News.'

'It's something I should tell Derek direct.'

'He'll be in touch with me.'

'Direct,' Harpur replied. They talked on the doorstep. Harpur hardly ever questioned the precept that you did not sniff around villains' steady women. If you wanted disaster there were less disastrous ways of getting it.

'I could tell him,' Melanie said. 'He'll contact you then, I know. I've heard him speak of you. I expect he has your numbers.'

'When?' Harpur asked.

'Oh, often. Speak of you favourably. Quite favourably. On television you always look as though you think you'll win but wouldn't worry much either way.'

'No, I meant when is he in touch with you?'

'Oh, you know Derek, I expect. It's unpredictable. I don't mind it in him. What personal? A police officer – senior police officer. It's . . . grave?' She spent a while picking the word.

'Is he working for Ralph Ember somewhere?' Harpur replied. 'That might be a way of reaching him.'

'Ralph? Oh, Derek does do some work for him now and then. Not on a regular basis. Ralph has various enterprises.'

'Well, yes. Sometimes he makes a business call down near the Isle of Wight. Did Derek go with him this time?'

'How do you mean, "this time"? Do you know Ralph went there recently?'

'If Derek mentioned it,' Harpur replied. 'I've spoken to Ralph about this, obviously, but he can be very guarded – the way of business people.'

'Derek moves about quite a bit when he's doing things for Ralph Ember.'

'Have you been crying?'

'Crying?'

144

'I thought you might have been crying. Can I come in? Is he missing?'

'Derek?'

'We might be able to help you.'

'What, my face is a bit puffy, is it? Only lack of sleep, I expect.'

'Why?' Harpur asked. 'Troubled?'

'I get spells.'

Yes, puffy, bedraggled, perhaps helpless. 'Can I come in?' Harpur replied.

'Of course.' She opened the door wider. He entered and she led him to a tidy, high-ceilinged living room with sunny, silver-framed, still-life prints on the walls and a suite of easy chairs with a three-seater settee in ivory loose covers. There was a dark blue fitted carpet, no television. Harpur liked the room. It had serenity. Ambrose Street was built at around the turn of the century. Most of the houses were divided and their flat seemed very spacious and light. Melanie and Beau had taste. Or Melanie. It was heartening to think of Beau coming back from some grubby and maybe hazardous job for Ralph Ember and finding relaxation with her here. Perhaps she had been thinking something like that herself and it had made her sad. Was it over? Most people were amazed Beau could land a woman like Melanie, but Beau probably had his bit of magic as long as you could wait around for it to show. And he was short on malice. If Denise had seen Harpur alone in this room with a woman whose body was as well maintained as Melanie's, she would have got nervy. Denise feared older women. Harpur often tried to reassure her, and so did the children. Through her studies Denise had apparently heard of very mature French actresses who did well sexually and she seemed always alert in case one of them turned up.

Harpur sat down. He did not like to think of those meaty Beau fingers on the ivory material covering these chair arms. Melanie went to the kitchen and came back with two bottled beers, an opener and no glasses. She opened the bottles and they drank. Melanie sat at one end of the settee, her face slightly turned away from Harpur, as though she were conscious now of the drag of sadness in it. Harpur said: 'Were you in the other night when I called with Derek's stepfather? There's a judas window in the door, isn't there?'

'You came here?'

'Were you in?'

'His stepfather? Is this to do with what you want to see him about?'

'Gurd.'

'Yes. To do with his mother, maybe?' Melanie said. 'I've met Mr Gurd.'

'In the past we've watched Derek and Ralph Ember call on a business associate in yachting country on the Solent,' Harpur replied. 'Surveillance.'

'You've got your job to do.'

'We think there might be changes in how the trade is run here,' Harpur said. 'Derek could have been affected some way.'

'Does it matter?'

'What?'

'How the trade's run. It's run and will go on running.'

'Did Derek mention the possibility of changes?' Harpur replied.

'When I said he spoke favourably of you I meant it. He told me you really understood things and cared. All right, you were fucking Iles's wife, but she might have felt neglected – him in the big job – and needed consolation. Derek was very unjudgmental about that. You've got two daughters, haven't you, and their mother killed? This featured on TV, too. But fucking Iles's wife before *your* wife was killed. Even so, Derek was tolerant, more or less. I admire that.'

'My feeling is that if people wanted to get at Ralph Ember they might do it through Derek,' Harpur replied.

'Do you know what I mean, "get at"? This would be a commercial matter.'

'Derek speaks favourably of you and he speaks favourably of Ralph Ember, too. He says Ralph would always do what he could for him – that's in an emergency or generally.'

'Ralph's going through some stress. And now this commercial matter on top.'

'Stress?'

'Ralph's sensitive – the family and so on.'

'Yes, I heard he's a man of feelings.'

'I don't know if you've come across a lad who's balding a bit but with hair that's gingerish where he has any and driving a Subaru Impreza,' Harpur replied.

'Is this part of the changes you mentioned? I'm hopeless on cars.'

'Did Derek mention changes?'

'I can see you'd really need to keep tabs.'

'Of course, while I'm sitting here, I'm wondering all the time whether Derek might ring – I mean it would be so convenient if he called when I'm present and I could talk to him direct about his mother.'

'This would be a true turn-up,' Melanie replied. She clapped her hands gently, silently, in hopeful excitement. 'It's possible. He rings very as and when, as you'd anticipate from Derek if you know him at all. I expect you do. It *is* about his mother, is it?'

'And the rest of it.'

'Ralph, the changes, all that?'

'Right,' Harpur said. 'A mobile?'

'Derek won't have one, no matter how people plead with him. He says he refuses to be on the end of an air wave for anybody. He has to call me, not vice versa. A streak of awkwardness. Frankly, I like it in him.'

Harpur thought she might weep again and waited in case she did. When women cried they could often be sympathized with lavishly and eased into talking. But she

147

put the bottle into her mouth and distracted herself like that. He felt pretty certain it was empty. His own was. She did not offer a replacement. She stood. Harpur stayed in the chair. 'It's possible this ginger bald lad has killed Derek,' he said. 'Or one of the ginger bald lad's mates has.'

'Yes, I did get that,' Melanie replied.

'This would be in a big room upstairs in the Solent house – maybe for darts and other games – or more likely the hall. And now he could be here to work on Ember.'

'Yes, I got that last bit, too,' Melanie said.

'Will you keep the flat on?' Harpur asked.

'For the present. It's expensive.'

'Beau brought in quite a bit, I expect.'

'Derek,' she replied, 'his name's Derek.'

In the evening, Harpur had a phone call at home. Jill answered first and yelled: 'Father dear, a voice from another world.' Lately, there had been a bit of discussion in Harpur's house about how his daughters should refer to informants who telephoned him, or even came to the front door or appeared in the back garden, though these actual visits were rare. Both girls felt a true contempt for most aspects of policing and liked to make it known. Some of this poison they had absorbed from their mother. The girls detested grasses. In the past when she took a call, Jill might shout, 'One of your finks on the phone, dad,' without covering the mouthpiece, of course. Informants were a jumpy lot, and had plenty to be jumpy about. They were into dark risk. They wanted secrecy, sensitive treatment, discretion. Harpur's daughters handed out blare and insults. Tipsters might give up trying to get in touch. Harpur had spoken to Jill about it: explained that without informants there would be no detection, just as opera would die without its singers, too. 'So?' Jill had replied. But she was getting towards fourteen now. Responsibility might be creeping in. This possibly explained the new formula. She probably still did not cover the mouthpiece.

When Harpur took the receiver, Jack Lamb said: 'You and I – the same quest, Col.'

'Truth, honesty, lawfulness. I hope so, Jack. Always.' Jill made a suffering saint face.

'No, I mean asking the same questions,' Lamb replied.

'Which?'

'We should meet,' Lamb said.

'Where?' Harpur never refused Lamb.

'Number Five.'

'Right.' Harpur never argued with Lamb.

'An hour?'

'Right.' Harpur never quibbled: an informant had his skin to think of and cater for, and you let him do it as his judgement said was best. You had to rely a lot on an informant's judgement, and so did he.

They worked to a list of supposedly secure rendezvous points, approved of by Jack in the past. Number Five was a small motorized passenger vessel, *The Imperial*. Several times a day when the weather was in favour it took sightseers on an hour's trip with commentary around the newly created centrepiece lagoon in the docks marina development. Harpur liked Five best. It seemed to him more secure and anonymous than the rest. One of these was a supermarket car park, another a launderette. There were also two former military posts: a foreshore block-house and a one-time anti-aircraft gun emplacement on a hill overlooking the city. Harpur had an idea that the blockhouse might be used for briefing meetings and splits by villains, as well. Uncomfortable. Lamb liked to dress up in army surplus gear whenever they met at either of the military spots, as if to merge with the setting. At his height and weight he was already conspicuous, and wearing a khaki cape or goose-step boots made it worse. For the boat tour, Jack generally appeared in ordinary clothes. The bulk of people on the excursion would be tourists from outside the city, unlikely to recognize either Jack or Harpur.

They bought tickets separately and met at the stern, as ever. Most passengers liked to crowd the bows and gaze ahead. As they pulled out from the jetty, Lamb said: 'Daphne Charlotte Trueblood-Maine, Col.'

They were looking back towards the massive barrage between Proconsul Dock and Chanty headland, completed a year ago to produce the lagoon. 'The chief adores all this,' Harpur replied. 'It helps his morale. I can understand it.'

'What?'

'Marina, barrage, lake. He sees it as the future. Rebirth. Something worthwhile for him to guard. Yes, rebirth. The chief and his wife have done this trip half a dozen times.'

Lamb stared out over the brown water. 'People will fight him for control of the city. More so now. It's a jewel.'

'Of course they'll fight him. We fight back.'

'Yes?' Lamb asked. 'Has it started, the fight for control?'

'Why do you ask that?'

There was a party of schoolchildren on the tour today and a few of them began some chasing game and dodged about between Harpur and Lamb, using them as shields. Lamb said: 'If I'm quizzing the police computer about something and I'm told that Colin Harpur has been putting the same questions earlier I know I must be on to a main topic.'

'What topic, Jack?'

'Daphne Charlotte Trueblood-Maine.'

'How are you able to ask the fucking police computer anything at all? You're not police. The police computer is confidential.'

'And imagine you on to something before me, Col!' Lamb replied. He put his open hand affectionately on Harpur's head for a second. Harpur was big but Lamb made him look paltry. People expected grasses to be slight

150

and slippery. They would be shocked by Jack. 'Rebirth,' he said. 'That brings us to Daphne Charlotte Trueblood-Maine yet again. Her transformation.'

'This sounds a damned expensive name, Jack, sold by the metre,' Harpur replied. 'Which computer cop do you pay?'

It was the kind of question Harpur would occasionally ask Lamb and which Lamb always ignored. Any informant would ignore it. Lamb was one of the greatest informants in Britain and the EU, or possibly worldwide, and his greatness came in part from knowing how to protect sources and in part from hearing plenty. Lamb talked exclusively to Harpur. It was a beautiful and possibly unique arrangement. Harpur would never risk it by too much curiosity. A procedure had to be observed and disposed of, that was all. Police asked questions. It was their mission. Jack's mission was to ignore them, mostly.

He said: 'I've a friend who's deep into anxiety, Col.'

'If someone's flogging stuff from the computer to you that's bound to be. They're sure to catch him, or her.'

'No, this is another friend altogether. I do manage more than one, you know. He and his wife keep a boarding house. They let a room to the driver of a Subaru Impreza. Heard of that make at all, Col?'

The little boat swung around for a closer look at the barrage. A loudspeaker voice gave stone and concrete tonnages and water statistics. It explained sweetly that wader birds which previously used the flooded mud flats would find alternative mud just as environmental further up the coast. Glancing across the perimeter wall of the lagoon and into the heart of the marina, Harpur could see the masts of that floating restaurant and sometime drugs emporium, *The Eton Boating Song*. Lamb said: 'He hates reading intrusive material about you, Col.'

'Who?'

'This other friend, the boarding house owner. I mean,

151

really intrusive. For instance, about Denise. Not exactly bust measurements, but her degree courses.'

'Sartre? That's intrusive,' Harpur replied.

'In a folder.'

'That right?'

'Have you seen it?'

'I already know her degree courses,' Harpur replied.

'And her bust measurements, I expect.' Lamb frowned and struck the stern gunwale with his fist. 'Forgive me – the coarseness. This is a lovely young girl who –'

'Thanks , Jack.'

'You might marry her one day. I should be respectful. She deserves it.'

'Denise won't have marriage. Would you want to take on two kids like Hazel and Jill? I'm a bit on the side, Jack.'

'Men are often but playthings, Col. A pink folder. Plus material on Iles. Found in the boarding house room.'

'How do you mean, *found*?'

'You *have* seen it, have you?' Some of the children were still about the stern and Lamb let his voice fall. 'Is Iles truly still going to young ethnic whores, Col? Well, in a way it's lucky that he is. We get the benefit.'

'Who?'

'You and I.'

'That right?' Harpur asked.

'Young ethnic whores were cited for Iles in the pink folder, of course. But they were famous, even without this, weren't they, Col?'

'Of course.'

'You've seen this stuff, have you?' Lamb said. 'My friend, the boarding house keeper, asked me to find out what I could about the Subaru driver, Col.'

'Why was that, Jack?'

'This driver began bringing a young ethnic whore back to his room, Col. The same one, each evening, admittedly, but, even so, my friend was not keen on this. It wasn't to do with the ethnic aspect. Not racial. He dislikes any kind of whore brought back to his place. And his wife dislikes it even more.'

'Reasonable.'

'But before he considered making trouble about it with the Subaru driver, he had a worry or two. He knew the assistant chief was into young ethnic whores. As you say – of course. Everyone knows that. The folder's only confirmatory.'

'How was the pink folder found, Jack? This was the driver's private room, wasn't it?'

'What troubled my friend, the boarding house keeper, was that the young ethnic whore might be one of Mr Iles's young ethnic whores. Do you see the sort of potential protocol difficulty, Col? He wondered whether the Subaru driver was a police colleague of Mr Iles to whom the ACC had recommended this young ethnic whore, as a hospitality gesture. My friend thought the Subaru driver might be an officer from out of town here on duty whom Mr Iles had kindly decided needed worthwhile night company. My friend would not want to offend someone who is a colleague of Mr Iles. He has a way of getting back at people who upset him or upset his friends. I don't know if you had noticed this.'

'The boarding house owner and his wife asked you to ask the computer who the Subaru driver was?' Harpur asked.

'I owed him, Col. Well, I'm told, up comes the name Daphne Charlotte Trueblood-Maine. As you know. Where did *you* get the car registration from, though?'

'But Daphne Charlotte Trueblood-Maine obviously doesn't match the name the Subaru driver is booked in as at the boarding house?' Harpur replied.

'Anyone can see why you got on in the police, Col.'

'So, then your friend and his wife went into the Subaru driver's room on the quiet and found the pink folder, with the information about Iles and whores in it that your friend and his wife knew already.'

'Plus the information about you and so on. They felt entitled to see whether anything in the room gave a name for the driver.'

'He *had* a name for him.'

'He had *two* names for him, Col. One, from me, was Daphne Charlotte Trueblood-Maine. The one in the signing-in book downstairs was Vincent Milce.'

'Doesn't sound right,' Harpur replied. 'Did you ask your other friend, your computer friend, to trawl the database for the alleged Milce?'

'Nothing.'

'No, I suppose not.'

The little boat was nearing the jetty again and the end of its trip. Lamb said: 'It's the pink folder, isn't it, Col?'

'What?'

'Significant. Something big's moving. Why all these facts about you and so on? There were figures in it, too. My friend thought like a year's accounts for a couple of businesses. He's good at all that. He wondered if they were to do with a club.'

'The Monty?' Harpur asked.

'He said a club. He couldn't do better than that.'

'Did he speak to the driver about the girl?' Harpur replied.

'He and his wife thought at the end that Vincent Milce was probably not a colleague of Mr Iles – not a *police* colleague.'

'Which other sort is there?'

'Is this the beginning of something new, Col?' Lamb asked. 'You know I don't come talking to you just for the sake of it.' Almost always there would be a justification from Jack for his informing. He knew how despised a grass could be, knew it even without Jill's help. Harpur invariably let Lamb state his philosophy of grassing. There was his ego to think of, as well as his skin. 'But if we're

154

watching an upheaval – a huge upheaval, possibly – and these files on you and Iles and . . . I mean, what is it, what, in God's name, Col?'

Here was Jack far out of type – asking. Harpur liked it. *Harpur* usually had to ask. Jack provided, and required Harpur to appreciate what he provided. Harpur never paid him for information, but Lamb ran a brilliantly profitable art business which drifted between the legal and the not. Occasionally some blind-eyeing was needed about where works came from, where they went. This was the arrangement.

They walked up the stone steps to the quay wall. 'Your friend said nothing about the girl to Vincent Milce?' Harpur asked.

'The girl herself, if she sees Mr Iles, might speak about what she would regard as harsh treatment from my friend, had he objected. He's scared of a fire bomb through the window or the slaughter of his labrador or razoring of his wife, something like that.'

'A fire bomb from an assistant chief constable, for God's sake, or killing of a pet, or razor work?' Harpur replied. 'What kind of police service would that be?'

'Everyone says Mr Iles is very considerate to his girls, don't they, Col? One called Honorée?'

'This was Honorée?'

'I don't think we have a name for her.'

'Well, yes, your friend could be right. Best not upset Honorée.'

'To upset Mr Iles via Honorée,' Lamb replied.

'Right.'

Chapter Twelve

Ember did not really want Melanie in Low Pastures again, and yet how could he have decently kept her out? The Saab stood in the drive and she must know he was at home. He had heard her tread on the gravel, could tell it was a woman and could also tell it was not Margaret: too brisk. Of course, he guessed Melanie. She would imagine some connection now. He could have gone to the side window again and peeped out around the curtains, but it did not seem worthwhile and, in any case, Cosmo York had been able to pick him out there. To Melanie, it might appear furtive, ungentlemanly. Ungentlemanliness was odious to Ralph above many other faults. He let her knock twice, then went to open the door.

In that stretch of time between hearing her steps and opening the door, Ember had a rush of thoughts. Somehow he had to make her accept that what happened between them the other night and in the morning was a grief occasion only, a support occasion. It gave no indicators to the future. He was glad to help her then, and she had helped him, too, he would admit it, but he would not think of a relationship, could not. For one thing, Margaret might be back shortly. She was his wife. True, there had been very full arrangements with other women while Margaret was still with him, but Melanie had been Beau's, and Ember could hardly submit to a long-term follow-on from someone like Beau Derek. It might seem unfeeling to say it now, but women indelibly marked themselves socially by the kind of men they slept with as established partners. The way Ralph saw it, although bed could certainly be a comforter, it was also a categorizer. Melanie was handsome but labelled. If she had wanted to be considered in a major way by Ralph she should never have gone full-time and blatant to Beau. She would appreciate this, surely. Melanie was a bright woman and knew about status. She must be familiar with the position achieved by Ralph through ownership of the club and Low Pastures, through his daughters' top schools and gymkhana activities, through Ralph's civic letters to the Press.

Ember felt he had done well by Melanie. This had been not simply taking her for consolation into his bed and sharing a fine, reasonably paced breakfast, but giving her that true, non-sexual yet entirely caring embrace in the car before he deposited her near Ambrose Street in the morning, together with heartening, genuine words about Beau. She was an admirable woman and he sincerely wanted her to be . . . to be . . . not happy, of course – that was impossible while she mourned, but to be unhysterical. Although it would have been gross to offer her money at this time, there were earned fees due to Beau and before long Melanie would certainly have them, and with good additions. Money pressures might gang now she was alone. Flats in Ambrose Street were not cheap. If it ever came to the confidential funeral for Beau that Ralph had in mind he would naturally deal with all costs, including a coffin, probably. This was not going to be the type of inevitably raw burial he had given Reid and that loud sod, Harry Foster, near Winchester. When a colleague was killed alongside you, and you could do nothing to save him although armed, you were certain to feel dogged by responsibilities. You would be a dismal creature if not. Ember had always been famed for looking after his work force and their dependants, and, surely, the point was, never had he made the smallest attempt to set up a casual affair with Melanie while Beau was alive, although Ralph had certainly noted her pull, and she might have been willing. Some boundaries were almost holy to a man like Ralph. Certainly not all men were so fussy. Think of Harpur and Detective Chief Inspector Francis Garland involved with Mrs Iles, wife of a senior colleague, at admittedly different stages of her life. Occasionally, recalling Harry Foster, Ember used to wonder what happened to his quite promising-looking girlfriend, Deloraine.

Before Ember had closed the door behind her, Melanie said: 'He knows it happened in that house Southampton way.'

'Who?'

'Harpur. Coss's place, where you used to take Derek on buying jaunts.'

She made it sound like an offence. He had taken Derek only because he had been made to take him by Barney and that women entourage. 'Coss?' he replied.

'Don't mess about, Ralph. Derek talked a bit to me, you know. This might be urgent. Harpur knows the spot.'

'Well, Coss's house is –'

'Not just the house, the *spot* in the house.'

'Spot?'

'The hall. Or possibly a games room. Is there a games room?'

'It's impossible.'

'*Is* there a games room? Is there a hall?'

'If he knew anything there'd have been media reports. We'd have heard of bodies by now.'

'Plural? Is Coss dead as well? And there were women, weren't there? Did you go back, looking for Derek? And Harpur saw you there?'

'He's bluffing.' God, Ralph recalled the sudden fear that he was watched there near the hall last time.

'*Was* Derek killed in the hall, or perhaps a games room?'

'I couldn't save him, Melanie.'

'Yes, you said.'

The sharpness unnerved him. 'In the hall,' Ember
replied.

'A ginger, balding man did it? Drives a Subaru Impreza
– one of those hot cars.'

'Three men were –'

'Is he around now?'

'Around?'

'Harpur seemed to think he was around. Was he the one
who came here the other night when we were . . . together?
You thought it was Margaret and the children.'

'Here?' Ember replied.

'Oh, fuck off, Ralph. I looked out of the window when
you went downstairs. Some sort of smart, sporty car.
I wouldn't recognize a Subaru. He ran to the house, didn't
he, and you let him in? He might have been half bald. Late
thirties? At the time I thought maybe some dealer. Not
Margaret, and so no trouble. But he's something bigger
than a dealer, is he? Where are the other two? You said
three.'

'Will Harpur arrest him?' Ember disliked the notion, at
this point. Although he wanted the end of York and the
other two, it must be when he was ready. He had to think
about immediate supplies. There were other kinds of
responsibilities – responsibilities to a fine network. Ember
took Melanie into the drawing room. Although it was full
of splendid period furniture, some Regency, some early
Victorian, Melanie did not seem to notice the elegance. She
could not be impressed. For a second, assaulted by her
indifference, Ember felt his life's accomplishments might
be tawdry and banal – the building of wealth and reputation, his beautifully diversified businesses, the eternally
clever sidling into survival. This woman did not rate them.
He found her unbelievably hard to handle. It was as if she
had taken over. He wanted to think of Beau's woman with
kindness, he wanted to be considerate, but she did not
seem to need anything like that, nor to be seeking it. He
felt she was turning him into a subordinate or someone

159

under interrogation. She might be used to treating poor Beau like that, but didn't she realize this was Ralph Ember and that they were in Ralph Ember's noted property? Her behaviour seemed hugely unsuitable. He recalled the moment in bed when she had mistaken him for Beau. Always this damn reduction. Ember longed to resist the way she trampled him now but could not find the power. In these new conditions, even his honourableness in never scheming to have her while Beau was still alive appeared cruelly diminished. She had become more than a bed person, and more than a shack-up for Beau Derek. There was a mind present – a *mind*, not just a brain, which he had always been aware of in Melanie – and there were cheek and authority, too.

'What was he here for?' she asked.

Ember had not said Cosmo York *was* here. She made up her own answers and had them right, the pushy bird. 'Who?'

'You're in association with him? He kills Derek while you watch yet you're in association with him?'

'Not the word, not the word, I swear, Melanie. Not association. And, no, not while I *watched*. A lapse of vigilance, that's how I would put it.' Christ, a woman – a woman who had cohabited with Beau – *she* could bring on one of his panics. His voice fluted. He rushed his excuses. He was pouring some claret for the two of them and could not trust himself for the moment to carry both glasses from the long sideboard. Melanie was sitting in a gold and grey re-covered Victorian armchair. She stood and went to his rosewood table on which lay monogrammed writing paper in a leather folder. She took a sheet and put it on the side of the table nearest to Ember. 'Draw it for me, Ralph, the hall scene, the hall scene when Derek died. I want the detailed geography of it, the disposition of people.'

He hated her for the fluency of this – that word, *disposition*, like a fucking military manual. It was much worse than *association*. Someone worked up and sad should not have *disposition* on call.

'Disposition?' he replied. He wanted to make it clear, to himself, mainly, but also to her that he could say it, regardless, all the s's in the right place and the query tone right.

'Draw where Derek was, where you were. Put D and R, if you like. The other three, X, Y, Z. Any doors or stairs, so I can try to see it complete.'

Ember wanted the best for her. He said: 'I understand why you might be . . . well, preoccupied by this awful scene, even obsessed, Melanie, but perhaps it does not help in dealing with grief to itemize the circumstances of a death, the death of someone loved.'

'Did you say they came out of a door behind you?' she replied.

He had to grab at that. He did not like the direction of her questions. In any case, what she said was true. 'Yes, from behind us. Utter surprise.'

'I don't understand how you were in the house at all. Where were Coss and the women? For God's sake, weren't you ready for a possible attack?'

He knew what she was asking him. She thought he might have intentionally led Beau into this: an upheaval in the trade was due, Ember wanted his corner kept intact, Beau might have objected to the readjustments. So, goodbye Beau and hello Mr Subaru and others – *associates*. 'We could have been more ready,' he said. 'It was slack. But this is a big house. A lot of doors. I don't know why, but I didn't expect them from that spot. I dozed a moment and then I was helpless.' His voice had returned to its ordinary pitch. He was speaking the truth. Melanie seemed to recognize that. He could walk all right now and carried the two glasses of wine unspilled to where Melanie waited. She took hers and drank a little. A jar of pencils and Biro pens stood on the table. She put down the glass, chose a pencil and began to sketch on the sheet of writing paper

161

herself. In her drawing, an outline Beau, marked D, lay on the floor face down. The three men stood on one side of him, pretty much as they had really stood. She had the R figure for Ralph ahead of the body, as though hardly part of things, Judas keeping his head down. A pistol was in the figure's right hand, but it pointed hopelessly or calculatedly to the floor. Ember said: 'No, I bent over Derek. I wanted to reassure him.'

'Of?'

'I didn't know how bad he was.'

She pushed the drawing towards Ember. 'Which one is Subaru man?'

He pointed to Z, the one closest to the body. He thought that correct. But he was not certain York did the killing. Hadn't he supposed Merryweather?

'And now Z is in town to run you,' she said.

'He's in town.'

'How does Harpur know?' she asked.

'Harpur gets a lot. Whispers.'

'Does he watch this house?'

'What, Low Pastures?' Ember asked.

'Subaru man has to be taken out, hasn't he?' she replied.

Ember saw the question was a test. It asked if he had been welcomed into an alliance with the Subaru driver and the other two. 'Of course he has to be taken out,' Ember replied at once. 'All of them. They killed a good man.'

She drank, mulled what he had said. 'Would you have told me about Subaru man if *I* hadn't told *you*? Or is he a pal now?'

'There was no need to tell you. I've my scheme for him and for his mates.'

'You'll do it? For real?'

'It was decided before your visit, believe me.'

'If you can't do it, I'll do it,' she replied.

'I've already begun –'

162

'I don't mean I'll do it, not personally, of course, but I'll get it done. I know people. Or Derek knew people.'

'What people?'

'There's some money in the bank. These people would do it. They were fond of Derek.'

She took her glass of wine and went back to the armchair. In the other hand she held her drawing. 'They value you, do they?'

'They value the business structure.'

'Hostile takeover bid you might say.

'People have tried before.'

'The structure's no good unless *you're* looking after it,' she replied.

'They like the alliance with Mansel Shale. They think they might be able to get him to take bulk from them, too. That's a possible bonus. They adore the tranquillity of the streets. Unhindered dealing. This is the Garden of Eden compared with, say, Manchester or Liverpool or Cardiff.' God, how could he be discussing commerce with this woman, Beau's woman?

'Do they want the Monty?'

'Why say that?'

'It seems obvious. You're known through the Monty. Have they scared you, paid you, promised you, into opening up the Monty to the trade at last?'

'They'd know they'd never get the club. I've other aims.'

'Oh, Lord, Derek used to talk about that. You're going to turn it into the Beefsteak, aren't you, Ralph, or the Athy?'

'It has fine potential.'

'They're taking the Monty, are they?' It was a question but she made it sound like a fact, an obvious fact. The calm intelligence in her face and the aura of foresight he found loathsome.

Chapter Thirteen

Iles said: 'Col, there's a girl I know quite well called Honorée.'

'I think I've met her, sir.'

'Certainly. She's a girl who stays in the mind. Ebullient.'

'I'd say so, sir.'

'Bright.'

'This would be the type of girl you'd go for,' Harpur replied.

'There's an ease of communication between us.'

'This is understandable, sir.'

As he sometimes liked to do, Iles was lying on Harpur's desk, his head in the mock wood out-tray. He had on his fine pale blue ACC uniform for some parade or ceremony later in the day. He said: 'Ease of communication may be one thing, Col, but Honorée is certainly not a girl who would divulge matters about one client to another, such as myself. Although she has a fondness for me and knows my interests, professional and other, this does not entail blab.'

'Confidences are important, as with a doctor or lawyer.'

'Except where the circumstances are totally unusual, Harpur.'

'Right,' Harpur replied.

'Possibly some present circumstances involving Honorée and a certain ginger yet balding client *are* totally unusual, Col.'

'Right.'

'A written profile of myself comes into it.'

'I'd like to read that, sir.'

'You've seen it, have you, you sod?' Iles raised his head a little from the tray. He was frowning. Hurriedly he said: 'Mind, Col, I'm not implying there's no ease of communication between my wife and myself, obviously.'

'That definitely would not have to follow,' Harpur said. He took in a reserve of breath. Harpur was always prepared for a siege when the ACC mentioned his wife.

'For instance, Sarah and I can talk now about the interludes she had with you and Garland.'

'Yes, you've told me about this, sir.'

'I call them interludes, because they were nothing more. They lacked all significance, Harpur.' Iles's voice dived towards throatiness and blur and then climbed to the routine baying of the impaled. 'We can talk about those episodes without stuttering or hesitation or dark silences. Not without rancour though – how could it be without rancour, Harpur? Even you will understand that.'

'I'll concede rancour's to be expected, sir.' Harpur could see that his office door was decently closed. He had the idea that some people who noticed Iles enter this room and knew of his spasms would deliberately hang about in the corridor as close as they could get to the door. They held bits of paper supposedly for rooms in this part of the building, and they listened. 'What sort of unusual situation involving Honorée and the ginger yet balding man, sir, plus the profile?' Harpur asked.

'That kind of easy conversation between Sarah and me can concern, for instance, your or Garland's method of dressing after rushed fucks in public places,' Iles replied. 'Yes, we can get amusement from this. It will show you how detached we have become. Such as whether you put your socks on first before other garments or leave these till almost last, apart, that is, from shoes. I don't say there's a hell of a lot about personality to read into this, but you'd be surprised how ritualistic and invariable the procedure can be. Sarah observed you never put your socks on until you were otherwise fully dressed, except for shoes. Had you noticed that, I wonder? People tend not to be self-aware about dressing. Garland's was a different procedure, as it happens.' Iles still had volume, but a terrible flatness and mock rationality now controlled his voice, like a post office loudspeaker telling customers the grille to get to. 'With Garland, there did not appear to be any pattern. Perhaps whiz-kiddery demands impulsiveness. Sometimes it would be socks on more or less first, sometimes virtually last, sometimes at a middle stage – say shirt and vest on but no trousers, and socks put on *before* trousers and pants, though not shoes, obviously, because this would make putting trousers on difficult and slow everything. This is the sort of *logistics* of fornication. Do you see what I mean?'

Iles liked answers, and it would be good to have something at normal sound level – that is, something from Harpur. He wanted to keep his reply going for as long as he could, perhaps giving Iles time to defroth his mouth a bit, get the tumult out of his eyes, and slip back into sanity and the facts about Honorée and Subaru man. Harpur was sitting behind the desk, Iles flat in front of him on it. Harpur said: 'Seemingly insignificant physical acts can have quite considerable implications, sir. Naturally, I'm thinking of how Gideon was told by God to select his army in the book of Judges.'

'Ah, Gideon, so true, Col,' Iles replied.

'It was the men who lapped water from the river with their hand – these were those Gideon was told to choose for his army, not the ones who bent down and drank straight. Now, this seems to me like the socks, sir.'

'Arguably.'

'Hard to see that the way a man drinks from a river would show whether he'd turn out to be a good trooper,' Harpur said. 'In the same way, the priority – or not – given

166

to socks in that kind of, well . . . situation, might be indicative of something fairly crucial, even core, but what exactly it is difficult to define. A profile of you, personally, sir? This is an impertinence.'

The assistant chief adjusted his head slightly in the tray and a couple of witness statements rustled. 'Because we have this happy frankness, Sarah and I, it does not necessarily mean I press her for every last physical detail of what happened between her and you and Garland,' he replied. 'I hope I'm not prurient, Harpur. I mean, the nature of arousals, duration, frequency.' Iles had not taken the chance to do anything about his lips and spit drifted on to the desk or beyond to the floor. 'True, now and then we have discussed the way you in particular –'

Harpur said: 'So, as far as this ginger yet balding man is concerned, did Honorée –'

'One thing she cannot tolerate is finding herself referred to as "a very young ethnic whore".'

'It's damn coarse. This was in the profile, listing your tastes?'

'She's an intelligent kid, Col.' His rage at this labelling of her made him twitch mildly along the whole of his body and he began to sit up on the desk, as if needing to look more assertive. Then he sank back. 'Do you know what she says to me?' Iles asked.

'It will be something intelligent, sir.'

'Ethnic,' Iles said.

'She –'

'She brings that word to me and asks what it means, Harpur.'

'Well, it's –'

'"Isn't everyone ethnic, Des?" she asks.'

'This is a point, sir.'

'"What does it mean, ethnic?" she demands.'

'I think I'd be wrongfooted, sir, but you probably –'

'"Ethnic means belonging to a race or a group, doesn't it, Desmond?" she asks. She had quite a sprinkling of education, Harpur. Beyond yours, obviously. "Tell me, Desmond, don't for instance *you* belong to a race or group? Doesn't HM the Queen? Doesn't Stan Gaston Helm-Waters?"'

'Who's that, sir?'

'Does it matter, Harpur?'

'She must be a bracing girl to be with. Intellectually, I mean, as well as –'

'*Ethnic*, Col – this word offended her so much that she felt freed from the usual restraints of confidentiality affecting clients. Tell me this, Harpur, would *you*, yourself, like to pick up a pink folder and find yourself described in it as "a very young ethnic whore"?'

'This is –'

'And yet you are as ethnic as she, no question. I feel you wouldn't dispute that. You've seen this pink folder, have you, and heard of the ginger yet balding man?'

'It would come as a real shock to pick up a pink folder and find papers about yourself in it,' Harpur replied.

'You've seen this pink folder, have you, you secretive shit?'

'A girl like Honorée is entitled to be startled,' Harpur answered.

'This was in good faith, Harpur,' Iles said.

'What, sir?'

'He goes out of the room for a piss, or something like that. It's a run-of-the-mill boarding house he takes her back to each time, The Mildew, or something like that.'

'Maidrew?'

'Not en suites. This is a girl left alone in a room with, for the moment, nothing to as you might say occupy her. She's almost bound to turn to a pink folder for a read if there's one lying about or in an unlocked case. A thinking girl like Honorée naturally wants to know the context in which a man friend moves. Would I, for instance, deny her the information that I am an assistant chief constable?' Iles detested the word assistant when applied to him and always almost swallowed it, or emphasized satirically the slimy, bum-sucking s's. Today he swallowed. 'And yet not specifically about her as a very young ethnic whore. Honorée was not the subject. Specifically about one's self, Col, with the mention of very young ethnic whores as a sort of life feature of mine. As you suggest. Honorée decided that discovering this profile of myself was another reason why she was entitled to breach client confidence and tell me what she had found.'

'She's well up on protocol.'

'I'm dear to her. You've seen this fucking stuff, have you, Harpur, know about the man?'

'Was she jealous?' Harpur replied.

'Honorée?'

'If it attributed "whores" to you, not "a whore". Is it odd, sir, that he knows you favour very young ethnic whores, yet he picks one himself?'

'People have always yearned to walk in my footsteps,' Iles said, 'so to speak. There were other dossiers in there, but, obviously, the one with my name on it shone for her, burned into her attention. It's possible there was one about you, Col.'

'Me, sir?'

'You've seen this fucking folder stuff, have you, Harpur?'

'He came back before she could read it all properly, I expect, did he, sir?' Harpur replied. 'She wouldn't want to be caught going through someone's case, even if unlocked. That's too much like what some would regard as typical whore behaviour, not necessarily very young ethnic whore, just whore.'

'Late thirties,' Iles replied. 'Drives a Subaru Impreza. Passable payer. Honorée admires the car. She brought the registration for me. She couldn't get an identification from the pink folder for this lad, nor in his clothes or the rest of his luggage. Honorée's not a girl who would normally invade a man's clothes, of course. I'd say pretty definitely she's never been through my pockets. But this was not a normal situation. She thought I might be able to do something via the number – find out who could be so interested in me, and, of course, why.'

'Why's the crux. As you say, sir, bright. Is she seeing him again?'

'I find, of course, Col, that you've been asking Lord Database about the same registration and have the same maiden lady owner. I've been down to the Maidrew, naturally – worried about Honorée associating with what looks like a through-and-through alias man – and I get the name Vincent Milce. That the name you have, too, Harpur? Are they moving in here big, Col?'

'Who, sir?'

'This is a polished operation.'

'The pink folder, you mean, sir?' Harpur asked. 'The research and knowledge of your individual ways.'

'Someone who has removed any piece of genuine ID evidence from all his clothes and luggage. This boy has work skills.'

'Is he clean, sir? I mean, in view of –'

'"Gifted", "incorruptible" were terms applied to me in the folder. These are damn clued-up people.'

'It would upset me to think of someone wearing a beautifully cut uniform of stupendous cloth yet, behind it, poxed, sir,' Harpur replied.

'Oh, a single pill these days, Col. Don't grieve.' All the same, Iles unzipped himself to check he was all right. He gazed for a while, sitting up a little and manipulating to get a range of scrutiny angles.

There was a gentle knock on the door and then it was pushed open a few inches. Iles whooped joyously and jumped down from the desk, re-zipping himself in the same movement. 'Why, it's the chief, Col,' he said. 'Here's a treat for us, sir. Wouldn't you say a treat, Harpur?'

Iles would require an answer. Harpur said: 'Mr Iles and I were just discussing –'

'Attempting a kind of overview, sir,' Iles said. 'We do it occasionally. But now we can enjoy a *real* overview.'

Lane obviously was not going to the same ceremonial duty as the ACC later. The chief had on one of those darkish suits that Iles said were made by convicts in Zaire as a break from mail bags, but showing like skills. He came into Harpur's room the way he did sometimes, a kind of shuffle, a kind of half stumble. Around the building he did not always wear shoes. He was in heavy navy socks today, one of them stretched out loose ahead of his foot by five or six inches. He looked like someone you wanted to press a pound into the palm of, hoping he'd spend it on soup not a can. Iles remained standing.

The chief said with a kind of pleaful urgency: 'Colin, are you able to promise me continuing peace in our streets?' He sat down on a straight-backed chair against the wall. 'I've been looking at our budget and –'

'This is what I meant, sir – the overview,' Iles said.

'I can't afford the manpower ever again to deal with that old-style gang warfare, turf disputes,' Lane replied. 'I have so many other needs to cover. Oh, God, yes, so many.'

Harpur felt appalled. The chief was offering a kind of capitulation, raw, total and pathetic. Peace on the streets was Iles's policy, never Mark Lane's, not till now. Always he had tried to reject compromise: would not accept a tranquillity bought by toleration of the Ralph Ember-Mansel Shale business alliance. The chief had believed it a duty to fight drugs commerce however it presented itself, and no matter how unbloodily run. Catholicism and his own nature had made Lane an absolutist who used to despise and shrink from all treaties with evil. Yes, used to. Had lack of funds begun to drag at his moral certainties? Zero tolerance of the drugs game would cost too much. Iles and despair and relativity had won: almost anything for a quiet life. The ACC, pacing mildly, looked sickened and ashamed. He would be horrified by such a devastating victory. Although Iles continually worked to squash and

171

limit Lane, he never wanted to bring utter collapse. That would suggest the whole system was wobbly, and Iles needed the system. He was part of it. Harpur had seen him draw back before when the chief looked liable to disintegrate under Iles's clever brutalities.

'I have cause for special anxiety, you see,' the chief said. 'Certain rumours.'

Iles said: 'Sir, whatever you may –'

'*Two* rumours, you see, but very credible rumours, both of which might mean our admirable period of non-violence is imperilled – as single items or taken together.' The chief was crouched forward, head over his knees. He spoke at just above a steady whisper. Iles stared down at him. Watching the ACC, Harpur thought of Wellington after Waterloo – something like, *Only a battle lost is worse than a battle won.* Shoeless, huddled, desperate, Lane recalled an Eastern Bloc political prisoner waiting for interrogation in Wall days.

'My wife,' the chief said.

Iles bucked up a bit. 'Mrs Lane has some views on the future, sir? Wonderfully perceptive woman, no question, but I wouldn't necessarily –'

'She hears things,' Lane said. 'It just happens.'

'Ah,' Iles replied.

'Oh, look here, Desmond, perhaps this will sound absurd,' the chief said.

'I'd hardly think so, sir – not involving Mrs Lane. Hears things where, sir?' Iles asked.

'The hairdresser's,' Lane replied. 'But unisex.'

'Ah,' Iles said.

The chief lifted his head and faced Iles properly. It looked as if Lane had suddenly decided not to cower any longer. His voice strengthened. There were reserves in Lane. Oh, God, if only they could have been got on tap more often. 'A man called Gurd has apparently called in, making inquiries, fishing for information about Derek Millward,' the chief said. 'This is a hairdresser's near

172

Ambrose Street. I gather Millward lives there. We, of course, know him as Beau Derek, lieutenant to Ralph Ember. Even a chief constable can be familiar with this much of the scene. Beau, apparently, is missing. Mr Gurd, his stepfather, has been looking for him because Beau's mother is dying, wishes to see him after an estrangement.'

'People like Beau do wander, sir,' Iles replied.

'Perhaps. Mr Gurd told the hairdressing people he has asked everyone who might know Beau's whereabouts and is now simply knocking local doors and calling on shops in case of sightings.'

Iles said: 'I'd bet Beau will –'

'And then something else,' the chief replied.

'Also at the hairdresser's, sir?' Iles asked.

'There's a buzz,' the chief replied.

Lane would do this now and then, pick some piece of slang, to show he had not soared too far above the world. He was good at it and could launch a word like buzz without any pause or emphasis.

Iles said: 'But specifically at the hairdresser's, sir, or is this a more as it were general buzz?' The ACC did give buzz a bit of projection. He seemed to have decided Lane was not wholly reduced after all and could therefore take some jollying along.

'That Ember's wife has left him,' the chief replied. 'She broke an appointment.'

Iles must feel it was necessary to deny anything that disturbed Lane. What disturbed him in his present state could annihilate him. 'Hairdressing appointment?' the ACC asked. 'Oh, but I'd imagine women do break –'

'The school has been informed that the younger daughter will not be attending any longer – just like that, no notice. One of the teachers uses the hairdresser's. Somebody saw their Volvo, very loaded, Mrs Ember and the two children in it, one child clutching a teddy bear, as if needing what the woman called "a comfort toy". An upheaval?' The chief lifted a hand and counted on his fingers: 'Beau. Mrs Ember. These are important changes. Do you see why I fear possible instability, Desmond, Colin? Ember does some playing around, as we all know, but he also prizes his wife and family. How will this affect him? Not the most stable of men. Will he remain controlled enough to maintain a business understanding with Mansel Shale? Beau was integral to that confederation, wasn't he, could prop Ralph when he wavered? And he *did* waver if things grew oppressive. Now, Beau's apparently removed. We don't know how. My wife wondered whether Mrs Ember and Beau might have gone together, a love thing. What implications here? Serious dislocation of the whole business scene?'

Always the chief expected chaos to disrupt his realm – at least his realm: perhaps it would begin here and then spread at unstoppable pace to the county, to the country, the cosmos. Lane saw his responsibilities as infinite. In a way it was wonderful in him, this willingness to accept the burden. In a way it was crazy, egomaniac. The chief harboured his own personal chaos theory, part scientific and sociological, part religious. Perhaps mainly religious. Hadn't failure in the Garden of Eden soon corrupted the world? Lane feared similar pollution might seep from his ground because of some carelessness or disability in him. These anxieties had once brought Lane to full and terrible breakdown. He had recovered but remained mentally fragile, and there were times today when he looked once more on the way to collapse. It might be worse now. After all, for the sake of order he had defiled his principles, embraced dirty appeasement. The results of even this seemed to be coming unstuck. Only catastrophe was left.

Iles said: 'They'll be back, sir. No, with all respect to Mrs Lane, I wouldn't think Beau and Margaret Ember have eloped. Consider Beau's skin.'

'Are there potentially anarchic realignments under way on our ground?' Lane cried.

There were. Harpur thought so. And, on less information, Iles did, too. But Harpur realized that neither he nor the ACC could tell Lane any of this. He had to be protected, shielded, preserved from rough facts and forecasts, shepherded safely towards retirement and honorary secretaryship of a charity. Harpur stayed silent out of humanity and respect for Lane as he had once been. Iles stayed silent because he could exist only in a settled hierarchy. Lane headed that hierarchy and somehow held it intact, although he might be feeble, bewildered and kept three-quarters in the dark. No, not somehow: held it intact by the insignia on his shoulder straps when he was in uniform, and by the ludicrous, obsolete faith the system put in him: held it together by conferred rank. The chief's rank Iles hated and lampooned and envied and understood and was sustained by. And Harpur thought the ACC knew in his soul he was sustained by it.

Lane forced himself to sit more upright in the straight chair. It was a planned effort, Harpur could see that. The chief tightened up his face muscles, made his eyes resolute. This was bravery. He said: 'I would like a meeting scheduled with Ember. Perhaps also with Mansel Shale. But at least with Ember. Colin, I take it you can arrange this? You have good contact with them?'

'Good contact?' Iles asked.

'A familiarity,' the chief replied. 'A familiarity in the course of Colin's normal work. I suggest no more than that. No devious hand-in-gloving, nothing illegal.'

'A formal meeting – Harpur, Ember, Shale, sir?' Iles said. 'May I ask, with what agenda?'

'No,' Lane said patiently, 'an unofficial meeting with me. Personally. Colin can be there if he wishes and perhaps you, also, Desmond, but this has to be above all a meeting of the principals in this situation.'

'Situation?' Iles replied. 'Which situation, sir?' Iles had probably understood entirely that the chief meant a meet-

175

ing with himself, but wanted to treat it as unthinkable. Harpur, too, saw it as unthinkable.

'This would be a session of reassurance,' Lane said, 'its purpose above all to comfort and sustain Ralph Ember at his time of strain and to try to save him from breakdown, from turning into Panicking Ralphy but Panicking Ralphy long-term, with hellish results – the fabric of accord ripped and trampled upon. This manor cannot be properly policed if the gangs re-emerge and slip into warfare again. My resources are not up to it.' He coughed and spoke more hurriedly: 'That is, *our* resources are not up to it, I mean, of course.'

Iles could not pace. He seemed to be paralysed, though he could still speak. 'This is . . . fu . . .' Perhaps he had been going to say fucking demented or fucking suicide or fucking *folie de grandeur*, but he amended it. 'This is fortunately only one way of reacting to the situation, sir, if I may say.'

'How I want it, Desmond,' the chief replied.

These moments would come now and then. Lane could take on a kind of fierce, addled authority, and even a kind of dignity. He had that now, the dignity. It was remarkable for someone in that hopeless suit and without shoes. Briefly, Harpur could feel workmanlike power radiate from the chief and forethought and decisiveness: all those qualities which for most of the time seemed to have been worn away or kicked to death in him by Iles and the mounting impossibilities of the job. Lane had once been a great detective on a neighbouring patch. Harpur occasionally worked with him then and was impressed. Harpur could still be impressed by him, though much less often now. Harpur felt something of that gifted, methodical brain at work in Lane's review of the Beau and Mrs Ember developments. Generally these days, though, he allowed other brains to dominate, and especially the brain of Iles. Allowed? Was compelled to. Promotion had almost ruined the chief. It was eerie to hear Lane talk of the need to save

176

Ember from breakdown when the main mission of Iles and Harpur was to save the chief himself from breakdown.

Harpur saw Iles's pain and fright rapidly increase. The ACC would dread to visualize Lane touched by dirt. A rendezvous with Ember and Manse Shale was dirt. Iles himself, and Harpur even more so, could operate in that off-colour, blighted region between order and lawlessness without bringing deep injury to the system of things. Perhaps they *had* to operate there, Harpur in particular, and do a bit of what the chief called hand-in-gloving. Lane, no. Lane, never. It was crucial he stayed out of it, above it, or wholesale discord would follow. The ACC's policy of peace on the streets had never been a spelled-out policy. It had happened, and Ember and Shale had observed it happen over the months and gratefully accepted it. There were no spoken deals, no itemized agreements. Laxity had been let develop, this was all. Ralph and Shale understood that unofficial tolerance might be withdrawn at any time decided by Iles. The ACC had given and the ACC could take away.

But if Lane parleyed with these two there would be a kind of contract, understood or actual, a contract between what the chief had called 'principals'. It would cease to be nod-and-wink, between-the-lines, reversible. It would be enshrined, and monstrous. Iles said: 'Sir, a man's wife leaves him, a nonentity aide disappears – do we really need to respond at this stage so profoundly? Is it proportionate?'

'I feel it may be opportune,' Lane said. He spoke levelly, no bark or snap, just inflexible, off-beam, perilous reasoning.

Harpur said: 'There's a chance Ember might want to come out of trading, sir, go legitimate. I was going to talk to him.'

'Who says there is a chance?' the chief asked. It was close to a bark, the bark of someone almost in charge.

'The word's around. The buzz,' Harpur replied.

177

'No, don't talk to him,' Lane said. 'I would fear the gap if Ember pulled out. Who, what, would fill it?'

God, yes, the chief had begun to think like Iles all through. Lane was in scrambling retreat from everything he believed and lived by. He was destroyed. His orderly tone showed only that for the moment he could hang on to control even when routed. The ACC said: 'I know this might seem not altogether to the point, sir, but would Mrs Lane want you to involve yourself with crud like Ember and Shale? I hate to think of her in your lovely drawing room having to digest news like this.'

'Desmond, my wife's views would *not* be relevant, whatever they were. It is a policing matter. However, I do know she favours this move, as a matter of fact.'

'She suggested it, sir?' the ACC asked.

'It is *my* decision, Desmond,' the chief replied.

Chapter Fourteen

Of course, Ralph Ember recognized at once that the slaughter of someone like Cosmo York, ginger Subaru prince, was bound to produce an extra bonding between Melanie and him, Ralph. God, how she had gone at York, though. Where did a woman like Melanie learn knife-play?

A special sort of partnership established itself through a killing together. The old acquaintanceship with her via Beau, and then the bunking together for mutual consolation that night – these were important, yes, but really quite slight in comparison. To a degree the new relationship might be sexual, and yet it was also bound to surpass that, even dwarf the sexual, though Ralph and Melanie did, of course, make love immediately after the stabbing, and in the same room as York's untidy body.

As a matter of fact, Ralph had held back from desire earlier tonight because he still wanted to resist the sly growth of commitment. Couldn't women get all sorts of big, stupid notions from a couple of pleasant intimate meetings? Too often he had been on the end of such misunderstandings. But, once the wasting of York happened, an unrushed time of deep closeness on the floor with Melanie had seemed right to Ember, despite the thick blood everywhere about, or possibly because of the thick blood everywhere about. It was a kind of thanks for what she had done and an endorsement of it. As he went tremblingly into her then, he had thought of that scene in

The Postman Always Rings Twice when Jack Nicholson and Jessica Lange very understandably want each other on the hillside just after pulping her husband in the car. Murder would always bring a raw, hotted-up feel to things. And yet, suddenly, flesh was not the whole of the case with Melanie. She brought him solid and inspiring companionship, as well as all the rest. Now, he found it very hard to recall his empty, frantic state when biting the teddy.

The fact that it was Melanie who actually got the knife into Cosmo York all those times probably made her more troubled afterwards about what had happened. And the blood on her clothes and shoes seemed to upset her for a couple of moments. Naturally, Ember urgently got the garments off her as soon as they checked York was thoroughly dead: urgent to free her from the muckiness of them, but also urgent because it had suddenly become that kind of emotional situation. For a moment she had remained tense, almost reluctant to join him on the floor. She was worried about how to get rid of York's body. He reassured her. That apparently fruitless detour around Winchester after the Tiderace trip not long ago acted as a morale builder: it proclaimed Ralph's efficiency. At the time he had been a bit disappointed not to find Foster and Gerry Reid. But didn't this prove he knew how to lose awkward deads for ever?

During the attack on York, streaks of blood had been bound to stain Ralph also. It did not fret him. No, he'd definitely say there was something aphrodisiac to it. He saw strung-out blood in one of Melanie's eyebrows – the right – which had been closest to Cosmo when she struck the first couple of blows, so the more likely to be sprayed. The hairs were dark and his blood sparkled there under the lights, vivid and dense, too wholesome-looking for someone like Cosmo. Looking down on Mel where she lay beneath him, Ember was thrilled by the unusualness of it.

Some women's horror of blood always puzzled Ember.

Their cycle should make them much more used to it on skin and clothing than men. Yet, given an incident like this with York, even a character as sure of herself as Melanie could become very briefly almost disabled by worry, poor, dear girl. Their lovemaking was in part a therapy again. He wanted to remind her and remind her and remind her that violence could also be sweet and rewarding. The grunts she uttered were happy grunts, give-it-to-me, give-it-to-me, give-it-to-me, Ralph, grunts. He would, he did, he did. Ember thought it vital they should remain in the same room as Cosmo. This was not just a matter of containing the spread of blood in one spot. To have it gloriously away with York's body in view signalled a perfect victory. Ember could not recall a comparable experience with Margaret or any other woman. Almost certainly he had never made love before when a knifed corpse was so close. He searched his memory. It was probably an experience very few men could claim. He felt ashamed of treating Melanie coolly earlier. She had not hesitated with the blade. Why had *he* been negative? He tried to compensate. York's glowing baldness was only a metre or so away from Ember when he climbed on top of Melanie, and for him it made Cosmo look almost comic, despite everything. They were beatable, York, Merryweather, even Bridges.

Odd that Mel should be more bothered than Ember about York's body, because it and the general mess were in the drawing room of Low Pastures, and unquestionably a nuisance. They had not covered Cosmo yet, and the disorganized way he lay and his open eyes could have made the scene ugly. It would all be put right. Ralph knew he owed Melanie his full entombing skills after what she had done.

But, for God's sake, it was wrong . . . it was slippery to think of this death as 'what Melanie had done'! That sounded as though he would stick blame for the attack on to her alone, a Panicking Ralph twitch. Although she had carried out the knifing, this was a shared moment, surely.

181

After all, was the most violent act he could manage to get his teeth into a teddy bear, for Christ's sake? Hadn't he helped line York up for her?

Strange, too, that Ember had been wondering how they would deal with Beau's body if found, and now Beau's woman had presented Ralph with another body altogether to get rid of. Also, he found it bizarre that she should be celebrating naked on the sealed boards with Ember the death of an enemy, when York was really only an enemy for Mel because he had killed her beloved partner: Cosmo's death was revenge, proclaiming her grand loyalty to Beau, and for her to be marking the event in this style with Ralph would surprise some moralists, no question. It might seem even more dubious than going to bed together just after he learned Margaret and the children had left, and Melanie heard about the end of Beau at Tiderace. Sex could be damn various.

The lovemaking with Mel was not the only surprise tonight. There had been several. She had called in at the Monty around closing time, obviously looking for Ember. It shocked and angered him to see her there. Women rarely came alone to the club. It was not that sort of place. She was bound to be conspicuous. In any case, this kind of mixing of his two lives Ralph always struggled to prevent. He did not like people from the trading side of things to appear here, and the trading side was where Melanie came from: he knew her through Beau and Beau had been part of the firm.

Ember had watched her tonight but for a while stayed at the little accounts desk behind the bar. The barman served her with a drink and she went to sit down at a table in a shadowy corner. Ember realized it could be awkward if Cosmo York heard he was getting into something close with Melanie. Or he might see it for himself: York dropped into the club whenever he felt like it, keeping an eye, the intrusive slob. Wouldn't it look like an alliance between Melanie and Ember? And in Cosmo's eyes wasn't that bound to mean a vengeance alliance against the man who had killed the partner of both of them? York was sure to be alerted. He might turn rough, and bring Bridges and Merryweather to help him turn rough.

Melanie had not stared about, kept her eyes down on her drink. It was a poor night for her to see the club, except that York was, so far, absent somewhere. A sullen, boozed group played the fruit machines, a set who talked forever about some big 'operation' they would bring off, but which never came to anything. Their shoes and clothes proved it. Looking at them, Ember could accept that it would take a while – years, not months – to bring the Monty up to the quality of the Carlton club in London. This scruffy team would recognize Melanie, know she had been Beau Derek's. Perhaps they thought she needed a grief drink. At least they would know she was not a street girl and leave her alone.

As if occupied only with gathering glasses Ember eventually went over. She spoke down at the table. 'I've been in touch with some people,' she muttered.

'What people?'

He had known what people. She was telling him she did not believe he would ever get himself to do anything about York and had begun her own arrangements. She meant he was Panicking Ralphy, all wind and promises and dodge. She had big neck, Melanie.

'People,' she said.

He cleaned the table and left the duster on it. The keys of the Saab were underneath. He moved on. After ten minutes she went from the club. After ten more he closed up. When he reached the car park she was lying out on the back seat, so as not to be seen. He drove immediately to Low Pastures. 'It's best if we talk at home.' He had meant it, and only that. He had given her the keys to get her out of sight: no romantic invitation. He hated involvement, unless he wanted involvement. At Low Pastures he led her into the drawing room and poured drinks. They sat down

183

in armchairs facing each other. Oh, he would never deny she was desirable. 'I'll take you home in a little while,' he said. 'I don't think we want taxis repeatedly out this way.'

He had watched but could not read her, was not sure whether she felt hurt at being told again she would have to go. Many women had had to learn this: although he might be available one night, it did not mean he was for ever available. He still expected Margaret back. 'What people?' he said.

'Rex Sallis,' she replied. 'Rex and Les Cater.'

Oh, God.

'They knew Derek.'

'I know they knew Derek.'

'I mean, *knew* him – liked him. They helped one another. They'd help me, if he was . . . If he's dead.'

'Sallis and Cater don't do hits. They're little-men burglars.'

'They can put me in touch. Obviously, I can't find my way direct to executioners. I needed go-betweens.'

'You *can* find your way direct to someone like that,' Ember told her. 'You have.' He believed it. He would do it. He spoke without blah. It was a statement. York had killed Ember's friend and still menaced the Monty. York would die. Ralph must work out how and do it. He drank a little Armagnac and gazed at her some more. Did she think a house like this, a room like this, furniture like this, came from dreams only and bullshit? He was not the same as that fucking lost, big-mouth crew in the club tonight.

'This was a kind of fall-back, that's all, Ralph,' she said.

He could see his words had got to her, perhaps scared her. 'And how much is all this going to cost you, the go-betweens and the unnamed specialist?' he asked.

'They wouldn't want much, Rex and Cater. This was friendship.'

'There was a figure?'

'They said a hundred each, for the facility. Like entrepreneurs.'

'But the main figure – for the one they're go-betweening with?' Ember asked.

'Maybe ten grand.'

'Yes, maybe. And Rex and Les would get a nibble at that, too, from him. For the *facility*. I'd see them in the club celebrating, most likely.'

'I'm not committed, Ralph.'

'You've got ten thousand around, plus the hundreds?' he'd asked. 'You'd blow money like that on a revenge spree?'

'Derek would want me to.'

'Derek would want you to keep it all very near, not talk to nobodies and outsiders.'

'If you'll do it, Ralph, of course, I –'

'I hate impatience.'

'Derek always used to praise your patience.'

He did not like that. It made him sound slow. 'Derek knew how things can be done, and how they can't be done.'

'Perhaps I misunderstood how things are. What you –'

'I think you did.'

'Look,' she said, waving a hand to show no problem, 'I'll tell Rex and Les, Sorry, boys, second thoughts – say I can't find that kind of money after all. They won't make trouble, Ralph.'

He had shrugged to signal that people like Rex and Les were not the kind who could make trouble for Ralph Ember. He downed the rest of his Armagnac. He had wanted her to know the meeting was more or less over. She did not finish her own drink, though, or move. Ember said: 'I'm a business person and the people I deal with are business persons. But, of course, it's a certain sort of business – mad to deny that – and now and then certain sorts of action are needed, some of them dark. I have to be prepared to carry out that kind of action. I am. I –'

She had held up a hand, telling him to listen. He felt infuriated at the way she took charge, but he listened. He heard a car on the gravel. This time, Ember thought he could recognize the engine. York must know Ralph's time-table, expected him to be recently back from the club. Melanie stood. 'I'll disappear,' she said.

'Go upstairs.'

'But it could be Margaret. She might want to –'

'No, go upstairs.'

She left quickly, taking her glass. He replumped the cushion in her chair and when York knocked the door went to open up, a fresh Armagnac in his hand. 'This is my routine,' he said, 'a nightcap after the club. Perhaps a video.'

'The Volvo still in dock?' It was grunting not talking.

Ember took him into the drawing room. He left the door open so that York would get the idea this had to be brief, whatever it was. Ralph poured him a drink and stayed standing. York had remained on his feet, too. He was wearing a county-style sports jacket of tremendous quality and cut, full of subdued reds and greens. With it he had on tan slacks and heavy brown brogues. Perhaps he bought the gear for calls on a place like Low Pastures. 'Ralph, I need to move in here,' he said. 'I've got trouble at that fucking boarding house. This is true trouble I'm getting there.'

Perhaps he was thinking of more than just calls at Low Pastures then, the fool. 'Taking girls to the room?'

'This is racial. I can't stand anything like that, not racial things,' York replied.

'A black girl?'

'Sweet kid.'

'Which black girl?'

'Called Honorée. Nice?'

Christ. 'Do you talk much?' Ember asked. 'Do you leave any papers around, anything like that? ID?'

'This is a steady thing – the same girl. Like a relation-

186

ship. Steady. They wouldn't make trouble if she was white, I know it.'

Ember had been facing the open door and over York's shoulder saw Melanie cross the hall quickly and silently. She must have come back downstairs. Had she decided to get out of the house? He hoped so.

York smiled, as if he suddenly saw more clearly. 'Oh,' he said, 'you're scared it might be a girl who goes with Iles? It's in the dossier he likes young pussy this colour, I know. But I asked her, obviously. She's never met him. Never even heard of him. There are a lot of black girls down the Valencia district.'

'Yes.'

'He can't get through them all. I mean, he's Iles but he can't get through them all. She said she knows the girl he likes best.'

Yes, she did. 'You're still not coming to live here,' Ember said.

'I wouldn't bring the girl. Well, naturally I wouldn't. This is a home. *Your* home, Ralph. She's got a place.'

'No,' Ember replied. He watched York for any quick movement. But he sipped his drink, that was all, so far.

'There's nobody here. I know it,' he said.

'Where?'

'In the house.'

'How do you mean?' Ember replied.

'Only you. Your wife – gone. Kids, gone.'

But, yes, there was somebody in the house, besides York and Ember. Melanie appeared behind Cosmo in the door-way, moving beautifully and with a very hefty knife from the kitchen in her right hand, her face full of a lovely, unfrightenable blankness. Although she could not have known that Beau was stabbed in the neck at Tiderace, she went for York's neck now herself with the first blow and the second and fourth and so on. This gave a sort of neatness to the vengeance. It would be luck. Probably she had picked the neck only because it was bare skin and

187

would need less effort than if she had to get to him through the excellent jacket. The thinking was good. To kill with a knife takes a lot of strength or a lot of precision. Ember didn't see how she could have either. She was not built like that or trained like that.

The first dig at the neck, though, was profound but clean so she could pull the blade out and get another jab in before he was doing anything much to protect himself. At the second blow he yelled and would have turned to confront her. He attempted to raise an arm, maybe to go for a weapon in a holster or pocket, maybe to hand-fight her for the knife, but this was when Ember did act and reached out to the shoulder of the jacket and pulled York around to face him again. It gave Mel the full area of Cosmo's back as target. She went at it with a downward movement from high up, placing the dig to the left and just under York's shoulder blade. Maybe she did know something, then. Cosmo yelled again, or it was more a shriek, and took one dodgy step towards Ralph, trying to get distance between her and him. Ember was still holding a bit of his jacket and felt the terrific material yanked away from him as York tumbled.

Once he was on the floor, Melanie could really work on him, and especially the neck again. She actually knelt alongside York like a nurse with a road casualty and slowly gave him three more lengths of the blade, putting out a kind of thin whistling sound because of the effort. Mel was probably at her nearest to him as she knelt there, but most of the blood on her, including the eyebrow blood, came from the first blow, when York was upright. Maybe she had hit the artery. Yes, it was possible she knew quite a bit. Ember felt what he had felt almost from when he first met her, that she was too good for Beau Derek. He had decided he must have her now, as soon as she put the knife down. It was an occasion.

Eventually, she stood. Ember said: 'There are other people. They'll come looking for him.'

'You can deal with them, Ralph. I know it.'

She spoke as if he was the one who had done what was done to York tonight, not herself. Ralph wondered if he was being soft-soaped. But, perhaps when you looked at things properly he *had* been the one who coped with York. Who brought him into the drawing room, arranged him with his back to the door, rearranged him a little later with his back open to Melanie? It could be argued that she had had the easy task, the simple soldier's role. Ember's was generalship. She had seen this more quickly than Ralph, and he admired her for that. Mel *was* a mind. There might be a problem about her stained clothes later. Possibly she would not want to get back into them and would use this as an attempt to stay until they had been given a bit of a cleaning. He could look out something of Margaret's for her.

Chapter Fifteen

Iles said: 'A friend of mine tells me Subaru man must have left our duchy, Col. He doesn't come cruising, looking for her, salivating, any more. This is almost a week.'

'Poor Honorée.'

'He was devoted, in his lousy way.'

'She deserves the best he could offer.'

'He's given up. I mean on everything, not just Honorée. The business aspect.'

'Is that so, sir?'

They were in the ACC's room at headquarters. Iles, standing at the window, looked out possessively now and then at what he termed his duchy, the terrain. Harpur had been called to the meeting. He was seated in an armchair underneath a framed colour photograph of Sarah Iles holding their baby daughter, Fanny. To Harpur, Sarah looked as if she had been dragooned into the pose. But he knew he was biased about Sarah and did not like to think of her in family settings. She might have been really happy. Iles had probably taken the photograph. That was intimate, in a way, and Harpur always resented it a bit. But, then, Iles had fathered Fanny, and this was even more intimate. Harpur could get an unpleasant vision of that happening whenever he looked at the portrait. Perhaps this was why Iles had hung it there. In all the visions Iles was on top. Harpur always fought off any gross alternatives.

The ACC said: 'It's retreat, Col. He comes here with his fucking pink folder, no doubt looking to make some sort of

190

trade takeover, but when he arrives and glances around he finds he can achieve zilch. All right, he has already heard from the pink folder about my integrity, but that's mightily different from discovering it for himself.'

'This would be integrity personified, sir. Integrity in the flesh rather than as a statement.'

Iles turned and gave Harpur a small, Reichsmarshal stare, obviously wondering about a head-butt for the kid-level mockery. Something quietened the ACC, though. Was he beginning to age? The notion dragged at Harpur's spirits. Decay everywhere?

Harpur said: 'How did he come upon it – the actuality of your integrity, sir?'

'Oh, the buzz around the city, obviously. I'm known as "Iles the Untouchable". You'll have heard that. And possibly he's discovered about you, too, Col. You've got a sliver of integrity somewhere behind that joke suit.'

Iles was in a majestic, very unjoke, grey suit, probably bought at one of the OK spots in London, not Hackney market. He turned from the window to face Harpur and give him the full analysis. 'Imagine his situation. He comes here – is sent here, possibly – to case the place trade-wise, maybe for his superiors. He has certainly *read* about the difficulties he will run into – my incorruptibility and to a miniature extent yours – that kind of thing – and then he finds from inquiries in the as it were field that the pink folder actually understates my unswerving probity, Col. This is easy to do. Fear would be sure to fix on him. Fear of the spotless. Fear and the wish to run. I think he *has* run, run back to his associates with a no-no message: *call it off, try somewhere else.* He might also have approached Ember and/or Manse Shale and found similar unbreakable resistance. Say Subaru and chums wanted to put drug selling through the Monty, for instance. Many have fancied that. Almost certainly, Barney Coss and the women did at one stage. Anyway, Subaru and chums might be thinking that way but are abruptly confronted by Ralph, eternal, obsessed custodian of the club's slimy' soul. However flimsy in general his morale is, when it comes to the Monty he is steel, Harpur, steel.'

'Yes, it could be like that.'

Iles sniffed around these words busily, like a cat with a dud plate of food. 'What – you *know* Subaru saw Ember, do you, you smart, deceitful jerk, Col? You've been watching this invader? So, how the hell did you get on to him, Harpur?'

'We might be able to keep business things as they are, then, sir,' Harpur replied. 'The status quo. Mr Lane will be delighted. No destructive stress.'

Rage made Iles's thin face thinner. 'Unforgivable,' he snarled. He clutched at his throat, as though choking. Almost instantly, though, he released the grip: Iles hated his Adam's apple and the feel of it must have sickened him more.

'What's unforgivable, sir?' Harpur asked.

'For Mr Lane to be pleased.'

'But *you* want things are they are, sir, the status quo.'

'Yes, I do, but he's the chief, for fuck's sake, Harpur. This is a holy eminence. A chief shouldn't connive at big-time drugs dealing on his ground.'

'An *assistant* chief does.'

'I make a balanced choice. But I can do that because I'm not the system. The chief *is*. Lane embodies all our love and regard for order, Col, all our morality, all our integrity, all our –'

'You have your own special integrity, sir. It says so in the pink folder.'

'It flows from, is bestowed by, the chief, as the fertilizing Nile flows from high ground to the otherwise parched delta. Think of that word, Col – chief.' His voice grew matter-of-fact but reverent, as if the points he'd made were so built-in they needed no arguing, only routine acknowledgement. 'This is position, this is leadership, this is responsibility, this is our *gloire*. Yes, for us the chief is de Gaulle, is an archangel.'

'As well as the Nile? I've heard you say such things before, sir.' And Harpur, of course, had, though not given such colour and force. 'I've never understood your thinking, sir. You –'

'Of course you've never understood it, Col.' Iles smiled and damned sympathetically.

'I might be able to bring Ember out of the drugs game,' Harpur replied.

'Yes, his cool wife said so, didn't she – that you, *only* you might manage it.' Iles sat on his desk and back-kicked it with one heel, not energetically enough to break anything yet. He was just taking solace from the din. 'You fucking specifically, Harpur. Not one's self. I was present, if you remember, when she said this, but naturally, naturally,' the ACC trilled, 'it's dear Colin Harpur who can work this transformation, not Des Iles. Have you ever witnessed such insulting behaviour before, Col? Was it humane?' The smile had vamoosed. Iles began to hiss: 'I look at you now, wearing those damn clothes as if they were totally normal, and sitting in unashamed proximity to a picture of my wife – my wife and our lovely, innocent –'

'Do you want me to turn Ralph legit, sir – try to? I'll tell him Margaret might come back, if he quits the trade. He probably knows this, but I'll underline it.'

Iles looked out at the city again. His power and reputation endlessly sang there. He needed to listen, hear assertive, adoring anthems raised about himself in detail, though skirting the Adam's apple.

Harpur said: 'Turn him legit and possibly make a hole in the trading firms to be contested by new gangs and –'

'Street chaos again.'

'Possibly, sir.'

'People, my people, deserve other,' Iles replied. He went quiet for a while, stopped clobbering the desk. Then he said: 'Yes, bring Ralph out of it, Col. You *are* the only one who could do it. I'm forced to say she's right.'

'Thank you, sir.'

'You have the same sort of grubby ethics and creepy brain as Ember. You wavelength each other. You'd be unique, Harpur, if it wasn't for him.'

'Thank you, sir.'

'I can't allow the chief to dirty himself, reduce himself, by accepting my tainted strategy. This would probably strike you as ironic if you knew what irony was, Col. Mark Lane is not made for *realpolitik*. You might ask what he *was* made for and –'

'Or I suppose *you* might, sir.'

'And I'd not know how to answer. But I dare not permit the collapse of lawfulness and the true values of the *system*, Col. It would be a disgusting endorsement by the man put over us of that seductive gospel, the end justifies the means. This might be *my* gospel, or even yours, if you understood what it meant, Harpur, but it cannot be Mark Lane's, or his puppet mistress's, Sally Lane's.'

Harpur said: 'I'll go and see Ralph.' He felt moved and baffled and relieved by the ACC's brilliantly contradictory assessment. Buried in it somewhere lay a statement of what policing would be if it could be but it couldn't. Iles was only able to operate his intelligent, murky variants of that ideal as long as he knew Mark Lane's authentic dream remained intact, as dream. It must be cherished and guarded by the chief, their appointed, crumbling, desperate figurehead. Or at least by him and Mrs Chief. But it was Lane himself who bore all that real and glorious insignia on his epaulettes. There had to be system, *system*.

Early afternoon was the best time to see Ralph Ember at home in Low Pastures. He would get back from the Monty at just after 2 a.m. and sleep until midday. Harpur drove

194

out there and parked on the gravelled forecourt alongside Ember's Saab. There had been times in his career when Harpur felt like the White Knight, fighting evil alone. He enjoyed that once in a while. To be morally white was a bracing change from all the greyness and worse he usually lived and worked in. Today, though, he saw himself more as a missionary or even a Messiah. He would bring Ralph Ember the glowing prospect of salvation.

When he knocked on the door it was opened by a small, thin, very pale girl of about eleven dressed in jodhpurs, a tweed jacket and brown boots. She said: 'Oh, I thought it was – My dad is here but not my mum.'

'It's your dad I wanted, I think.'

She turned and bellowed: 'Dad. Someone. My mum's doing a big shop or she'd be here. We've been away for nearly a week, to see my grandma. But now we're back.'

'Just away on a visit?' Harpur replied.

The girl looked doubtful.

'You all came back?'

'Who?'

'Your mum, your sister, you.'

She giggled. 'Well, yes. I suppose. Here I am, aren't I? Venetia's upstairs. My mum's –'

'Out on the big shop.'

'My grandma's old. She likes people going to see her.'

'I expect so.'

The girl said: 'I don't see how a teddy bear could get hurt in a week, even if it's only an old one.'

'No,' Harpur replied. 'It's not something that usually happens to teddy bears.'

'If it wasn't put back on the shelf properly it could fall. That's what dad said.'

'It could.'

'I was going to take it and leave the other one because although the other one – I mean the other other one – although that is older I like it the best. I'm eleven which some would say is old to have teddy bears, I know that, but there are men, really grown-up men, who collect teddy bears, you know.'

'Yes. I don't think eleven is too old.'

'But then I thought that if we were going away for ever I'd better take the new one, because the old one would get older and older and might wear out. Of course, *I* would be getting older and older as well, and I might get so I did not want *any* teddy bear any longer. But I could not be sure, because of grown men who have teddy bears. So I put the old one back on the shelf, but perhaps I didn't put it back properly because of the rush and it fell and cut its stomach.'

'You thought you were going for ever?' Harpur replied.

'Even if it fell, how could its stomach get cut? Dad said perhaps he fell over it.'

'Did he?'

'Perhaps dad went into my room when we were away to see things were all right, no spiders' webs and that. He could have stepped on Justin by accident.'

'Did he? This could damage a stomach. But stomachs can be repaired.'

'Oh, I think so. I'm going riding with a friend in the paddock. When you knocked I thought you were her mother bringing her.'

'No school?'

'My friend's a bit ill. Whooping cough. She mustn't go near other kids because of catching it, the germs. I've had it, so I won't. Me, I haven't been going to school because of going away. But next week, I expect. Mum will tell them I'm coming back. Worse luck. Here's dad.'

Ember said: 'Well, ask Mr Harpur in, Fay, for heaven's sake.' He had on green tracksuit bottoms, a brown, high-necked sweater and trainers. He looked triumphant, nimble, in no need of salvation. He could have auditioned immediately if they wanted a well-made star for an epic.

'I just thought, talk to him about Justin, the teddy, and gran,' she replied. 'I didn't know who he is.'

'A police officer, Fay.'

'Oh, not things at the club again, is it?' she asked. 'Not people with their ear chewed off in fights?'

'Of course not,' Ember replied, with a grand laugh. 'I expect it's a business matter.'

'The club *is* a business matter, isn't it?' Fay asked.

'Come, Mr Harpur.' Ember shooed Fay off to a different part of the house and took Harpur into the fine drawing room. Ralph went to the sideboard and poured a couple of Armagnacs. He brought one to Harpur and they sat down. 'I can't do your favourite here, I'm afraid, not gin and cider mixed. No cider.'

'Are you all right, Ralph?' Harpur replied.

'Well, fine, fine. The family all around me, you know. My older daughter's with us on a break from Poitiers, France.'

'We thought maybe changes.'

'What kind of changes?' Ember said. 'Is this to do with Beau and that Mr Gurd, his stepfather?'

'The chief gets anxious.'

'A fine man. I'd like to think he can keep his health now.'

Harpur said: 'Do you ever consider coming out of the business, Ralph?'

He sighed. 'Well, I suppose we all would like to quit work, wouldn't we, Mr Harpur? But . . .' He waved a hand towards one of the drawing-room windows. Harpur could see Fay and another girl in the paddock trotting circles on nicely cared for, tallish ponies. 'I've got a place to keep up, a family to look after. The Monty has a lot to pay for. I don't think I could sell up and retire yet.' He stretched out in his armchair, maybe to get the sports gear into prominence and declare his fitness, and the idiocy of retirement talk. 'Few of us are like the police, you know, able to retire when you're still only spring chickens.'

'No, I meant the *business*, of course, Ralph, the other business.'

'Oh, the little bits of buying and selling. That comes and goes, very as and when, believe me. No great strain. No great loot, either, I'm afraid.'

Harpur said: 'I was wondering –'

'You were looking for Beau, were you, at Tiderace the other night?' Ember asked very gently.

'You saw me?' Harpur was sure Ember did not. Melanie talked to him?

Ember said: 'Both of us illegally on someone else's property, so I suppose we're not going to shop each other. Anyway, in a good, humane cause.'

'Did you think he might be there?' Harpur replied.

'It's a mystery.'

'And the people who live at Tiderace – Barney Coss and so on? A big house, deserted like that.'

'These are yachting people. They do what they like when they want to. They handle a bit of buying and selling themselves, of course – how I know them. But they'd never let that interfere with their leisure. Never. They'll just cut loose, go. They might be crewing for someone. Their own boat's still there. An invitation and an instant decision. They've got the money to make it feasible. I'll have to settle with Barney for the broken window! He'll be annoyed, I expect, but he'll understand.'

'This is what I meant by changes,' Harpur replied.

'Sorry?'

'As if they'd gone.'

'Barney and the women? Well, obviously, they *have* gone, but only for –'

'Anything happened, do you think? Like Beau,' Harpur said.

'Do you mean Beau might have left with them on some long yachting spree? It's possible. He doesn't know much about all that. But, yes, it's possible. They like Beau. He'd make it a foursome. Those two women, I don't suppose either of them cares much who it is as long it's someone.'

'His partner, Melanie, still doesn't seem to know what's happened to him.'

'No? It's a mystery.'

'Do you talk to her much, Ralph?'

'She's quite a personality in her own right,' Ember replied.

'When I say changes, I mean on the street,' Harpur said.

'Hard to keep up with, I admit.'

'This is what makes Mr Lane anxious. I don't like to see him given stress.'

'He's got a plateful of responsibilities. He's lucky to have the backing of such a wife, especially when he's been ill,' Ember replied.

'We spotted some ginger-to-bald newcomer in a Subaru.'

'How do you mean, "spotted"?'

'Possibly looking at the scene,' Harpur said.

'What would make you decide that?'

'Probably a pathfinder. I'm getting an instinct for them, I expect.'

'All kinds of flash people have their eye on this city now, you know, Mr Harpur. It's what's called a growth point, I believe. That's why I think the Monty has such a future, and why it would be a mistake to give it up.' Ember stood and went to the sideboard for more Armagnac. But Harpur also stood to show he was leaving. There would be no born-again work of salvation achieved here. Not today, anyway. Ember had his family back. He was garrisoned. He was strong in self-belief, rich in double-talk. He was Ralph. Aplomb shone in his jaw scar.

He stood with Harpur in the porch of Low Pastures and they watched the two children on their ponies cantering line ahead now. 'Fay seemed to think she was going away indefinitely,' Harpur said.

'A week is like for ever to them, isn't it, Mr Harpur? Lord, the preparations for a little trip to their grand-

199

mother's! Which teddy? – all that. You heard about it, didn't you – Justin or Cedric! Thanks for your patience. I expect you understand, though. You've got daughters yourself, haven't you?'

'They were in Subaru man's folder,' Harpur replied.

'Sorry?'

Harpur went back to headquarters and now did launch a call for sightings of the Subaru. Towards the end of the afternoon he had a message that a wreck burned out at a hillside spot famous for such torchings might be the vehicle. There were no plates. Its chassis number was still readable and belonged to a Subaru stolen four months ago from an hotel car park in Devizes.

'Someone who knows our local bonfire sites then,' Harpur said to the Traffic voice who rang him. 'Anything at all recovered?'

'What sort of thing, sir?'

'A pink folder.'

'This was a very capable blaze, sir.'

'Yes, I expect so.'

Chapter Sixteen

Obviously, after the sudden return of Margaret and the children like that, Ember was alight with joy and gratitude for the lasting power of marriage and had to get hold of Beau's Melanie pretty urgently and tell her not to come out to Low Pastures any more, especially not creeping around the front door in the middle of the night like a lover. If she turned up during the day, he could possibly explain it to Margaret all right because anyone would understand Melanie's concern about the long disappearance of Beau and her wish to discuss this with Ralph, his business chief. In a way, it would be better now if Melanie did not have such a clearly fuckable body and come-on cheek bones. These might cause Margaret doubts, even if it was a day visit. Margaret knew how women would pester him when she was not about, and even when she was. The damned El Cid factor.

Ember definitely appreciated that the situation was sensitive and complex. He knew he could not just pick up the telephone and tell Melanie things between them were closed on account of developments, as he might have done at the end of a run-of-the-mill fling. After all, Melanie was much more than a sad woman he had allowed a consolation session or two to, upstairs and down. For God's sake, they had killed someone together in Ember's drawing room and with a knife from his own kitchen set. Or, at least, Melanie had killed him, but Ralph was undoubtedly in attendance and could to some extent be said to have lined him up for her. Although the knife was now replaced and purged, Ember considered he would never be able to use it again on roasts without thinking of Melanie and Subaru man's neck. Ember also considered that the experience of making love on the floor to a woman who had someone else's blood thick in the right eyebrow would be around in his memory for a fair time as pretty well unique. His life had been given an undeniable twist by Melanie. All his original estimates of her as an unslight piece were correct. She had to be the most unslight piece he had ever had real contact with. He saw himself as damn sharp about women. Hadn't he known Margaret would scuttle home, the dear, after a due bit of sassy gesture?

He arranged to go down and see Mel at the Ambrose Street flat. 'Ralph, I'm so happy for you,' she said as soon as he told her. She stood far from him, wearing a black T-shirt and denim skirt, as though aware he must reassume full husbandhood and would want to. This upset Ember. Why didn't she fight to retain him? He had expected her to be jealous and resentful, even to ask in a rage whether on her return he took Margaret immediately to the bed Melanie and Ralph shared that night he revealed Beau Derek was dead. He had readied up a heartfelt denial of this, in case. There were susceptibilities involved here which any man would have respected, and Ember above all did.

'She couldn't endure things without you, Ralph,' Melanie said. 'I understand. You and Margaret – a kind of permanence.'

'Everything looked OK,' Ember replied, '– the drawing room and his car gone, naturally.'

'Him in it?'

'That's not the drill at all, Mel.'

'Sorry. I don't know about these things.'

'Fire's never going to destroy a body totally, even with petrol. We don't want serious police inquiries started,

202

bringing publicity. A burned-out car's routine, but not a burned-out car with remains in it.'

'Where is he, then?'

'But you did know about what *really* counted – how to finish him,' Ember replied.

'Oh, I see that as quite joint.'

'Absolutely,' Ember said at once.

'As the grievance was joint.'

'Absolutely.'

'It's given you peril, hasn't it?'

'Some,' Ember replied. 'This has to be accepted.' He nodded and smiled very briefly, a comradely sort of smile. He wanted her to know he did not blame her in any final way for slaughtering someone on his property and leaving him to shift the body and vehicle and spruce up the place. If you were Ralph Ember, you *did* accept such loads. There would be inconvenient but worthwhile deaths and these had to be accommodated. Thank God, he still knew the meaning of *noblesse oblige*. He had lived by it when associated with Beau, and would live by it now when associated with Beau's partner. This was a woman with excellent breasts for her age and it would be crude to reproach her for a stabbing.

Melanie said: 'Possibly Subaru had told whoever ran him he was coming out to Low Pastures to see you.'

'Yes, there'd be a detailed, agreed itinerary with timings. That's basic.'

'This would be their last information from him, Ralph. A pointer to your place.'

'Right.' He had thought of all this on his own and did not really want it gone over again. Now and then Ember regarded Low Pastures as a hellish liability: impossible to defend when all those fucking fields and bushes and copses could give people like Andrew Cartier Bridges and Charlie Merryweather such an easy approach. Although they were not rural warriors, those two and their team, they could adapt. You'd need bloody radar and snipers in a bedroom window. Ralph's own shooting was below that standard, and handguns only, not a rifle.

Melanie said: 'So, when Subaru fails to renew contact with them –'

'*You* should be all right, Mel. They wouldn't know you were at Low Pastures.'

'No, but *you*, Ralph. Already a potential target and now this, even without media publicity.'

Because he had repeatedly lanced himself earlier with these jabbing thoughts he found he could resist panic as she pushed on, so sodding graphic and raw. Ember felt proud. He had come to feel protective about her voluntarily, no compulsion. Strength and gentlemanliness were his, gentlemanliness in its true, full meaning. He was all-round gracious and undaunted.

'In a way, bait,' Melanie said.

'What?'

'Subaru man – the removal of him. If he did tell his masters his programme, we know where they'll come looking once things seem to have gone wrong. A plus, Ralph. It fixes them to a location – Low Pastures. They could be met there, dealt with there. We want them as well as Subaru man, don't we? They did Derek, as much as he did.'

'They were present, yes.'

'The way *you* were present at Subaru man's death, Ralph. They are a part of it, as you so willingly recognize you were a part of *our* necessary murder.'

He'd heard that cut-price phrase, *necessary murder*, somewhere during the university foundation year. Auden? Orwell? 'True,' he said. Ember suddenly began to lose contact with that strength and gentlemanliness he'd thought just now were his. They seemed to go out of him, like air through a tyre gash. He felt as he had felt before with Melanie, that she would grab mastery, turn him into a traipsing follower only, knock him down to Beau level. Ember recalled a scene in *Some Like It Hot*, on TV so often.

204

In it, Jack Lemmon, dressed as a woman, wrestles the lead when tangoing with that old shrimp, Joe E. Brown.

'They have to be removed, too, haven't they?' Melanie asked.

Ember said: 'Removed? Well, in –'

'And first-class business reasons for it, also, surely. You've said so. I don't mean just saving the Monty, though that's immense – a sort of grail quest, clearly.'

Not what she'd said before, when she'd sensed they wanted the club. Fucking *grail*! She had talked about the Monty as a dump. This one could spin to a purpose. He knew that already, though.

'But, Ralph, if these people – Subaru and his string-pullers – or only the string-pullers now – if they're trying to replace the Tiderace group as bulk suppliers there's a chance for whoever blasts *them* – that's the string-pullers – a chance to clean up the lot, get *really* major, isn't there? This is dealing of a different category. This is mighty.' Her voice boomed with commercial vim and know-how. You would not think this a woman so recently more or less widowed. She was prettier than that dreary, dead old hamster, Maud, in the Tiderace group, but Melanie had the same sort of huge vision and ferocity.

Of course, she was giving him back his own idea of the possible future as if it was new. 'These boys are not push-overs, Mel,' he replied. *Tiderace*? She even had the name. Beau must have really gabbed. Ember could forgive him. Mel was powerful. She wouldn't tolerate secrets.

'I didn't expect they *were* pushovers, Ralph,' she replied. 'They're big, I'm sure. They are filthy and creepy and it takes three of them to kill Derek, but that doesn't mean their plans can't be massive.' She did a kind of grand chortle, vivid with devotion and sex. 'But, and such a but, Ralph, those plans will run against someone who's like nobody they've ever had to cope with before.'

For a second he realized he was seeing himself as a terrific amalgamation of not just Ben Hur and Moses but El

Cid and General Gordon of Khartoum and the fire chief in *Earthquake*, too. 'Oh, look, Mel, I –'

'Ralph Ember,' she said.

It counted large, this kind of testimonial from someone as perceptive and staunch as Melanie. There might be a buttering element to it, sure, yet he felt she also had a true belief in him, and not just cock-based. He would make it deserved. Ember said: 'Plainly, that kind of general business thought occurred to me – the opportunity.'

'You've schemed a fine opening, Ralph. Derek was always on about your tactical genius.' She gave him a small, apologetic smile. 'Frankly, I used to feel a little sceptical. But now I've seen it operating for myself.'

'All good tactics depend on the ability to compel others to do what you want them to do, Mel. Consider D-Day – making the Germans think the invasion would be Calais way, not Normandy, and put their armies in the wrong spot.'

'Set them up.'

'That's one phrase to describe it.' She would even chop his damn words about, as if he were flowery and indecisive. He'd run across snotty women like this on the university staff.

'And now here's the chance to get the bastards in our sights, Ralph,' she said.

'I think so, Mel.' He longed to fuck some humility into her again, as he had longed to fuck the arrogance out of those niggling, college wonder-girl lecturers, get their book-buggered, egomaniac eyes rolling. But he knew he might be able to use Mel's brains, and he had tried to use the university women's brains, too. Unquestionably, women were entitled to be seen as more than pussy in current times. Ember hoped he would always argue this.

He and Mel were in the living room at Ambrose Street. Ember had been there before and thought it a surprisingly OK room for a struggler like Beau to have: light, unpoky and the furniture solid, not glue triumphs. There were mild coloured prints and pictures. Ember did not feel it unseemly to be discussing policy in such a room, even with someone not fully of the trade. It might be reasonable for him to pay the rent of the flat for a period, on top of whatever he sorted out for Melanie as those supposed fees owing to Beau. But did she *need* money? She had talked of being able to come up with a ten grand payment for someone to hit Subaru, before *she* hit him instead. And didn't she speak today as though she thought of herself as part of the firm from now on, and presumably coining? Occasionally she said 'we' and 'our', as though they were already colleagues. Oh, she flattered him, iconized him, as well, yes – made out he was the one who truly rated and scared all the opposition into helplessness – but that's what some of it was, flattery. She had a scheme.

Melanie went to the kitchen to make coffee. These were definitely legs for easing apart: their length, symmetry and slenderness, though no frailty to them. Oh, Jesus, was this nothing but a degenerate, leching, male reaction? After all, weren't these the legs of a woman grieving for one of his most reliable staff people? Couldn't he think of her legs as simply legs, for – obviously – standing her upright and getting her to places like the kitchen and back and the secret funeral if they ever found Beau?

She returned with the coffee and sat opposite him. 'But, look, Ralph,' she said, 'that fucking Low Pastures is troublesome. I know it and the surrounds well now.'

He did not mind swearing by women, and in any case she was in her own home, although speaking about his. However, the statement indicated another ploy in her campaign to control: she was the tough-talking chief now. 'I don't follow,' he replied.

'So wide open. Hard to lay on an ambush.'

'Well, yes.' He did not know if he wanted an ambush at all for Bridges and Merryweather, and, if he did, he did not want it at Low Pastures. Yes, wide open. And his wife and children were there now. They must be kept out of the cross-fire.

Melanie seemed to spot his fears: 'Not actually *at* Low Pastures, obviously. That would be stupid. You'd get pulled in and charged afterwards. But there are some nice bits of secluded approach road.'

God, she'd noted them.

'I was wondering about Rex Sallis and Les Cater,' she said.

'What?'

'Some backing for you there. They could be bought in – mercenaries. It might take a bit more money than they wanted for middling. We're asking them to risk getting shot at. But nothing outrageous. I mean, you're alone now, Ralph. Derek's gone.'

Beau Derek, the gun virgin, would have been no asset, anyway. And Ember was never going to allow nothings like Sallis and Cater on to his property or near it. Christ, imagine kitting those two out with weapons and letting them wander close to Low Pastures while Margaret and the children were there! He felt an immense tenderness towards his wife and daughters. It had been a rhapsodic moment yesterday in the early afternoon when he heard the Volvo estate approach over the gravel and then the voices of the kids yelling through the open windows of the car to tell him they were back. Quickly, he had run up to the bedroom and done a recheck, then come down and taken one more thorough look at the drawing-room floor.

After this, he had rushed out to greet Margaret. He did no questioning, just listened forgivingly to her account of going to see her mother and a description of the journey home. Obviously it was true that she had been there. He could not be sure, though, whether the stay at her mother's was originally to have been only the initial stage in a permanent desertion of him and Low Pastures. Apparently, that was what Fay had suggested to Harpur. He let the uncertainties remain uncertainties, however. Humaneness was his entire aim. He did not mention the money she had taken. That would be a bit much for a visit to her mother's, wouldn't it? He expected the cash to be replaced in the roof space, probably in full, but was he likely to quibble about a thousand or two, for heaven's sake, or even count what she brought back? To him it appeared the children had never been sure whether they were leaving on a visit or permanently. Margaret's farewell letter had said she put the choice to them about going or staying, but they might not have realized she meant going or staying for keeps. In any case, it had *not* meant for keeps, had it?

When the girls went out to check that the stable boy had been looking after their ponies right, Ember and Margaret hurried upstairs and all she said was: 'Too lonely, Ralph. It couldn't be done.' She had needed his body probably even more than he needed hers. He could understand this. She had the guilt.

So, yes, Melanie read things brilliantly right. There *was* a permanency between him and Margaret. He wanted to lean forward and touch Melanie now in thanks for that lovely insight, touch her somewhere totally unintimate like elbow or chin, not those deep and friendly thighs, not yet. Ember decided not to handle her at all for the moment. He said: 'Perhaps I'll talk to Mansel Shale.'

'To do what?'

'He'd probably like to be in on things.'

'Which things?'

'To wipe out Bridges and Merryweather – Subaru man's associates – and get the importation and bulk distributors' corner,' Ember replied. 'It's too big an operation to handle alone. He's got a nifty lad, Denzil, working with him, and other hard people. We should be able to put something useful together.' He deliberately brought in that 'we'. She would not know whether he was talking about himself plus Shale and his crew, or Ember and her. That was how he wanted it.

'Does he trust you?' she asked.

'Who, Manse? We're like partners. That's how the scene is run here now. You know this from Derek, Mel.'

'I think you're brave.'

'It's a matter of –'

'I don't mean just brave about your own position but your family's. If you draw those two – Bridges and Merryweather, did you call them? – if you draw these to Low Pastures, or near, looking for Subaru, your children and Margaret will get some danger, too, won't they, even if you bring in Shale and his heavies? And I do know how devoted you are to the girls and your wife. Ralph, it shines in you, so fiercely, so admirably.'

This damn testimonial wrongfooted him again. How could he do anything coital with her after that? Now, it would be seedy and glaringly treacherous to reach out and stroke her great legs progressively. He would not have objected to getting into a bed where Beau used to lie. Melanie was the kind sure to change sheets and pillow cases often. Squeamishness by him would have been insolent and stupid. But it could not happen today. Delicacy had intruded. He leaned forward and gave her elbow a maty squeeze. 'We'll win this one,' he said.

'We?'

'Yes, we'll win this one,' he replied.

Ember rang Mansel Shale and arranged to visit. Ralph did not like this much. Shale's place could be dangerous. And it must always be an error to let Manse know you needed help, because he would obviously want to scrag you via the weakness, as close partners in any business or priesthood or profession would. Ember remembered with contempt how they did Thatcher.

Obviously, Ralph could not tell Shale Beau was dead. It

would look like Ember's team had been half crippled and stood ready for slaughter. Shale was sure to ask how it happened, and why Ember did not stop it, try to. Or, no, he might not ask, just think. Manse could be like that. It would fix more frailty on to Ralph, invite more jubilant kicking. That well-known 'survival of the fittest' idea was invented for Manse Shale. Probably it had been former Shales who fucked up dinosaurs. But Ember did not see where else to look for aid. *Not* Sallis and Cater. Those were people with even less class than Beau. They were not made for such an enterprise. This should be a hijack in the true, original sense: a load of crooks like Bridges and the rest to be robbed of what they had just robbed from others. Manse was for ever loutish, yes, but he had the brain to appreciate the lovely possibilities of this scheme. Had they been given a glimpse, Harvard Business School would recognize its beauty and put it on the course. 'Ah, I thought you might come, Ralph,' Shale said. 'This *got* to be re Beau.'

'Beau?'

'You lost him?'

'Beau?'

'Lost him, Ralph? Is there a security problem?'

They were in what Shale called his den-room, not just his den, in case it made him sound too much like an animal. Ember could understand why Mansel would worry about this, with such eyes. And he had a heap of darkish hair which would be fine for a llama needing to beat mountain ice.

Shale said: 'Someone around asking and asking for Beau, I mean, *really* asking, digging, Ralph, asking some of my people on the street, calling him Derek – have they seen Derek lately?' Shale tried to make his voice softer, more refined and plaintive. He'd never get there. He sounded just oozy. '"Please do try to recall if you've seen him, it's *so* important," all that urgency – but they knew he meant Beau. This is pushers on the street – *on the street* –

211

he's asking. Them dross got no training in silence except about theirselves, Ralph. Have they heard of discretion? Discretion? Do me a fucking favour. It's mad to be bleating at them like this. This is some relative re a sick woman. I would of thought you'd make certain the sod didn't go about shouting names like that, associating Beau with the trade, disturbing the surface. Ramifications, Ralph. There's none of us safe from ramifications. That's one of the first lessons I got from the academy of life.'

'This Gurd?'

'It could be Gurd. Some name like that most probably. Starting G, most probably. That stuck in my head. Gurd or Snape. Short name. Denzil got it written down. He handles the clerking side and he's great with short names.'

'Beau's mother's dying.'

'Like that, yes. That was the gist. Some woman. It could be a mother,' Shale replied. 'All right, mention someone's mother and it's bound to reach my sentimental side, Ralph. You heard of decorum, at all? You won't find me saying a mother should not want to see her son, I hope.'

'I'm sure, Manse.'

'But where's the tact, where's the care in the search?'

'If Gurd's around again I'll suggest tact and care.'

'Suggest? *Tell* the fucker, tact and care, or, better still, tell him fuck off. I appreciate his kindly purpose. I don't want to put heavy treatment on someone looking for someone because of his terminal mother, do I? Like I said, decorum.'

'When I say *suggest*, Manse, if Ralph Ember *suggests*, people know they're getting an order, believe me. This is called man management. Like control without them knowing it's control.'

'Sew his mouth. Or scare him out of fucking sight, for keeps.'

Manse lived in what used to be a rectory and Ember certainly did not mind that as long as Shale rationed the talk about it. Once, Ember had made a joke about Manse living in a manse, the term for the home of a minister of religion, but of course Shale did not understand it, or pretended not to. He did seem to believe the place gave him a kind of mysterious spiritual link with all the clergy who had been there before, not necessarily like the Apostolic Succession, but what he used to call 'a happy, holy line'. Probably everyone needed something similar, some connection with what was good, even if you had to imagine it. Ember had the Monty and its future. Some people kept a picture of a saint or John Lennon.

'So, where is he, Ralph?'

'Gurd? I think he went –'

'Beau.'

'Beau? Oh, Beau!' Ember explained with plenty of good nature about Beau's little ways. 'You know Beau, he'll take off sometimes when he feels like it, tell nobody not even his woman.'

'You get amongst that when he goes?'

'Who, Melanie?' Ember replied. 'They've been together – well, I can't remember how long. Something really solid to it. Melanie's strong. She understands Beau. She doesn't –'

'I don't see how someone could go off when his mother's fading, not even Beau. He's in Acapulco or the Canaries and his mother's calling out for him from her bed as a mother is entitled to and repeatedly, "Derek, Derek, my boy!"' Shale had adjusted his voice again. 'Oh, this touches me, Ralph.'

'He didn't know she was fading, Manse. There was an estrangement.'

'Why do you say *didn't*?'

'He didn't know she was sick.'

'*Doesn't* know she's sick? Shouldn't it be *doesn't* know he's sick? He's dead?'

'I love this room, you know,' Ember replied. He did a gaze. 'The pictures. Taste. Dutch women from those times seemed made for art, didn't they, the hats and thick bodies and lips? And, yet, it would take an artist in the period to spot that these ordinary women were good enough for art reaching right into the new millennium, wouldn't it, Manse? I suppose this is what we term genius. A Dutch woman of that century like the portrait by the bookcase is so right for this room. It gives more than Dutchness.'

'I get a lot of comfort from art,' Shale said. 'Beau's dead somewhere? I got what's known as Pre-Raphaelites in the other room. You heard of them at all? Tresses, long frocks that can be blue, orange, real perky colours. Hughes, Prentis. Heard of them at all? Top league. A house like this *needs* art, and I don't mean fucking glossy muck about tulip petals or kittens. You want me to put out a search for Beau? That why you're here, Ralph? You're not one for visiting. You want Denzil to do some asking, some real asking, not like this, this . . .'

'Gurd.'

'Denzil asking people who might know if Beau been terminated hisself somewhere, never mind his fine mother, likewise slipping away.'

When Shale bought the house, he had also purchased some rectory furniture from the church authorities, including a vast, mahogany, MD-style desk. It was in this den-room. He used to work at accounts on it sometimes, the way Ember did on the small desk at the Monty. Once, Manse had told Ember it really thrilled him to be totting figures on the same wood where good sermons had been prepared and testimonials for people who became full-scale beauticians or schoolteachers.

'I thought just a tactics discussion, Manse,' Ember replied.

'My tactics are right already.'

'No question, but –'

'You saying I screwed up some way?'

'Never, Manse.'

'You ever seen that Welsh thing?'

'Which, Manse?'

214

'On TV in the afternoons sometimes. The Endless, is it called? When they're all dressed up like the KKK – robes, hoods?'

'The Eisteddfod.'

'And someone comes on the stage with a sword and shouts, "Is it peace?" But he shouts it in Welsh. I found out that's what it means. Well, I ask you now, is it peace, Ralph? Of course it fucking is. *This* is tactics. By clever policy we got serenity in all our neighbourhoods.'

'Unquestionably. But the need to develop, Manse. I don't say revolution, not put in peril what we've got. An advance, though, Manse.'

'What fucking advance? You change things, you got risk.'

The other matter Shale would often make a speech about was that Mark Lane, the chief, also lived in a former rectory, but out in the country. Manse believed it, too, set up a link, a law-and-order link this one, and not especially religious, though the chief was a devoted Catholic. Manse considered it could be because they were both in rectories that Mark Lane might gradually come round to seeing Shale's business as perhaps tolerable, particularly now a wise understanding existed with Ember. Occasionally Shale let a woman share St James's rectory with him for anything up to months, and Ember felt unsure how things were at present. Manse's chauffeur and right-hand rough-house, Denzil, occupied a flat in the attics. Denzil you had to watch.

Shale reached out and ran a couple of fingers along the edge of the big desk. This item and the art and occasional live-in floozies could bring Manse quite a bit of calm. Ember thought he deserved that. Shale had also told Ember this desk showed that ultimately every aspect of life – religion, civic duties, crack, the Health Service, cosmetic shops, poppers, education, smack, the UN, needles, service industries and Ecstasy – ultimately, all were part of the same general structure. Apparently, some churchy girl who moved in with Shale for three weeks a while ago told him about a doctrine called 'the principle of plenitude', meaning life actually *needed* all its completely different elements in order to be full. For Manse, his desk proved it. Fucking gibberish, obviously, but that wasn't something you said to an ambitious thinker like Shale if you wanted to preserve an alliance. And especially if you wanted Manse in a new aspect of the alliance, a double-killing aspect, with luck.

'I suppose Denzil might be able to get somewhere with a hunt. Do you *want* him found, though?' Shale asked.

'Beau?'

'What tactics?' Shale replied.

'Yes, I call it tactics, I think that's the word. Of course, yes, you certainly have your tactics already, Manse. But no business should mark time.'

'Is this something . . . like . . . something *major* between you and Beau's woman?' Shale replied. 'I heard your wife's gone, tired of it all, I mean the extra ladies. Did you get rid of Beau yourself so you can take his girl permanent? Look, is this a body going to show up sometime? I know you're ace at disposal, but all the same a body could show up by misfortune, could it? You're out here now to prepare me? Maybe you don't want Denzil to look for him at all, you're just saying if Beau gets found somewhere I shouldn't worry – it's not about the trade, just you and his woman fixing things up nicely for yourselves, which your wife has left you because of. This makes me anxious, Ralph, definitely anxious.'

'Margaret gone?' Ember said, with a true laugh. 'Where does that fiction come from?'

'I hear.'

'Maybe we should have met at my place instead, Manse, and then you could see Margaret and the children about, just as ever.'

Shale said: 'Of course, Ralphy, I know you could ask, why the hell do I go on at you about banging Beau's woman if he's away but I have girls for myself in here.

216

I want to be fair. One here now. Carmel, a grand kid. She been here before on a semi-longlasting arrangement. I'm not somebody who just gets rid of a girl and that's the end, Ralph. Unfeeling. I can go on having affection for a girl, and if there's a blank spell I'll get in touch again and say, "Oh, come back, Carmel, do. There's a place reserved for you still." Or Lowri. Or Patricia. Favouritism is not in my nature. I'm off-and-on with names but I don't ever forget the name of a girl who's lived on these premises. These are *people*, Ralph, not just items. They should be give consideration.'

'They're fortunate to have run into someone like you, Manse.'

'But doing it with the girl of a business colleague who could still be alive, only absent – I see possible upsets there. *Is* he still alive, Ralph? The love side might get out into the commercial side, and this is a peril for everyone. This isn't the same as with Carmel, you see. Or Lowri, or Patricia. I hear she's something you wouldn't think some-one like Beau would ever get near, that right?'

'Who, Melanie?' Ember replied.

All this talk around things – it meant Manse was not relaxed. Anyone looking at him sitting there near the desk now could tell he was still edgy because of all sorts but especially because he was the one who liked to have the ideas and make the proposals and did not know how to act if someone else came along and mentioned tactics. Shale could be very various, quite jumpy, but just the same Ralph would have regarded it as vulgar to enter his home on this kind of mission with a pistol aboard. It had nothing to do with the house being religious as an ex-rectory. Ember considered that only where meetings were likely to become genuinely bloodstained might it be right to go into somebody's domestic setting armed. This was the same sort of sensitiveness he had felt about waving a pistol about at Tiderace. Too much fondness for firearms was primitive, like Mussolini. All right, Chuck Heston headed an important gun club in the US, but Ralph did not have to imitate him in everything, just because of the physical resemblance. And, as Ember had told Melanie, he and Mansel Shale were more or less colleagues. Certain tensions existed, as in all vibrant business associations, but nothing to justify weapons. Manse was in a red leather armchair and looked fairly all right, although short, his feet only just on the floor. He had on one of those zip-up fleeces, around these days to de-naff the cardigan. It was loose, but Ember felt pretty sure it did not cover a pistol. Shale said: 'A body such as Beau's bob into sight somewhere and we got police boots all over, Ralph. Probably Harpur and Iles theirselves. Iles loves the tranquillity we give him, but all the time he's wondering if war will come back, and if Beau gets found dead Iles is not going to realize it's just because of you and eternal pussy, he'll think gang feuding is here again, and he'll be on to us like the Panzer Corps.'

'I'm glad you mentioned this. What I'm saying is we can deliver even better, safer peace, Manse,' Ember replied. 'We'll have every side of the business between us. I mean *every* side.'

Shale needed a spell to think about this and try to work out what Ember had in mind. He stood up and went out of the den-room. Soon he came back with a bottle of white wine, two goblet glasses and a corkscrew. He opened the bottle and poured a glass each. He handed Ember his. Ralph saw the label was Montlouis, which might be all right, from down Vouvray way in France. It was a bit sweet and soft, but probably suitable for a discussion where very serious things about the lives of crud like Bridges and Merryweather would be considered.

'This is a dream project, Manse. We can get into control of everything, from importing right through to street and rave distribution,' Ember said.

'Importing? Your importer's Barney Coss, isn't he? So, where's he in this?'

'Yes, where is he?' Ember replied. 'And the women.'

'Out of it?'

'I've already dealt with a third of the opposition. He's gone, and no body problem, believe me.'

Shale could not understand one fragment of it. Well, of course not. It was lovely to watch him in the big armchair trying to keep his snub face looking bright and in charge, but his ferret eyes a mist for now. 'Which third is that, then, Ralph?'

'This was someone who came poking about.'

'You mean that Gurd, or Snape?'

Ember sighed. 'No, no, Manse. Gurd is just a family thing, a humane thing. This was someone flashing a Subaru and making sick remarks about the Monty. So, you'll see he had to go. Leaving another pair. It's what I meant by developments. This is an operation planned in very tidy stages, Manse, the way you like. Famed for that. I think you'll appreciate it when I give you things in full.'

Naturally, Shale hated to be talked to like this, like to a pupil, so fuck him. He had to respond with a knocking remark. 'I don't want to be dragged into anything problematical, Ralph. Not something I, personally, haven't once-overed.' But you could see he was gasping to know the picture, and not one with a fucking fat Dutch woman with fat lips in it.

Chapter Seventeen

'People who feel hurt and put down, Col – always they're the ones to talk, aren't they? They're the whistle-blowers.'

'Are *you* hurt and put down, Jack?' Harpur said. 'You talk. You blow whistles like a virtuoso.'

As far as Harpur could make out in the four-fifths dark, Jack Lamb's mighty face assumed some pain. His voice went into a patient, lecturing tone: 'I listen to people who are hurt and put down and who talk,' he said. 'I give them an ear and sometimes sympathy and sometimes cash. Then, if I think it's matter suitable for *your* ears and will damage only those who deserve to be damaged, I talk to you, not because *I'm* hurt and put down, no, but because I feel . . . well, I feel a duty. My mother forever stresses duty.'

'A lovely woman. Shall we see her again soon?' Harpur prepared himself for Jack's routine long-winded testament of grassing once more. But it did not come. Perhaps Lamb realized he had put all that in front of Harpur often enough over the years. 'Which people have been hurt and put down, Jack?' Harpur said eventually – that kind of question Harpur always asked because police were supposed to, and the kind of question Lamb never answered, because informants didn't: sources were still sources and sources still dried if someone were wet enough to disclose them: dried and now and then still violently died.

'This was two minor lads lined up for a little of what's

called "middling" work and then the commission is withdrawn. Abruptly. No excuse or explanation. D'you know middling work at all, Col? Go-betweening.'

'Which two minor lads, Jack?'

'Only one of them spoke to me, an acquaintance from, oh, such a way back,' Lamb replied, 'but they're both feeling hurt and put down.'

'Who was it spoke to you, Jack?' Harpur asked.

'I can understand their resentment,' Lamb replied. 'Wouldn't anyone? In their lowly way, professional people, with expectations that contracts are honoured, Col.'

'Little villains?'

'But entitled to proper treatment.'

'Contract? What kind of contract, Jack?'

'A professional agreement.'

Lamb paced a bit. He had called Harpur to what he thought was most likely Lamb's favourite secret meeting spot: the concrete foreshore blockhouse dating from 1940 and built to throw back Hitler if he had tried it by sea, this bit of sea. Lamb liked to step about inside and also frequently crouch to peer through the weapons slits, as though the German pocket battleship *Bismarck*, and a family of landing craft were ready to sneak in and molest him. All the same, Jack seemed to feel more or less secure with the thick, old concrete swathing him, although Harpur had the worrying idea that the place sometimes acted as rendezvous for criminals splitting loot, or planning the next job, as much as for him and Lamb. Jack appeared to find a womb-like quality in the blockhouse: he revered his mother and, although she made twice-yearly visits, her home was in the United States and he probably missed her. Jack was getting on for six feet six inches and nearly nineteen stone. He took a good slice of the blockhouse's area, whether pacing or crouched over a loophole. Harpur kept to one wall, his face turned towards the door space and decent air. The blockhouse had had sixty years of very basic uses and Jack's bulk moving about got the wafts going. He was wearing some army surplus to chime with a military setting again, and would have been a deterrent to invaders even without the blockhouse. This time the outfit was grey and looked to Harpur like German tank corps stuff. Jack did not go in for detailed accuracy. Any uniform would do, as long as it was a warrior's, not a doorman's. He adored epaulettes.

'What sort of go-betweening, Jack?'

'This was to put someone in touch with someone,' Lamb replied.

Harpur waited, but Lamb was squinting at the dark horizon for a World War II restart. Harpur said: 'Isn't that what go-betweening usually is, putting people in touch with someone?'

'Don't get fucking satiric with me, Col, or I'll wipe you out.'

'Right.'

'Then suddenly the assignment's off,' Lamb said.

'Why?'

'Many possible answers.' Lamb turned back, paced a bit more as he considered them all silently.

'Which one do you like the best, Jack?' There was a rigmarole when Harpur talked to Lamb, or at least listened to Lamb. Jack gave whatever he had to give very slowly, rather roundabout and teasing. He offered Harpur time to appreciate properly the excellent quality of what he was getting. And Harpur did appreciate it and would always keep coming. There was no grass quite like Jack. His performances could be an ache, though.

Lamb said: 'Which possible answer do *you* like the best, Col?'

'Jack, I don't know anything about the task, for God's sake. How can I pick?'

'No, but taking tasks as a general thing – the *concept* of tasks – if someone cancels an instruction why would that be?'

'They've changed their mind,' Harpur replied.

'Oh, so brilliantly true!'

'Don't get fucking satiric with me, Jack, or I'll wipe you out.'

'Right. Yes, they *have* changed their mind. But why?'

'This is where the many possible answers come in,' Harpur said.

'Name one.'

'The job's already been done, or handed to someone else,' Harpur replied.

'I knew you'd get there,' Lamb said.

'Which job's already been done?'

'These two were engaged to put someone in touch with a hit artist, Col.' The word *hit* hit the concrete wall near Harpur like a bullet and bounced off and echoed, hitting and hitting more walls until the life of *hit* was hit out of it.

'Ah, you did say a contract,' Harpur replied.

'These two weren't going to do it, just find someone distinguished who would do it.'

'Which two is that, Jack?'

'If I tell you who commissioned them you'd be able to work out who they are because they were both good friends and colleagues of his/her partner, Col.'

'Which?'

'Which what?'

'His or her?' Harpur replied.

'They were never told who was to be hit, just to put him/her in touch with the artist. Customary drill. Need-to-know basis only.'

'Which hit artist?' Harpur asked. '*I* need to know.'

'Someone from away. Expensive. This would be for a fee, the putting one side in touch with the other. Ten grand is a figure in the air. Overall. The go-betweens would get a cut.'

'Right. A normal entrepreneurial task, really. So then the instruction is cancelled and the fee with it? That how it went?' Harpur asked.

'Someone could be dead, Col. Hit before the hit artist was even approached.'

'Who could be dead, Jack?'

'Here's a problem. But I think an *important* death.'

'Why?'

'I said these two were hurt and disappointed.'

'Well, yes, they lost a job,' Harpur replied.

'They lost *two* jobs.'

'How's that?'

'This is what I mean when I say an *important* death.'

'What?' Harpur replied.

'This death is enough to make big changes in the scene.'

'Which scene?'

'There's some recruiting going on,' Lamb replied. 'I pick up murmurs.'

'Well, you always do, Jack. The best. What sort of recruiting?'

'Recruiting. Fighting men. Are we into a war situation?' Lamb crouched and glowered out at the darkness again, damn ready for whatever they could throw at him.

'*Are* we into a war situation, Jack?'

'My informant and his associate –'

'The hurt and disappointed ones?'

'They have not been asked to join.'

'Join what?' Harpur replied.

'The war. This is what I said, *two* jobs lost. They miss the middling, and then they're cut out of the battle build-up. They're hurt and disappointed a second time. This is two possible fees.'

'But why?' Harpur asked.

'Why not asked? Because Ember doesn't think much of them.'

'It's Ember who's recruiting?'

'And Shale. A combined force.'

This was real information. Always, Lamb produced, as

224

long as Harpur could wait. Always, Harpur could. 'Recruitment for what?'

'My tipster thinks Ember considers him shit. Knows Ember considers him shit. And his mate. Regards them as no class. And has told Shale they're shit.'

'That doesn't help with identification of the two. Ember thinks most people are shit. He looks at them from an El Cid eminence. Most of us *are* shit seen from there. He thinks I'm shit, no class.'

'Well, yes. Do you see the line?'

'Which line?' Harpur replied.

'The way the line of events develops. Someone gets hit. Straight afterwards Ember and Shale need to put a force together. Why?'

'Because people are coming to hit whoever hit the one who got hit and take over whatever work the one who got hit was doing?' The echoes coughed like a machine gun of Gunga Din's time. 'Mixture of revenge and commerce. No brew is stronger.'

'I knew you'd get there, Col.'

'Who hit the one who got hit? Ember? Shale?'

'Who would have a motive to hit the one who got hit, Col?'

'The one who was going to engage the two to put him/ her in touch with the hit artist before the one to be hit by the hit artist was hit by someone else, presumably him/her.'

'Clarity is one of your gifts, Col. I hear Subaru man has dropped out of sight.'

'That right?'

'You heard, did you?' Lamb replied. 'I understand his car was found.'

'*A* car was found.'

'Come on, Col. A Subaru found.'

'Yes, *a* Subaru. He wasn't in it.'

'Who did it knows the basics. Now, you'll tell me there

225

are a lot of people who know the basics, so this is no help with identification, either.'

'There *are* a lot of people who know the basics, Jack.'

Lamb moved towards the door opening. Harpur's audience with him was near closure. 'Change, possible upheaval, possible chaos, Col. Chaos I fear, Col. Chaos – the annihilation of all we believe in.'

'Who?'

'Why I felt it right to speak.'

So, here was the defence of grassing, after all, but at least short. 'The chief frets about impending chaos, too,' Harpur replied.

'People with a feel for civic life do, Col.'

'That right?'

'I do believe in progress, Col – dentistry, sunroofs and the unpluggable telephone – but it's got to be cherished, sternly guarded. Chaos is the natural, primeval state. It could come back if we're careless.'

'You and the chief, co-thinkers. This is some team.'

Yes, as to chaos, Mark Lane never ceased to sense this approaching foul shadow, and it was because he considered the death of Beau Derek meant the shadow had moved sickeningly closer that he insisted on coming to inspect the body. The chief would occasionally fix on an incident as symbolic of something vastly larger than itself and requiring personal, hands-on treatment from him. The discovery of Beau rated as one of these incidents. Maybe the ability to spot symbols, indicators, was a qualification of high rank.

With this body, there were identification difficulties again. Beau had been in the sea a long time. A fingerprint job. Beau did have a bit of a record. Nothing recent and nothing big, but enough for the matching machine to breathe his name. The naked corpse washed up on a beach near Sidmouth in Devon would have stayed a mystery, otherwise. Nobody had reported Beau missing. Melanie wanted to see him now but she would never have officially named him a missing person. People like Melanie didn't report things.

Harpur drove one of the big Rovers. Melanie was alongside him in the front, the chief and Iles behind. Iles always tried to be present when the chief attended these especially meaningful situations as he saw them, so that Lane might be told what the meaning of the meaningful situation really was. Iles could have a way with symbols, too, when wanted. Lane did not always listen to him. Iles would still scheme to be there, though. He felt a fierce obligation to protect Lane from ideas.

In the car, Iles leaned forward and spoke gently into Melanie's ear: 'My dear, if you decide finally you don't wish to see him, that would be all right. Perhaps nothing would be gained. Perhaps you would be further distressed. The prints will be enough. You're not crucial to identification.'

'I want to see him,' she said.

'That's all right, then,' Iles replied. 'I understand.'

'At some stage, I'd like to be alone with him briefly,' Melanie said.

'Of course,' Iles said.

'Whether he's recognizable or not,' she replied. 'If his mother's still alive, I'll say I've seen him. Not how he was. It's awful, but at least it would end her fretting.'

'That's kind,' Iles replied. He sat back again.

After a time, from his corner alongside the assistant chief, Lane said: 'We certainly would not want to badger you now, Melanie, but we're reaching out, reaching out, endlessly reaching out, trying to read the significance of his death. Forgive me. I know that to you it is a death, and this is enough. And yet if we can interpret what this death is saying it might be a comfort to us all. Can you give us any guidance?'

Iles seemed to want her left untroubled. Appallingly

227

unexpected streaks of tenderness would appear in the ACC now and then, confusing people. He said: 'Oh, chief, perhaps we could ask Melanie such things when –'

'No, no guidance at all, I'm afraid,' she replied, her voice final, flat.

'As to why he should be found where he was, for instance,' Lane said.

'Of course, we don't know he was put into the sea anywhere near there, sir,' Harpur said. 'Currents and tides are not really chartable.'

'So, where do *you* think he was put in the sea, Harpur?' Iles asked.

Lane said: 'I naturally wondered whether it was anything to do with his work helping Ember. He did occasional tasks for him, I believe. We will talk to him, but perhaps you'd know, Melanie, whether he handled any assignment for Ember lately.'

'Oh, Derek was a very private, very discreet person about his work,' Melanie replied.

'I see,' the chief said.

'Yes, that's how he struck me, too,' Iles said. He was telling Lane to drop it, to forget policing and get human.

At the mortuary they left Melanie with Beau for a while, as she had asked. Harpur, Lane and Iles waited outside in the hospital grounds. It was a tree-bordered, pleasant, lively spot with paved walkways and a fountain. Harpur thought of pictures he had seen of college quadrangles or secret gardens in country houses: places with secure pasts and probable futures. Visitors and hospital staff continually passed near them. Harpur, Lane and Iles hardly talked. Harpur found it simply a comfort to be out of the bare, dead room and away from the destroyed features. In a while, Lane said: 'I don't like to think of her alone like that.'

'She doesn't consider herself alone, sir,' Iles said. 'She'll speak to him, try to remember him as he was. As he was

228

wasn't much, but she'll want that. This is private, mystical, unforensic.'

'I'll go a little closer, in case she calls out, needing support,' the chief replied. 'She might have overestimated her strength.'

'She won't call,' Iles said. There was an outer office, anyway, and Lane probably would not hear her, even if she did. Simply, he seemed to feel guilt at being at such a distance from her and in such different surroundings – as if the prettiness and busyness of the piece of ground where they stood involved abandonment of her. Lane lived for responsibility. Perhaps he felt guilt, too, at having interrogated her in the car.

'But the body, the face – Oh, God,' Lane said and moved back towards the mortuary entrance. 'Don't worry, I will not intrude. I shan't return inside. But just to be near.'

Iles watched him go: 'Forget the garb, he's a glorious old thing,' he said, 'his instincts, as ever, noble.'

'Of course,' Harpur replied.

'He'd have made a superb warden for an old people's home,' Iles said. 'It would not be in him to starve anyone deliberately, no matter what age. She knows the fucking lot, does she?'

'Melanie?'

'Why he's dead, even *how* he's dead, and what happens next.'

'Beau thought so much of her,' Harpur replied. 'I can see why.'

'And *you* – you know the fucking lot, do you, Harpur?'

'I think the Tiderace people will turn up in the sea eventually. Different spots, I expect.'

'Sure they will,' Iles said. 'Cast thy dead upon the waters for thou shalt find them after many days in different spots. A putsch. They've been replaced, Col, haven't they? Subaru man was in our domain to fix the new supply arrangements, was he, check on outlets?'

'I think he's dead,' Harpur replied.

'Who says?'

'Yes, he could be dead,' Harpur replied.

'Who hit him?' Iles asked.

'Yes, hit,' Harpur replied. 'He would have been hit, anyway, but he was hit before he was due to be *officially* hit. Some special opportunity.'

Iles stared at him, untangling this. 'You're sure? Christ, of course you're sure. You know every fucking thing, don't you, Harpur, and keep every fucking thing under your helmet until you feel like opening up. Listen, Col, if he's dead his mates will come looking for who did it, and they'll want to carry on from wherever he finished. This is a mighty business matter for them. They'll ask around.'

'I should think so,' Harpur replied.

Harpur watched Iles's face as he worked out the further steps. The ACC grew anguished: 'They'll go to the damn boarding house to find his last movements. They might learn about Honorée. They *will* learn about Honorée from the rancid couple who run that place. These visiting thugs will probably locate Honorée and lean on her for inside stuff. I mean *lean* on.' Iles's voice soared and broke towards a sob. The chief, at the mortuary door, heard him and looked back. 'Get the fucking car, Harpur,' the assistant chief pleaded. 'Let's go home. Let me go to her. Now. This is a girl who needs protection. This is policing, Col, *inter alia.*'

'We can't rush a woman out of a morgue mourning a destroyed lover, or a man who's there to console.'

Iles considered this and spat. 'No,' he said.

'You could ring Francis Garland and tell him to make sure Honorée is all right until you arrive.'

'Garland?' Iles resumed yelling and waved an arm about, in a frenzy, waist-high, as if getting range on Harpur for a kidney punch. 'Is that some rotten joke, Col? Let Garland close to a woman of mine again?'

'Subaru man was close to her.'

'Subaru man was Subaru man, a paying guest in all

meanings. Garland is Francis Vandal Conquistador Garland.'

'Well, we wait.'

The chief called feelingly: 'What is it, Desmond? You look bad. Is all this too much for you?'

'I'm worried that a special tender-aged whore of mine might get slaughtered because of silence, sir,' Iles shouted. 'Irreplaceable. Chaos is coming upon us.' A couple of passing nurses in smart blue and yellow uniforms caught at least the end of this and glanced towards the ACC, possibly wondering whether he had slipped out from a psychiatric ward, or was a top-grade seer. He yelled again: 'Harpur's been sitting on some information, that sweet, murky way he has.'

The chief walked back from the mortuary entrance and unhesitatingly put an arm around Iles's shoulders. The chief had courage, Harpur never doubted this. That word *chaos* and the ACC's apparent anxiety about it would have gone straight to Lane's response machinery. 'I think you need me more than Melanie, does, Desmond,' he said. 'It's why I exist. Yet I *know* you will come through. You are still Desmond Iles.' Today, the chief made this sound a plus.

The ACC did not detach himself from the chief's hold but said: 'Never mind about me. What about my lovely, warm, youthful, black friend, sir? She is the future.'

'Perhaps we are already into chaos,' Lane replied.

'Sir?' Iles said.

'An assistant chief involved with a –'

'Not *involved*, sir. Some richer, more magical term.'

'Which?' Lane asked.

'Enthralled by,' Harpur said.

'Pitiably enthralled by, Desmond,' Lane said.

'Yes, enthralled by,' Iles replied. 'Good, Col, fine of you, very fine. *The* word. I toast it. You understand these things, you with your own access to lovely, young, titted, perky womanhood, your undergraduate bird, replacing at last –' Iles began to scream and twisted out from beneath the chief's wholesome embrace – 'replacing at last, Harpur, your deceitful, lewd, destructive obsession with the flesh of my –'

'Here's Melanie now, sir,' Harpur replied. Her face was strong. Harpur could see no trace of tears as she strode towards them. She led to the car and they took their places as previously.

For long stretches on the way back Harpur had the Rover up to 120 mph. At the edge of his vision he was conscious of Iles, leaning forward from the rear seat once more and making a kind of rolling movement with his right hand, to demand additional speed – the way instructors did with trainee drivers in Traffic Division. It was early evening.

'I'm going to ask Col to drive us straight to Dring Place, if you don't mind, Melanie, chief,' Iles said. 'A dear chum of mine walks there quite often at this time. It's her jolly routine.'

'Beat. Is it the same dear chum as you've just spoken about?' the chief asked.

'It is, it is, sir,' Iles replied. 'Shrewd. But I hope I know the meaning of constancy. Some of us loathe casualness in sex, don't we, sir? Oh, God, let her be there, and undamaged!'

'But why do you say this, Desmond?' Lane asked. 'Is she threatened? I mean, more than any of these girls is constantly threatened. It's their life mode.'

'Yes, more than any of these girls is constantly threatened,' Iles replied. 'But I love your phrase, sir – "life mode". I'll note it.'

'But why is she especially menaced?' the chief asked. 'Is there something I haven't been told?'

'Ah,' Iles replied. 'Dring Place, Col, off Valencia Esplanade. But, of course, you know.'

'It's one of our calling grounds when we need you urgently but you're unfindable, sir,' Harpur replied. He had slowed the Rover right down now so he and Iles could eye search the shop doorways and corners. Harpur said: 'There's Honorée, just finalizing a deal by the look of it.'

'Oh, but she's lovely,' Melanie said. 'So young.'

'Thank you,' Iles replied. 'But, of course, not at all *too* young. Entitled to consent. The chief would certainly protest otherwise.'

'I protest, anyway,' Lane said. 'Soliciting.'

Honorée was bent over, talking terms to a BMW driver, probably about to get into his car, her left profile, delicate, unaquiline and winning, towards the Rover.

'Passing the time of day, I think, sir,' Iles replied.

Lane said: 'Desmond, this is behaviour that –'

'Hazel on the other hand *is* too young,' Harpur said.

'Unquestionably,' Iles said.

'Well don't,' Harpur replied.

'What?' Iles asked.

'Question it.'

Iles left the car, muttering thanks to God, and to Harpur for the navigation and driving. He sprinted the hundred or so metres towards Honorée. She seemed to sense his approach, stood up at once and turned to face him. Then, joyfully, she ran to meet Iles, shaky but determined on her huge heels, legs endless and elegant, small black handbag dangling from her wrist like a smashed manacle. She opened her arms as they neared and in a moment embraced him, her left arm on the same Iles shoulder where the chief's had been, but possibly more welcome. Her face against the ACC's, she was chattering something wise and timeless to him, though Harpur could not hear it properly. This was blood speaking to blood, this was that inspiring, notional constancy Iles had mentioned, and might even believe in.

The BMW driver stuck his head out of the open window and began to howl jagged curses at Honorée for deserting him. Iles turned and seemed to acknowledge the justice of this. He freed himself from Honorée and gave a charming, apologetic shrug towards the car, raising two hands as though to say he could not really be blamed if a girl wanted him, Iles, more than she wanted the driver. He continued to shout and swear, now at Iles as well as at Honorée, something about the ACC's age and greyness and, possibly, his Adam's apple. Iles bent quickly, took off one of his black slip-ons and stepping quickly to the car hit the man three times about the nose and jaw with the heel of this first-class shoe. The tom tried to cover his face with his hands and leaned forward almost on to the steering wheel. Harpur thought he might be sobbing. With his free left hand Iles gave him two very short quick punches in the ear and the man immediately slipped down sideways out of sight. Then the ACC returned to Honorée, the shoe still in his hand, in case the driver recovered and had more to say. But Honorée drew the ACC away, talking eagerly to him again. She turned and waved to the Rover, her smile enormous and grateful, her eyes brilliant, even as seen from this distance. They turned the corner out of Dring Place and on to Valencia Esplanade, the main street, Iles inevitably up-and-down in his walk but eager.

'Oh, yes, but she's lovely,' Melanie said again. Harpur drove her home and then took Lane to his own car at headquarters. 'Can I really tolerate that kind of behaviour, Colin?'

'The kerb-crawler in the BMW, sir? We're getting rid of them slowly. This will have been a deterrent.'

Harpur drove out to Low Pastures. He thought he might just catch Ember before he left for the night stint at the Monty. Ralph opened the door himself and took Harpur into the fine drawing room. The two daughters, Margaret and Ember had been playing Scrabble at a rosewood table and Margaret was just clearing up after the game. Ember was in a suit, about to leave for work. On the Scrabble board, just before Margaret put the letters into a tin,

Harpur saw the words *status quo*. 'Social call only,' Harpur said.

'Oh, yea?' the older daughter, Venetia, replied. 'We'd better leave them to it, mum.' Her lack of manners reminded Harpur of his own daughters.

When the children and Ember's wife had gone from the room, Harpur said: 'Just checking you're all right, Ralph.'

'Why not, Mr Harpur?'

'I heard you and Manse were putting a defence force together.'

'Defence? Against whom?'

'You've seen them off already, have you, done them, while I was away – Subaru man's pals.'

'Subaru man? Pals?'

'Where did you do it, you and Shale and your boys? Down on one of the nice remote approach roads? Such an advantage sometimes to be rural, isn't it? You've cleaned everything up? I saw no wrecks, no corpses.'

'Did what, Mr Harpur?' Ember poured a couple of Armagnacs. 'Still no cider. You're going to think me a very slack host.'

'Did they want the Monty then, Ralph?' Harpur asked.

'Did who?'

'People are so stupid. They don't realize how near your central being the Monty is. How you'll fight for the Monty.'

'Oh, I've a few little plans for the club, yes. Away where, Mr Harpur?'

'Beau's dead. Did you hear?'

'Oh, God, dead? Beau? Oh, his mother. And that Mr Gurd.'

'You knew about the death, Ralph? You were there when it happened?'

'Where *did* it happen? This is terrible for Melanie,' Ember replied.

'She'll need some comforting, yes,' Harpur said. 'Deaths everywhere, aren't there? Are you moving into something much, much bigger, Ralph?'

'Oh, Low Pastures is big enough for Margaret, the family and me, I think.'

'I meant trade-wise,' Harpur said. 'As you know. Some very big-time vacuums to fill, wouldn't you say?'

'Vacuums? Something I learned from my university foundation year – how does it go? Yes – "Nature abhors a vacuum."'

'Right. You, Manse Shale, possibly Melanie, into importing? She's formidable. Would you say she's formidable, Ralph?'

'Poor Melanie,' Ember replied. 'She saw a lot in Beau, regardless.'